"Miss Grimsley, h   luct a
tour? Let me assure y   thing
but a disgraceful ruin

Sarah could tell Lo   wasn't too pleased with her,
and she tried to pacify him. "But, my lord, Mr. and Mrs. Proctor
showed me all through the castle. I thoroughly enjoyed their
stories about your great-great-grandfather. Besides," she said,
turning her back to him, "I am sure that you can make it sound
quite romantic—and that is what you want, is it not?"

His lordship now stood so close behind her that Sarah felt
his breath on the back of her neck. She was finding it very
difficult to keep her mind on the subject. "Tomorrow the ladies
will be escorted by your friends. It will give you an excellent
opportunity to interact with all three women without having to
spend all your time with one."

She could almost hear his mind working, but she wasn't sure
in which direction.

"By Jupiter! You may be right." He gave her a hug. "Miss
Grimsley, once again you have astounded me with your acuteness. Carry on with whatever you were doing. I must go back
to our guests."

With her back still to him, Sarah listened to Lord Copley
walk away, whistling. He was gone, and yet, the warmth of his
breath and the strength of his arms where he'd touched her still
lingered. Sarah wrapped her arms around herself and squeezed,
wishing she could feel that way forever . . .

ZEBRA'S REGENCY ROMANCES
DAZZLE AND DELIGHT

A BEGUILING INTRIGUE   (4441, $3.99)
by Olivia Sumner

Pretty as a picture Justine Riggs cared nothing for propriety. She dressed as a boy, sat on her horse like a jockey, and pondered the stars like a scientist. But when she tried to best the handsome Quenton Fletcher, Marquess of Devon, by proving that she was the better equestrian, he would try to prove Justine's antics were pure folly. The game he had in mind was seduction—never imagining that he might lose his heart in the process!

AN INCONVENIENT ENGAGEMENT   (4442, $3.99)
by Joy Reed

Rebecca Wentworth was furious when she saw her betrothed waltzing with another. So she decides to make him jealous by flirting with the handsomest man at the ball, John Collinwood, Earl of Stanford. The "wicked" nobleman knew exactly what the enticing miss was up to—and he was only too happy to play along. But as Rebecca gazed into his magnificent eyes, her errant fiancé was soon utterly forgotten!

SCANDAL'S LADY   (4472, $3.99)
by Mary Kingsley

Cassandra was shocked to learn that the new Earl of Lynton was her childhood friend, Nicholas St. John. After years at sea and mixed feelings Nicholas had come home to take the family title. And although Cassandra knew her place as a governess, she could not help the thrill that went through her each time he was near. Nicholas was pleased to find that his old friend Cassandra was his new next door neighbor, but after being near her, he wondered if mere friendship would be enough . . .

HIS LORDSHIP'S REWARD   (4473, $3.99)
by Carola Dunn

As the daughter of a seasoned soldier, Fanny Ingram was accustomed to the vagaries of military life and cared not a whit about matters of rank and social standing. So she certainly never foresaw her *tendre* for handsome Viscount Roworth of Kent with whom she was forced to share lodgings, while he carried out his clandestine activities on behalf of the British Army. And though good sense told Roworth to keep his distance, he couldn't stop from taking Fanny in his arms for a kiss that made all hearts equal!

Available wherever paperbacks are sold, or order direct from the Publisher. Send cover price plus 50¢ per copy for mailing and handling to Penguin USA, P.O. Box 999, c/o Dept. 17109, Bergenfield, NJ 07621. Residents of New York and Tennessee must include sales tax. DO NOT SEND CASH.

Charade of Hearts
Paula Tanner Girard

ZEBRA BOOKS
KENSINGTON PUBLISHING CORP.

ZEBRA BOOKS are published by

Kensington Publishing Corp.
850 Third Avenue
New York, NY 10022

Zebra and the Z logo Reg. U.S. Pat. & TM Off.

First Printing: March, 1996
10 9 8 7 6 5 4 3 2 1

Printed in the United States of America

One

Miss Sarah Greenwood checked the weekly menus with Cook for the second time that day, adding hot Chelsea buns to Thursday night's dinner. She knew them to be a favorite with her father, as they were with their king, George III. She then went into the kitchen courtyard and, ignoring the bone-chilling February cold, stood, arms akimbo, contemplating the vegetable garden. Cleave, the old gardener, stopped, hat in hand, patiently awaiting his young mistress's orders.

"I believe this spring, Cleave, it would be better if we moved the poles for the beans one row to the left and put the cabbages over nearer the hedge."

"Aye, mum, if you say so," the old man said, quite used to Miss Greenwood's constant changes.

Thinking that she must find Minnie to remind her to put less starch in her father's shirts, Sarah headed back through the kitchen to go abovestairs. Ever since the young, good-looking Albert had come into their employ, Minnie had become addlepated, prattling on endlessly about his dreams of going to America.

Sarah was a dependable young lady. Having spent her three and twenty years as the only child of a country squire, she was quite happy with her life and dedicated to seeing that Elmsdale Manor ran with the greatest efficiency. Her mother, not in the least organized in either her life or thoughts, had agreeably turned over the running of the household to her daughter.

However, Mr. Uriah Greenwood was not so content. Ever since his daughter tired of organizing her toy's and had emerged from the nursery, he felt that he had become less and less the master of his small domain.

It was enough that he owned a sizable amount of tenanted land in Devonshire and made a suitable living. This allowed his wife of twenty-six years to be comfortable with a house-keeper, a personal maid, cook, and two serving girls. For harder work there was the gardener, a stableman and Albert who doubled as butler and coachman. Sarah had her dun-colored, moorland pony, Sylvester; Mr. Greenwood had his horses, various smaller carts, a fine carriage, a stream full of fighting trout, and a well-stocked library. Their expenses were modest, for they found most of their needs met in the neighboring village of Herring's Cross.

Eleven years ago, to settle his wife's inheritance, Mr. Greenwood took his wife and daughter to London. They had traveled two days across the bleak moors and another three along the mail-coach road to reach the city where they spent a full week before returning to Devonshire. His wife and daughter proclaimed their excursion a great success, and Mr. Greenwood, having shown his generosity felt he had done his duty to his family.

Now, he sat in his comfortable den, rummaging hope-lessly through the pile of papers on his desk. "Mrs. Green-wood, where is the statement from the butcher?"

"Why, I cannot imagine, Mr. Greenwood," replied his wife, who was settled comfortably on a settee nearby, trying to stuff a bon bon into the mouth of the brown and white pug whimpering at her feet. "How can I feed you if you keep bouncing up and down?"

"I beg your pardon, madam?"

"Oh, not you, Mr. Greenwood—Pixie," she said, as the dog ran to the full-length casement windows and raised one paw. "I have no idea where your papers are. You know I have no mind for such matters."

"How, pray tell, can I pay our bills if I cannot find them?"

They both looked at each other and said in unison, "Sarah!"

At that moment, their daughter, her brown curls curling around her face, her cheeks still pink from the brisk outdoor air, looked into the room. "Really, Papa, if you would keep things orderly, you would not lose them. Did you try looking in the pigeonhole labeled *bills?*"

While her father tilted back his head and adjusted his spectacles to read the labels on each little compartment, Pixie raised her left paw and let out an ear-splitting howl.

Sarah rushed over, picked up the dog and ran to open the door onto the terrace. "Mama, I have told you that when Pixie raises her left paw it means she wishes to go out to relieve herself."

Mrs. Greenwood watched her daughter disappear. "Here I thought Pixie wanted a sweet. She is indeed a remarkable girl, don't you agree, Mr. Greenwood? Why, she even gets the ducks to march in order to the pond," she said, all the while wondering how she and Mr. Greenwood had come to turn out so tall and slender a child when both of them were short and stout.

The squire extracted a paper from one of the shelves. "If she is so remarkable, why isn't she married and arranging her husband's affairs instead of mine?"

"Now you know eligible young men are scarce in Herring's Cross. You said as much yourself, that none of them in the area is up to our standards." Mrs. Greenwood looked at her husband hopefully. "I don't suppose we could send her up to London for a Season. It would be much to her advantage. After all, that is how I met you."

"You know my living doesn't cover such an expense. What is wrong with the vicar? He has been wrangling invitations to dinner a lot lately and has a connection through his mother's sister to the Earl of Winningham."

Mrs. Greenwood sighed. "Sarah seems not to be attracted to him."

"Well, something has to be done. I lay out a sheet of paper on my desk and go look for a reference book, and the paper is put back in the drawer by the time I return. And when I go to retrieve my book, it has been shelved again. She needs a husband and babies to keep her occupied."

Mrs. Greenwood's thoughts ambled down another path. "Is not your own grandmother Huxley a countess and still living? She resides in the district of Mayfair, does she not? Surely she would sponsor her own great-granddaughter if you wrote to her."

"Never," Mr. Greenwood spouted. "My father broke the tie before I was born."

"A pity. Whatever for?"

"Have no idea," the squire said. "Can't recall."

"Well, I am certain if you cannot remember, it is highly unlikely your grandmother can either. Surely if our daughter just turned up on her doorstep, she would not shirk her duty. After all, Sarah is her own great-granddaughter."

Admiration showing in his eyes, Mr. Greenwood observed his wife as if she'd come up with the most brilliant idea he'd heard from her in twenty-six years. " 'Pon my soul, my dear, you may have the right of it. The worst she could do is send Sarah back to us. Heh?"

"Of course, I would miss her," she said, blushing at the look Mr. Greenwood sent her way. On retrospection, Mrs. Greenwood thought, it would be nice to have a respite from their daughter's organized ways. As much as she loved Sarah, it was a little wearying to be regimented all the time.

So it was that one week later, with little warning beforehand, Miss Sarah Greenwood found herself seated across from her parents in the family carriage which was to take them to Herring's Cross. Beside her sat Minnie. Mr. Green-wood had made arrangements for a local coach line to carry her and the maid, who was to accompany her, to Honiton where they would transfer to a finer coach on the London post-road.

Albert, looking quite grim, loaded the baggage on the boot, then climbed up into his seat. Almost all of Sarah's clothes were in that trunk. She shoved a small portmanteau containing her nightclothes under the coach seat.

Mrs. Greenwood inspected her daughter's dark blue woolen traveling pelisse for the third time. "The countess will probably think we are quite behind in the latest dress here in the country, but I am certain she will see that you have a fashionable wardrobe."

To Sarah, who had never ventured farther than twenty-five miles from home in her life except for their grand journey years ago to London, it was an adventure which she now faced with some hesitation. Especially after her mother's last words.

Mrs. Greenwood's sunny disposition quite overlooked her daughter's discomfort. "Just think, my dear, you will not have to plan meals, or see that the house is dusted, or worry yourself about the stables being clean. You will be waited on and fussed over . . . go shopping for pretty clothes to wear to all those parties and teas and balls . . ." Her mother's voice trailed off. "You did place your money in your reticule?"

"Yes, Mama." Sarah replied, thinking to herself that the whole Season sounded quite boring. After all, she'd already been to the city for one whole week, and she was certain she and her mother had seen and done everything of interest there was to do. She wished her mother understood that she enjoyed planning the meals and organizing the garden. But it was her duty to find a husband, and she didn't want to be a disappointment to her parents.

"Well, I am certain Lady Huxley will find you a suitable husband dear. London is full of nice young gentlemen."

Minnie, twisting her handkerchief into knots, burst into tears. If the squire or Mrs. Greenwood had any apprehensions about sending their daughter to London with no more than a maid, and a wailing one at that, they didn't show it. As Mr. Greenwood said, "After all, I showed her the way to go about it once before, did I not?"

When their carriage arrived at Herring's Cross, Sarah kissed her mother and father, and boarded the travelers' coach. There were already two other passengers seated. One was a large woman with a colossal green turban on her head. Her cherry-cheeked plumpness gave her an ageless appearance neither young nor old. The other occupant, a country gentleman, was sleeping, his chin resting on his chest. Sarah settled next to the woman who held a wicker basket on her lap.

Just before he'd handed Minnie up to take her place across from Sarah, Albert whispered a few words into the maid's ear. She blushed. It calmed her for a moment, but once the young man was out of her sight, she began to sob uncontrollably.

Sarah leaned over and patted the girl's hand. She hoped Minnie wasn't going to be a watering pot the entire trip. "Now, Minnie, it will be but five months before we are home."

Her words were said to quiet the child, but Sarah began to question the wisdom of forcing the maid to go with her. The couple obviously had affection for each other. Since Sarah had never suffered from that emotion, she speculated on what it must be like to be in love. If it produced this much misery, Sarah hoped she'd be spared ever becoming victim to the malady.

The driver cracked his whip and the horses were off, click-clock, along the gravelly rural road. The coach was not well-sprung and consequently, the passengers were bounced this way and that. Sarah tried to content herself with looking out the small window. The fields would soon yield their stalks of grain, and higher up in the rocky hills, sheep, no more than puffs of white, made a pleasing quilted design against the muted tones of winter. This was home and Sarah thought the countryside a pleasant sight, no matter what the season, but she loved the springtime best and regretted she'd miss it this year.

Minnie hiccuped.

Sarah was wondering if they all were to suffer the entire trip, when the turbaned lady held out her basket toward the girl and, like a magician revealing a treasure, popped open its lid.

"My dear," she said with robust generosity, "there is no better elixir for a woman than a sweet. Perhaps a little snack will soothe the pain of separating from that handsome fellow."

Sarah didn't know if it was the vast display of goodies or the kindness in the woman's voice which startled Minnie into silence. Whatever, Sarah was thankful for the interruption as the maid concentrated her gaze on the astronomical array of chocolates, nuts, sugar biscuits, cinnamon-covered dried apples and caramels. While Minnie was occupied in making her selection, the woman turned to Sarah.

"I am Miss Stanhope Grimsley. I hope you do not think me forward, my dear, but I could not but overhear your mother mention that you are going to London for the Season. You are undoubtedly very excited."

Sarah was still trying to think how to respond to that when Miss Grimsley continued. "We shall be riding together for the next two days as far as Danbury Wells. I am on my way to a new position at Roxwealde Castle by invitation of Lord Copley, the fifth baron. He has asked me to take charge of his home and act as his hostess for a party."

"A castle?" Sarah's wide-eyed gaze fixed on the elegant brooch adorning the green silk turban. Surely someone dressed so elegantly did not need to work. "But why?" she asked.

Miss Grimsley must have read her mind, for she leaned closer and said confidentially, "Alas, there are ladies of high birth, who for reasons beyond their control, are left to provide for themselves. For the last twelve years, I have been chatelaine at the late Duke of Warrick's hunting estate in Cornwall."

To Sarah it sounded like a fairy tale, and far more exciting than going to the city. But adding to the intrigue was the puzzle of why a well-born lady would ever be in a position to have to seek employment. Then Sarah remembered Miss Crumpet, her governess. She'd been just such a girl, but at the time, Sarah had been too young to analyze the situation. Oh, dear, she thought, it could happen to anyone—even herself. Would she wish to become a governess of someone's children? The idea frightened her, and she gave Miss Grimsley her undivided attention.

Now that Minnie chewed on a chocolate, Miss Grimsley turned the basket toward Sarah, who couldn't resist trying one of the dried apples. The gentleman continued to snore softly. Pulling the box back onto her lap, Miss Grimsley selected a caramel for herself. "I was to have my Season twelve years ago, but it was not to be."

Although Sarah didn't view that goal as anything to crow about, she thought she should make some sort of sympathetic response. "I am sorry."

Miss Grimsley gave a burst of laughter. "You need not be, my dear. Sometimes circumstances which seem to have gone sour, turn into cream puffs." After a quick glance to see if their male companion was still asleep, she again opened the box to Minnie, who eagerly helped herself. "I was only sixteen and looking forward to my come-out the following Season when my father died unexpectedly. He was Lord Grimsley, the twelfth baron. My mother was dead and I had no brothers or sisters. The title and all our property in Sussex went to a distant cousin, a foppish fool, totally wrapped up in the life of a London dandy. He cared nothing for being made guardian of a sixteen-year-old miss, nor did he want to use any of his newly acquired blunt to bring me into Society. And yet there I was, big as life, and I do believe he entertained all sorts of ideas to be rid of me."

Sarah thought of her own safe home and loving parents. "That was dreadful," she gasped. "Could he do that?"

Miss Grimsley didn't seem overly upset by this indignity and set about to pick another sweet from her basket. "My cousin was sorely in dun territory and used every bit of my father's money to pay his debts. I was helpless and my only recourse was to find a way to earn my own living. Book-learning held no interest for me and I would have made a dreadful governess. However, my cousin did find my father's house a convenient lair for entertaining his friends when they were visiting Brighton, which was my good fortune. That is where I met His Grace."

"The Duke of Warrick?" Sarah asked.

"Yes, he came to a party with Cumberland, one of the Prince of Wale's younger brothers. Warrick took pity on me and asked if I would like to move to his hunting estate in Cornwall."

"How kind," Sarah agreed.

Miss Grimsley slapped her knee and chortled. "I told him I knew little about taking care of a large house, and he said very seriously that if I learned all that I needed, I should be his chatelaine, the keeper of the keys, for as long as I pleased."

"You must have been an apt pupil," Sarah said.

A secret smile turned up the corners of Miss Grimsley's mouth. "Ah, yes, very quick indeed, my dear. I became the duke's favorite hostess. I spent twelve happy years there."

"Then why are you leaving?"

"The duchess has thrown me out."

Sarah shook her head in sympathy. "How terrible, and after you took care of their house all those years."

Miss Grimsley's lips puckered innocently. "The duke died a few months ago, and I was about to think I must try to live on the little substance I have accumulated when, quite unexpectedly, a letter arrived from Lord Copley, asking me to arrange a party he wished to give before the Season started."

At that moment, the coach came to an abrupt halt and the coachman called down, "Darrydell." The gentleman disembarked and as soon as a woman boarded with her three unruly children, they were off once again. For the rest of the morning, there was little time to converse for they stopped at every hamlet and country road. A kaleidoscope of colorful travelers followed: gentlemen, farmers, and a peddler with his pots and pans, who clambered up to sit with the young fustians seated amidst the baggage atop the windy coach.

Around noon, the coachman announced. "Ram's Horn Inn, Chalkton. Ten minutes for lunch and changing drivers."

Sarah chose instead to buy buns from a roadside vendor while she walked about the marketplace to stretch her legs. A now subdued but Friday-faced Minnie accompanied her. Sarah saw many of the villagers owned little moorland ponies, bay, dun, or brown. The animals were ideal for traversing the rugged moors and soggy boglands where dangerous paths could cause an unwary traveler to sink into the ground and disappear in a matter of minutes.

Sarah noticed a bulky-coated rider coming in behind them, his face swathed in a woolen scarf, astride a pony, similar to her own pet. Homesickness threatened to envelop Sarah, but she made a great effort to put a cheerful note in her voice. "See Minnie, the farmer over there is riding a pony that looks just like my Sylvester." Instead of calming the girl, Minnie started bawling again. With a sigh of resignation, Sarah pocketed the buns and pulled her maid back to the coach.

Only Miss Grimsley's disposition remained constant, sunny, in contrast to the darkening skies. By the end of the first day, the three women were the only passengers remaining when the coach pulled up for the night at the Ramshead Towers, a small, comfortable country inn. The little courtyard was crowded with people, animals and vehicles, one with a noble crest on the door, but mostly humble carriages, and even a dogcart with another dun-colored pony in harness. Sarah now knew better than to call Minnie's attention to anything which reminded her of Elmsdale and immediately sought refuge in the cozy inn where they were given a small room with a narrow bed and a cot.

"Come Minnie," urged Sarah. "You will feel better after a warm meal."

The girl stood looking down at her hands. "I really ain't hungry, miss."

Sarah herself was quite famished after having only bread and sweetmeats since morning, but nothing she could do would persuade her maid to go below to the kitchen, so she left her perched on her trunk.

Sarah joined Miss Grimsley and a few other travelers in a private dining room for a hearty repast. By the time Sarah returned to her room full of good food and bone-tired from the long day, Minnie was curled up on her cot, asleep, obviously too exhausted to undress. The steady symphony of rain drops on the window soon lulled Sarah into deep slumber.

The following morning, Minnie was gone, as was Sarah's trunk and reticule. Only the traveling outfit she'd worn the day before and her portmanteau remained. The light dawned on Sarah. It *had* been her dear Sylvester that she'd seen—and Albert. He'd followed them. Wherever the lovers planned to go, Sarah would not begrudge them the use of her faithful old pony, and she was sure her father wouldn't pine over the old hay-eater's disappearance. Although she surmised he might have a few words to say when he discovered his butler-driver had run off and taken his daughter's money as well.

"Oh, my dear," exclaimed Miss Grimsley as soon as she heard the news. "You will, of course, want to return home."

"No," Sarah said with determination. "I cannot disappoint my parents. I shall continue to London."

Miss Grimsley gave her a look of approval. "Then, please allow me to lend you some funds and offer my protection as far as Danbury Wells. I shall make certain that the replacement drivers are all compensated to see that you are chaperoned the remainder of your journey."

No amount of protest would change the magnanimous woman's resolve, and since Sarah saw no other way out of her predicament, she accepted her generous offer. When she arrived in London, she'd ask her great-grandmother to send a recompense to Miss Grimsley at Roxwealde Castle.

As the coach climbed the gloomy heights of the moors, the rain drove sideways and the driver and postboy pulled up their mufflers and collars. The skies forecast grimmer weather ahead, but inside the coach Miss Grimsley remained a ray of sunshine and her constant chatter helped take Sarah's mind off her troubles.

"Oh, yes, my dear," she said in answer to one of Sarah's inquiries, "my former employer was quite generous. He only visited the estate when he invited guests during the hunting season. But as long as I tended to the pleasures of his friends, he permitted me to do as I pleased the remainder of the year. The duke's residence had over eighty rooms and he let me change anything I pleased."

"Anything?" Sarah asked breathlessly.

"Anything," Miss Grimsley repeated. "Each year I tried to see if I could outdo myself in the number of rooms I redecorated. I understand Roxwealde Castle has over one hundred rooms."

Sarah's eyes glowed. "I cannot imagine anything so wonderful."

Miss Grimsley continued, "Lord Copley plans to have this party in only a few weeks time."

"What a great responsibility," Sarah said breathlessly.

Miss Grimsley whispered behind her hand, "I hear the baron is quite a rascal and rich as Croesus."

Sarah blinked, trying hard not to show her ignorance. She wasn't quite sure what one did to become a rascal. Her only knowledge of the goings-on of Society was confined to her mother's tales of long ago. Her father's form of education had been in showing her a robin's nest in the garden or taking her fishing.

Miss Grimsley, her eyes lit with some secret glow, gave Sarah a wink and a playful pat on the hand. "My dear, one is never too old—you know."

At that moment the carriage tilted dangerously, and Sarah left her speculations to try to keep from falling off her seat. The narrow rocky road was becoming more wretched and one wheel so uncomfortably unbalanced that her stomach began to roil.

Suddenly they stopped altogether and after much shouting, the coachman tugged open the carriage door. "The bridge is down over Devil's Gorge. We will have to detour."

After he slammed shut the door, Miss Grimsley chuckled and tucked her carriage rug tighter around her legs. "Can you imagine that? It looks as if we are in for more adventures before we arrive in Danbury Wells."

Later that evening they finally came to a halt at a fog-engulfed, out-of-the-way tavern called the Badger's Skull."

Miss Grimsley took one look at the exterior and called, "Driver, must we stop here?"

The coachman shouted over the wind. " 'Tis late, the iron ring on one of the wheels is badly damaged and must be fixed before we can go on."

"But however will Lord Copley's men know where I am

when they do not find me at Danbury Wells?" Miss Grimsley asked as she stepped down into the muddy yard outside the darkened tavern.

The coachman leaned forward to assure her, "We are near the village of Gilliam. In the morning, we will find someone to carry a message."

Finally after much pounding, the door of the tavern opened. Sarah could see the slovenly proprietor, his shirt smudged and torn, bottle in hand, was less than happy to be disturbed and asked to provide food and shelter for unexpected guests. He led them into the common room.

"Wait here," he grumbled. "Ain't had no customers all day."

Leaving the group, he entered a back room, where he threw a log onto the dying fire and poured more water into the still warm stew pot. It hadn't been cleaned since his wife ran off three days before and there wasn't enough in it to feed four more people. "Don't know why they has to come now," he said, looking around helplessly. Spotting the scrapings from the vegetables his old woman had cleaned before she left, he scooped up the lot off the earthen floor and threw them into the pot. He could tell from their high and mighty looks, them two females was ladies and would expect more than vegetables. He went into a back shed, unhooked a chicken carcass which he was going to use for fox bait and tossed that into the pot as well. Holding his nose, he dropped in a whole bulb of garlic to cover the odor. Supper cooking, he went back into the front room.

"Victuals be ready in a demmed minute," he said grudgingly. "Only has two rooms up the stairs for the ladies."

While the driver and boy made a trip to the coach for Miss Grimsley's trunks, the women were shown to two small connecting rooms. The back room was the only one large enough to accommodate Miss Grimsley's luggage.

There were no linens, only dirty quilts with wads of stuffing falling out. Sarah was almost too tired to care, but not quite. She shook out the comforters, smoothed the beds, inspected them for insects, then took her pitcher downstairs to find some water. She discovered a little boy behind the kitchen who fetched her some from the rain barrel. "Me name's Fibber," he said.

Sarah thanked him and carried the pitcher back upstairs to share with Miss Grimsley.

After washing as best they could, the two women went down to eat. It took only two bites for Sarah to say, "Excuse me, Miss Grimsley, but I don't believe I care for supper."

Miss Grimsley looked askance. "But my dear, you have hardly eaten a thing today. I know it is not what you are accustomed to, nor I, but you should take some nourishment."

Sarah glanced over at the driver and post-boy, sitting at another table attacking their food, and grimaced. "I am afraid I cannot," she said, rushing up the stairs, barely making it to the chamber pot. She managed to take off her dress and after splashing water over her face, crawled into bed in her petticoat and fell asleep.

In the middle of the night, Sarah awakened to find a very sick Miss Grimsley standing over her in her voluminous nightdress.

"I am afraid I do not feel at all the thing," the big woman said.

Sarah, still discomfited herself, nevertheless threw off the quilts to get up. She finally managed to light the stump of a candle on the table. "Oh, Miss Grimsley," she said, looking with great sympathy at the splotchy-faced woman, "do sit down."

Instead, Miss Grimsley crumpled onto the bed. Alarmed, Sarah wadded up the hem of her underskirt, wet it in the pitcher of water, and applied the cold cloth to her friend's burning brow. "You will be just fine in the morning," she soothed, relieved to see the woman had lapsed into a deep sleep. The effort had made Sarah so dizzy that she could barely stand. There was nothing for her to do but cover Miss Grimsley and leave her there. Sarah slowly made her way into the back room, climbed over the baggage and collapsed on Miss Grimsley's bed.

The following morning, the proprietor of the Badger's Skull tried to rouse the dormant body of the coachman from the common room floor. When there was no response, he rolled the man over. Large blind eyes stared up at the ceiling. "Bloody hell! The cock bawd's dead," the tavern owner swore. He turned and nudged the post-boy with his boot. The green-faced youngster groaned. The proprietor ran up the stairs and boldly threw open the door to the women's room. Cautiously, he approached the bed and looked down into the same vacant eyes he'd seen in the driver's face. He didn't take time to go into the other room.

"Fibber," he bellowed, clumping down the stairs. The small ragamuffin ran in from the back of the building. "Take me donkey and get ye down to Gilliam to the apothecary's. Tell him to fetch the constable over from Danbury Wells. We got us a bunch of dead bodies here."

Two

As soon as the wide-eyed boy disappeared out the door, the proprietor took the kettle and dirty bowls into the backyard and scrubbed them down with sand. Rinsing them in the rain barrel, he carried the dishes back into the kitchen and plopped them on the table, cursing, "The bloody gentry's brung the plague."

Abovestairs, time meant nothing to Sarah. She felt someone lift her up and pour a drink down her scratchy throat which made her once again cast up her accounts, though she had nothing left in her stomach. Voices talked too loudly. More nasty liquid. She felt herself being rolled over and over—warmer and warmer—and being carried. Clickety-clock, clickety-clock, the drumming sounded—as if she belonged to another time and place. Finally, sweet oblivion.

Then the voices started again. Sarah slowly came awake, but she could barely see a thing. Something covered her face up to her eyes. A steady tattoo of rain tapped on a window somewhere. She tried to raise her hands to remove the offending cover and found she was wrapped like a cocoon. The room was lit only by the few candles in sconces on the wall and flames from a stone fireplace. She was not in the tavern. Where was Miss Grimsley? Sarah turned to face a dark mullioned window on the far wall. All was black. It was surely nighttime. Her attention focused on three figures on the other side of the room, huddled like strange creatures in some gothic tale. Struggling to clear the cobwebs from her brain, Sarah strained to hear what they said.

A heavy-set man, hat in hand, spoke in solicitous, sub-dued tones. "The apothecary said he give her an emetic and then enough laudanum to render her unconscious. He declared she was lucky to have eaten so little of the rotten victuals."

Deep resonant tones came from the slightly taller figure in a gentleman's coat and ascot. "Then she will recover fully?"

"Aye, Lord Copley. He insisted she would be right as rain in no time at all, soon as she sleeps off the drug. Said she would recover much quicker if she was removed from the filthy inn."

Sarah caught her breath. Had she heard right? Was she in the house of the baron? The rascal? She struggled to raise her head to see better.

Lord Copley spoke again. "Thank you, Jacob. It was for-tunate you were in Danbury Wells when the report came in of the incident."

The woman scolded, "Lud, the way ye imprisoned her in that carriage rug, the poor thing canna move."

"I only done what the apothecary told me, Missus Proc-tor," the servant protested. "He said wrap her up warm and move her as little as possible."

The voice with authority spoke. "Well done, Jacob. I am sure Mrs. Proctor meant no accusation. She will take over from here."

"Aye, milord," the man replied in a more mollified voice. "Is that all ye wish of me?"

"I shall bring Dog out before my guests are to arrive. I expect you to take care of him as usual. You may go now. I have a few things to talk over with Mrs. Proctor."

Sarah heard a door close, then the baron spoke. "Dog will occupy his usual room, Mrs. Proctor."

"Yes, yer lordship," the woman replied. "His room be

ready and his bed made up with fresh straw in his mattress like before."

"Thank you. Don't forget to lay up plenty of wood for his fireplace. If need be, have a man deliver coal from Danbury Wells. I don't want Dog catching a chill on the bare floor. He is quite old and has rheumatism, you know, so make certain you have the stool for him to climb into bed."

Sarah rolled this statement around in her brain. Many an Englishman lavished care on his hounds, but a bed and room of its own? That could spoil an animal considerably. Someone had covered her head with an oversized nightcap and the frills fell so low over her brow, they nearly covered one eye, putting her at a decided disadvantage. She shook her head until the ruffle flipped back. Although she could see better now, the effort made her light-headed and she coughed.

At the unexpected sound, the man whirled around. In a few long strides he was beside the bed looking down at her. Small incandescent points of light reflected off his strong, sculptured features and made it look as if little flames of fire sprang from his golden hair. Shivers ran up her spine and this frightened her. Was this what a rascal looked like—so handsome it hurt her to look at him? Sarah shrank back into the pillow, eyes barely seeing over the edge of the blanket.

His deep voice electrified her. "Madam, I am Copley. I cannot tell you how sorry I was to hear of your unfortunate experience, but my man has told me that we can expect a quick recovery, thank God." Before Sarah could respond to his unexpected show of compassion, he held up his hand. "Don't try to talk. I must return to London, but I am certain I covered everything expected of you in my letters. Remember, you need not spare any expense. Good night, and welcome to Roxwealde, Miss Grimsley."

Shock held Sarah hostage for a second. Good heavens! The baron thought her to be Miss Grimsley. She opened her mouth to set him straight, but only a squeak came out. His highbrows shot up. Then before she could clear her scratchy throat, he turned and exited the room. Trying to make sense of what he'd said, strange thoughts spiraled through Sarah's head, leaving her quite addlepated. It had to be the drug, she thought, drifting off into a dreamless sleep.

For a moment after he'd entered the corridor, Andersen, Lord Copley, the fifth baron, leaned against the thick oaken door and shook with laughter. While he was in the room, it had been all he could do to contain his mirth. Rolled up in that coach rug, the *Honorable* Stanhope Grimsley looked like a big, brown potato served up on a platter.

He knew he should be ashamed of himself, for the poor woman had a near disaster, but once again the Copley charm had not failed him in gaining his prize. The Duke of Warrick's incomparable hostess was finally here. He had heard that Prinny himself was thinking of asking her to Brighton to arrange some of his stately affairs. Whistling, Andersen took the steps two at a time to his second floor apartment. He could now leave immediately for London, certain that Roxwealde was in expert hands.

Hours later, Sarah awakened and looked up into soft clouds draped overhead. Surely heaven wasn't covered with green velvet? On closer analysis, she discovered it to be a large, four-postered bed, so high off the ground that a small stepstool was needed to climb up and down. She couldn't imagine where she was for the last thing she remembered was falling asleep in that miserable hovel called the Badger's Skull. Hazily, her gaze roamed her surroundings. The rich aroma of hot buns and porridge teased Sarah's nostrils and she realized how hungry she was. While she struggled to release herself from her bounds, musty, but not unpleasant odors permeated her consciousness. A soft gray light floated in through the tall mullioned window which Sarah was certain she'd seen before.

The minute Sarah stirred, a smiling, chubby woman was at the bedside leaning over her. "Ye're awake." Sturdy hands loosened the blanket. "My, that man Jacob wrapped ye up good." As soon as she'd freed Sarah's hands, the woman hurried to a table set against the wall. "I be Missus Proctor, Lord Copley's housekeeper," she called back. "Me mister be caretaker of Roxwealde Castle, and I see to the small staff needed when the baron ain't here. But he says ye will be needing more servants."

She laughed heartily, chattering on, relieving Sarah of having to answer, "Law! Me and Mister have enough kin living hereabouts to fill two Roxwealdes. I cannot tell you how happy we be to hear that his lordship plans on opening up the castle for a party. He seldom visits before summer."

She came back carrying a tray which she placed on the bedside table alongside a reticule and a pair of spectacles which Sarah recognized as having belonged to Miss Grimsley. The enticing vapor rising from the spout of the china pot diverted Sarah's attention from the articles.

"I brought ye some victuals, but mayhaps ye only want a cuppa coffee wi' honey?"

As Sarah peered at the plate heaped high with crumpets, jellies, a bowlful of butter, bacon and who-knew-what-all, her stomach began to grumble. She felt as if she hadn't eaten in a week.

"Thank the good lord, 'twas not you who died, Miss Grimsley."

Sarah's hand gripped her sore throat. Good heavens, why did the woman call her Miss Grimsley? Then slowly snatches of the strange conversation she'd overheard the night before came back to her. The compelling gentleman with the flames in his hair, saying, *"Good night, and welcome to Roxwealde Castle, Miss Grimsley."*

So it wasn't a dream. Her jovial traveling companion was dead. Tears came to Sarah's eyes and she opened her mouth to speak, but little more than a croak came out. "And . . . the others?"

Mrs. Proctor handed her a cup. "Now, now, don't ye be trying to say a thing until ye have yer coffee. If I know those apothecaries, they overdose everyone." The woman shook her head sorrowfully. "The driver died, too. The post boy, sad little beggar, will be all right. The authorities will question him when he is feeling more the thing, but 'tis unlikely he can name the passengers, him just being put on at the last coach stop. The poor woman was not so fortunate. They dinna know who she was for she had no identification and only a portmanteau what had some lady's things in it."

Sarah drained her cup. The hot soothing liquid ran down her parched throat. She had to tell the baron who she was and straighten out this whole affair. Her voice sounded absurdly like a frog. "Ahh . . . L' Copl'y?"

Mrs. Proctor shook her finger. "Don't ye be trying to talk now, pet, til ye get yer voice back. His lordship went off to London last night. He thought mayhaps ye could tell the authorities who the unfortunate lady was, but I told him that it weren't likely she wouldna told anyone the truth. If ye asks me, the gel was running away, so she wouldna given her real name to anyone now would she?" She pointed to a door leading off the farside of the room. "Yer three trunks are over by the wall."

Sarah grabbed her stomach. After drinking the hot liquid, her urgency to answer the call of nature suddenly became apparent.

Mrs. Proctor, her face turning pink as she comprehended Sarah's gestures, wiped her hands down her apron. "How amiss I be, Miss Grimsley. Ye'll find the chamber pot in the commode behind that screen and warm water in the pitcher on the stand. Shall I send a maid up to help ye dress and put away yer clothes?"

Sarah needed time to think. Shaking her head vigorously, she held her hand to her forehead.

Mrs. Proctor's brow furrowed, then her eyes brightened. "You need more rest?"

Feigning weakness, Sarah nodded.

"Ye eat what ye can and then lie down a bit. We don't want ye tiring yerself now." Mrs. Proctor hurried toward the door. "I'll come check on ye in about an hour."

As soon as she was alone, Sarah threw off the heavy woolen blanket and the old quilt from the tavern and took care of her needs. Hungrily, she stuffed a cinnamon bun into her mouth, and after picking up another, crossed to the window. Surprisingly, considering all that had happened to her, she felt in fine fettle.

From her vantage point on what must be the first floor. Sarah could see two other wings, their old stone walls covered with ivy. Rounded turrets at each corner guarded an army of chimney stacks standing at attention across the slated roofs. Beyond the building itself were pale shadows of the barely discernible moors still wrapped in morning fog. This magnificent castle was to have been Miss Grimsley's domain.

As she tried to stir up some enthusiasm for the social life her mother had described to her when telling her of her own youthful entry into London Society twenty-six years ago, a bad case of the dismals descended upon Sarah. She found herself inexplicably becoming more and more dissatisfied with her circumstance. When it came right down to it, it seemed distressingly dull to contemplate spending one's time going to endless assemblies and balls which someone else had arranged. The longer she thought on it, a Season with a great-grandmother whom she'd never laid eyes on loomed more and more depressing.

Sarah looked down at her rumpled petticoat and stockinged feet. In her present state of dishabille, she couldn't very well continue on to London. Perhaps she could borrow a dress of Miss Grimsley's. Heaven knew that the vivacious lady was not about to object, now was she? On the other hand, perchance she could persuade the baron to let her stay here. Then, she'd return to Elmsdale at the end of the Season and tell her parents that she did not take. At first they would be disappointed, but Sarah was sure that in time they would forget altogether about her finding a husband.

Sarah crossed the room and opened the first trunk. A colorful array of splendid fabrics stared back at her; silks and satins; velvets and warm marino; lacy undergarments; fans and feathered turbans. If this was what well-dressed ladies wore, Sarah's plain frocks were sadly out of fashion.

Unless she could think of another solution, she would have to beg the mercy of the wealthy baron to underwrite the expense of her journey to London. Or, embarrassing as it may be, ask him to arrange for her to return home. Her parents would, of course, be disappointed, but they would never reprimand her. But Sarah would feel she had failed them.

She held up a deep green silk dress, then pulled it down over her head. She and Miss Grimsley were of a like height, but that was where the similarity ended. The gown hung like a tent. Disappointed, Sarah continued to search through the trunk, hoping to find something which might fit better. Underneath several layers of elegant gowns and lush chemises, she uncovered a packet of letters bound with a purple ribbon and addressed to the Honourable Stanhope Grimsley in Cornwall. When Sarah attempted to remove them, one slipped its binding and fell open onto the floor. It was on seeing his signature that she recalled Lord Copley's words, *"I am certain I covered everything expected of you in my letters."*

Sarah did not consider herself a person wont to hatching wicked schemes, but desperation forced her to reappraise her situation. As she realized she had less than one hour to think what path to pursue, excitement raced through her mind. Pursing her lips, she placed a finger on her chin and gave the problem her deepest concentration. She envisioned what it would be like if she were mistress, planning a party in the castle. How dreadful it would be for Lord Copley to return with his guests to find things at sixes and sevens, because there was no Miss Grimsley.

Determination being one of Sarah's strongest characteristics, her decision came swiftly. She shed the dress and wriggled into one of Miss Grimsley's corsets. It was so large she didn't need to undo the lacing. A feather pillow stuffed into the undergarment filled out its contours. She covered herself with three petticoats to ward off the chill, then struggled back into the green gown. With a sound pat on her stomach, she viewed her inflated image in the cheval mirror. It will do, she thought, puffing out her cheeks to make her face appear more rounded.

Miss Grimsley was dead; there could be no gainsaying it, and Sarah was extremely regretful. But as her plans took shape in her mind, she had a notion her benefactress would approve the masquerade. Miss Grimsley had a commitment to Lord Copley, a responsibility to discharge, and Sarah intended to see the good lady didn't fail. It was, she reasoned, the least she could do.

Picking up a length of orange gauze, Sarah twisted it into a turban over her brown curls, and secured it with a brooch the size of an egg. She plunked Miss Grimsley's spectacles on the end of her nose, so she could peer over the rims, and thus transformed herself into the new mistress of Roxwealde Castle.

As she stared into the looking glass at her new self, a knock sounded on the door.

"Miss Grimsley? Are ye up, dear?"

Sarah glanced at the letters. She'd read them later. Clearing her throat, she called out huskily, "Yes, I am, Mrs. Proctor. Do come in."

Lord Copley, slumped down into the comfortable leather wing-chair in his South Kensington townhouse, stretched his long legs toward the burning logs in the fireplace and took a deep breath. He much preferred the smell of a wood fire to that of coal. One hand clutched a half-empty glass of wine, the other dangled over the armrest, his fingers digging deeply into the thick hair on Dog's head.

He'd been back in London for nearly three weeks. For one of those, he'd entertained the euphoric illusion that preparations were going well for what was to be his farewell party to his bachelor days—a week-long romp with a fine selection of aspiring actresses from Drury Lane. His rapscallion cronies, Mr. Henry Smith, Mr. Basil Ripple and Ernest Lance, the young Marquis of Wetherby, had embraced the idea of the anticipated gambol with enthusiasm, while at the same time expressing sorrow over losing one of their liveliest revelers to the marriage mart.

This was the year in which Andersen intended to enter the Season's activities with the sole purpose of selecting a wife. Up until a fortnight ago, he'd thought he had the entire Season to make his choice. Then, while his fiancée made preparations for their wedding, he'd planned on keeping the castle open for his little country parties—far enough from London not to cause any gossip. Once he married, Andersen had every intention of settling down to play the dutiful husband—for a while anyway. Without removing his gaze from the flames, he raised his glass to the gentleman seated opposite him.

Mr. Peter Trummel, Andersen's best friend and companion in all things devilish, sat in a similar chair, as he did many an evening when he was in Town. "What's the great emergency, Andy? You sounded like a demmed potentate summoning his vassal."

Andersen shot him a brooding glance. "You've changed, Peter. You were always the first one to accept an invitation to any festivity. Why did you turn down this one to Roxwealde?"

"Truth of it is, all the madcap activities don't excite me as they used to. Now that I've inherited the small estate in Yorkshire from my grandmama, I've had the whole winter removed from Town to think about it. Becoming a country gentleman isn't all that bad. I've been giving serious thought to settling down and starting my nursery."

"Well you haven't a sword dangling over your head like I have, so I am entreating you to help *me* find a wife first."

"That should be easy for a bloke like you—rich and passable-looking enough to fetch a decent sort of female." Peter's arm covered his face as if to ward off an imaginary cuff from his handsome friend. When he got nothing but a scowl, he said, "So, why the long face?"

The baron continued to stare into the fire. "Tooley called me to his office week before last."

Peter relaxed and sat back with a grin. "That usually brings a smile to your ugly face. Never did see anyone so surely born with the touch of Midas as you."

"Not my man of business, Endicott, but old Tooley, my solicitor. He reminded me I turn thirty in two months."

Peter raised his hands, an expression of mock horror upon his good-natured countenance. "Oh, indeed, that is devastating news. Shall I start funeral arrangements?"

Andersen shot him a withering look. "I thought you knew the ghastly terms of the entail on the Copley estate."

Peter raised his eyebrows.

"No, I suppose you do not," the baron said. "Don't like to think about them myself. That's why I stopped paying attention to birthdays years ago. I missed a year somewhere along the way. I thought I was eight and twenty. If I am not married before I turn thirty, the entire estate goes to my nephew Rupert who incidentally is only four years old."

His friend remained silent, his expressive eyes asking for answers.

"I am afraid my father was a true believer that the family curse had passed down to me as well."

"The curse?"

"Copley men seldom talked about it. Let me just say, I must find a wife."

Peter fell back, laughing. "For a moment there, I thought you were serious. By Jove, that should prove no problem for you, what with all the single ladies throwing out lures for a well-heeled husband. Just let it be known you're looking, and I wager they will be stepping on each other to get in line." Peter got nothing but a glare, so added, "It isn't as if you need to give up your lifestyle. You have this house here in London to escape to. Being shackled doesn't mean a man has to be tied down. Just be a little more discreet. Cheer up, the ladies will all be in Town in another month and you can take your pick."

The baron shifted uneasily in his chair. "I cannot wait that long, for another unexpected bend in the river has loomed up. Endicott, my man of business, came to see me three days ago. Last year, I talked him into putting nearly all my assets into India bonds with the prospect of doubling my fortune. I expected the Port Royal fleet to arrive any day loaded with silks and spices from the East."

"Zounds! Clemantis and Routers made fortunes last year in spices alone."

"Unfortunately, Endicott told me word has arrived at the Exchange that the entire fleet went down in a storm off the Canary Islands."

"Surely you had it underwritten."

Copley's face betrayed him by turning red. "With my history of good luck. I did not think it necessary. Had only a little coverage. What I will retrieve will not pay a trifle of my debts. There, my friend, is the reason for my dismals. You are looking at the bankrupt Lord Copley."

"Good God! Is that why you called me back to London? You know I'd give you a loan if I could, Andy, but I am not exactly running in the roses, m'self, at the moment. Being a fourth son, my allowance has never been all that great—and now with trying to refurbish my country house . . ." his voice trailed off.

Andersen stared into his glass. His plan had been to acquire a finer house in a more fashionable area such as Mayfair when he married in another year. Until then his present, convenient location was satisfactory. It was a typical bachelor abode, cared for by a small male staff, a cook and a housemaid who came in during the day. When he wanted to extend his hospitality overnight, it could accommodate any number of his rackety friends.

As if seeing it for the first time, the baron glanced around at his surroundings. True, the house wasn't as tidy as it would have been had he hired a housekeeper, but he didn't judge a residence by how neatly the furniture was arranged or how well the tableware matched. As long as he had a comfortable bed, good companions, and his man kept the wine flowing freely, he was satisfied.

Pulling himself away from his musings, Andersen met Peter's gaze forcefully. "That is not why I asked you to come. Since Endicott does my investing for me, as yet no one knows that all of my blunt was in on the venture. I see this as only a temporary setback, but if my creditors hear of my dire straits, I'm afraid they will call in my notes. It follows that if all the papas think that they will have to dig into their pockets to keep their future son-in-law out of debtor's prison, they will lock up their daughters."

"Don't sound like you to give up, Andy."

"Dash it all, Trummel! A few days ago the thought of losing my capital and that old castle in Devon wouldn't have perplexed me overly much. Since I came into my inheritance, I have multiplied my living a dozen times over by persuading Endicott to invest the interest in what he hailed as *dubious schemes*. I don't understand why my intuition failed me; because up 'til now they have paid off handsomely."

"Is it not possible to hold off your creditors a bit longer?"

"You know that ordinarily I would look forward to the challenge of recouping my loses, if it weren't for this little matter of having to marry quickly. Therefore, I must keep my present financial situation from being found out, and it is requisite that I find a wife with a substantial dowry."

"Time is your nemesis."

"You have the right of it. But let me assure you, if my bride comes with a goodly portion. I plan to reward her handsomely for the part her blunt will play in my recovery. She shall have the finest houses money can buy, and never will she have to ask for wardrobe or spending money."

"I don't question your generosity, Andy. And now, too, I understand why it is imperative that you make your move before the Season starts. Do you have any particular lady in mind?"

Andersen drew a scrap of paper from his pocket and glanced at it. "Actually, there are several."

"Why don't you offer for one of them? I can think of few women who would refuse you."

"Thank you, Peter. Your faith in my powers of persuasion is touching. However, the more I gave thought to the matter, the more the notion of being legshackled the remainder of my life to someone I don't rub well with was not something I relished. My number of possibles decreased considerably."

The baron looked as if he was giving it great thought, "I don't expect great affection, but a fairly pleasing nature is preferable. My wife does not have to look like Aphrodite, for ofttimes raving beauty creates a selfish nature. But a pretty face will be most welcome. Neither am I attracted to the corpulent women that prevail in our Regent's crowd, nor one who looks as if she is nothing but a walking skeleton. A spiteful disposition could run me from my own house and would pose a threat to creating an heir to the Copley clan."

Peter shook his head. "Not very particular, are you? I thought you said you had to find a bride quickly."

"I do, but my choices are scattered from one end of England to the other and would not be coming to London for another month. One lady lives in Gloucestershire, another in Hampshire, still another in Cheshire, and so forth. Since time is of the essence, I perceived the only possible solution was to gather them all in one place."

"Good lord! Have you lost your mind? I never heard of anything so preposterous.

Andersen raised his eyebrows and stared at Peter. "Indeed, I thought it rather an admirable solution."

"God, Andy, you make it sound like such a complicated affair, you fairly scare me away from attempting the parson's trap myself."

Andersen patted the sleeping animal sprawled out beside his chair. "You certainly see that there *was not* enough time for me to visit each one separately."

"I don't like the sound of that *was not*. What have you done? And what about your party at Roxwealde?"

The baron looked from his nearly empty glass to the dying embers in the fireplace and reached for the bellrope. "Before I tell you what I have done and what I wish you to do for me, let me ring for more refreshments."

Peter had no time to respond before their conversation was interrupted by the door opening.

A bleary-eyed scarecrow, his black suit rumpled, his hair the consistency and color of dried straw, shuffled into the room. "D'chew ring, m'lord?"

"Ah, there you are, Fletcher," Copley said, not unkindly, pushing aside the stack of dirty dishes on the table to make room for his glass. "The fire is in need of logs. And we could use more brandy—perhaps a snack of bread and cheese before we retire?"

Dog awakened at the sound of Fletcher's voice. As if he was used to the routine, he withdrew his paws from the servant's path to the fireplace before falling back to sleep.

Fletcher gathered the smallest sticks from the pile stacked against the wall. In a matter of minutes, he managed to trip over his own feet, sending his armful of wood clattering across the hearth into the burning embers. Sparks popped onto the carpet, slowly burning holes among the ones already there. With an apologetic look at his master, he danced about trying to extinguish the spots of red sending gray specks into the air, before finally making his way out the door.

Peter brushed particles of soot off his knees and said in exasperation, "Andy, why in God's name do you put up with that inebriated valet . . . or butler . . . or whatever he is supposed to represent? He doesn't do anything right. Look at this place."

Andersen let his gaze follow the path of Peter's eyes as they glanced from the tufts of hair that had fallen off Dog to the sooty footprints tracked by Fletcher from the fireplace to the door. Feeling his personal circumstance was being attacked, Andersen responded defensively. "What is wrong with my house? It is satisfactory enough for me."

Regardless of his indifference to his untidy surroundings, the baron was particular about his own appearance. He prided himself in maintaining a certain impeccable dress, thanks to his tailors and his own good taste, not to any help from Fletcher, who was in his cups most of the time. Why he put up with the sly knave he had no idea. No, he did know. It was the same impetuous nature that Peter accused him of which had made him acquire Dog.

Late one night several months earlier, Copley had returned to the Earl of Brickleigh's after a jolly night on the town with several friends only to be met by the earl's valet,

Fletcher, obviously as cup-shot as his master. As the servant tried to assist his lordship, both men had fallen in a heap on the marbled entry floor, and Brickleigh, known for his short temper, threw the bewildered servant out onto the street in front of everyone.

The baron had helped Fletcher up off the cobblestones and taken him home with him. After all, he was in need of a houseman. It was unconscionable, of course, for a servant to rifle his master's wine cellar, but the sight of any creature huddling pitifully in the rain, was more than Andersen could stand. He hadn't known at the time the extent of the man's drinking, but when he was sober, Fletcher was a halfway decent valet. The baron only wished the reprobate wouldn't try so hard to please when he was foxed.

Now, Andersen's fingers kneaded the thick ruff around his pet's neck. When a cacophony of rattling sounds came from the direction of the corridor, he knew it was Fletcher trying to return with a tray of food and the brandy decanter all at one time. The noise increased, and Andersen tensed for the disaster he anticipated as inevitable. A terrible crash was followed by a drum roll, which had to be the pewter decanter rolling down the tiled hallway.

Before either Andersen or his friend could rise from his chair, Dog, startled from his slumber, raised his huge leonine head and roared.

Clutching the arms of his chair, Peter, his eyes the size of full moons, stared into the cavernous mouth of the large African lion only a few feet in front of him. "God, Andy! Must you keep that wild beast in the house? Someday, he will devour us all!"

Three

For the first time that evening, Lord Copley laughed and affectionately pulled the cat's ear. "Dog is as harmless as a kitten."

The big animal licked his master's hand, then rolled over to have his belly scratched. Andersen recalled his sense of injustice the day he'd visited the Prince's menagerie at the Tower of London and heard that the animal was to be killed for no other reason than that it had grown too old to be entertaining. There was talk of closing down the menagerie altogether. The monkeys had been removed years before when one had bitten a small boy. The on dit spread that an eccentric dowager had given them a home. That was what gave him the idea of adopting Dog.

Peter didn't take his gaze off the lion. "You still have not told me what you intend to do. Surely you don't plan to cancel your party."

"Not cancel—only change my intentions. Instead of our little demi-reps, I shall be hosting some of the most eligible females of le beau monde." Andersen smiled roguishly. "Which, is where, my friend, you and the others will come in. If the four of you endeavor to keep the young ladies occupied, it will give me the opportunity to court each in turn."

"And the others agreed? Henry, Basil and Weatherby? Gad! You all belong in Bedlam, but I suppose you may as well count me in."

"I knew I could rely upon you. Thank you, Peter."

The men stopped talking as Fletcher entered and set his tray down on the long sideboard before offering the men a plate of crumbled biscuits. Andersen raised one eyebrow, and looked inquiringly at the poor display.

"Cook's already retired, milord, and the serving gel's gone home. I did m'best," the servant mumbled, looking soulfully at his meager offering.

"It is of little consequence, Fletcher," Andersen replied. "After all, it is not one of your duties." Then, seeing that his valet wasn't going to be much use to him anymore that evening, he added, "You may retire, too, as soon as you refill our glasses." While his man turned to comply, the baron continued his conversation with Peter. "As you can see, out of necessity, my assembly will be entirely of another kind than I first envisioned."

"You always have been impulsive Andy. It is madness to throw a country party in that god-forsaken part of the moors during the coldest time of the year. How can you hope to persuade any of the fine ladies you expect to woo to accept such a preposterous invitation?"

A slow smile spread across the baron's face. "My plight has not rendered me completely witless, Trummel. Can you name one woman who can resist the fascination of a gathering in a faerytale castle?"

Peter grinned. "That's all very well, but like as not, they shall turn about and leave as soon as they see the place. The paramours we've invited previously, may have thought it quite a friendly atmosphere, but they visited in the warmer months. No offense, Copley, but need I remind you that Roxwealde sits on two thousand acres of rock and is in a terrible state of disrepair. Beams are rotting, tiles are missing from the roof, and weeds fairly choke the carriageway."

Andersen's eyes narrowed to dark pools. Perhaps Peter was right. Few ladies he knew would abide the old monstrosity his great-great-grandsire built in the Devonshire moors to resemble a Norman castle. Beyond the park, the house was surrounded by rocky soil covered by bronzing bracken and mottled bramble, treacherous boglands and granite outcroppings that dropped off to nowhere. Its sinister-looking twin towers were enough to terrify the bravest souls.

Percival, the first baron, Lord Copley, built the castle in 1689 with a large family in mind, and Andersen didn't believe it had had many improvements since that time, because heir after heir, including himself, made occasional visits, but refused to live in it.

Even as a child, Andersen found very little to like about thorns that tore one's clothes and dripping moss that grew in dark oaken copses. However, he did discover the heath a perfect place to set free the helpless creatures he kept rescuing.

Now the baron dismissed Peter's negative description of his ancestral home with a wave of his hand. "The ladies are not aware of the castle's poor condition."

"They will be once they arrive."

"I strove to make it sound quite romantic in my missives to them."

"God, Andy, that dreadful old gothic will need more than a bit of beeswax before it will be presentable for such a gala as you suggest. As I recall, the staff at Roxwealde isn't the fanciest either," Peter said, kicking a piece of biscuit across the floor toward the lion, who lapped it up in one gulp.

"That is why I have engaged Miss Grimsley," Andersen said smugly, glancing about his jumbled den.

Peter stopped his glass halfway to his lips. "Who?"

The baron's mouth twitched. "The Honourable Stanhope Grimsley. It is true that we have had the shortest of acquaintances, but from her reputation as hostess for the late Duke of Warrick for twelve years, I have every confidence that the lady will be my *coup de maitre,* my master stroke in this campaign. I hear her father was a baron who at one time was in much the same straits as I. But more about her, later."

Peter scoffed. "Our friends aren't going to be too pleased when they find out they have to leave their doxies behind to keep your guests amused for an extended stay in that ice house. They promised the girls a frolic."

"I have already made a deal with those raspscallions. In exchange for their assistance, I've agreed to hire their little bits of muslin as chambermaids for the duration of the party. After all, they are aspiring actresses, are they not?"

Peter slapped his knee. "Gad, Copley! I have never heard of anything so outrageous—if the ladies find out the truth, it will be the biggest scandal to hit England in a decade. I wonder you dare."

Andersen winked. "There is still time for me to enlist the services of a companion for you—just give me a preference—Druscilla, the little redhead, perhaps, who plays the part of the lost lamb?"

"I shall pass up your generous offer," Peter said.

Andersen sat forward. "But I will need your level head to make certain our friends stick to their bargain and do not mix their society manners with any rackety behavior."

Peter's eyes twinkled. "I am certain you will have their compliance with or without my help, but you can count on me to come to the gala. I would not miss it for the world. I only meant that I have no desire for Druscilla's company."

The viscount grinned back at Peter, a sense of relief running through him. "I am glad to hear you do not mean to desert me, for I already sent out the invitations to six of last year's debutantes."

"Why am I not surprised?

Andersen ignored his friend. "Unfortunately, one lady is traveling in France and another is already engaged and begged to be excused. But four have sent word that they will attend."

Peter looked amused. "You are quite sure of yourself, aren't you? But excuse me for saying so, old chap, there are more tantalizing fish in the sea than a viscount. And one that is now empty in the pockets."

Andersen threw back his head and laughed. "Trummel, are you trying to challenge me as Wetherby has always done? Lady Caroline's acceptance was one of the first to arrive. Not only that, but her father plans to accompany her entourage to Roxwealde."

"Andy, you jest! Lady Caroline? Don't know how you can think the Earl of Favor will take to his only daughter lowering herself to marry a baron when the fair Caroline has had several titled, young bucks seeking her hand for two seasons. If I'm not mistaken, our chum Wetherby caught her eye last year. By the by, the bets at White's weigh heavily toward Wetherby succumbing eventually. The way he runs through his allowance, he could use the blunt her dowry will bring. Aren't you afraid he might cut you out?"

"Not at all." Andersen didn't reason why his self-confidence still ran high, even though, his fortunes had gone downhill.

Peter looked at him suspiciously. "Does Wetherby know that Lady Caroline is one of your special guests?"

"No. I didn't know myself until a few days ago precisely who would be coming."

"You don't think that creates a problem?"

"Why should it? Wetherby is but four and twenty. He doesn't want to get married yet, and besides, he knows I am a better shot with pistols than he."

"You had best wipe that grin off your face, Andy. Caroline may be beautiful, charming and moneyed, but being a marquis does have advantages over a baron. Why don't you aim for some woman not so top-lofty?"

Andersen's smile disappeared, and he rose from his seat so quickly that he quelled any further response his friend planned to give. "It is late. Tomorrow I ride to Roxwealde Castle to inform Miss Grimsley that instead of the previous small group, she can expect several of the most eligible debutantes and their attendants to come to my pre-season rout. Fletcher and I shall be gone by the time you rise in the morning. You know, of course, that you and your man are welcome to stay here while you are in Town."

The lion yawned and stretched. Andersen's humor returned when he saw Peter's wary gaze cut to the lion. "Don't worry, Dog will be going with me."

"What in the world are you going to do with him when you have your party?"

Andersen looked down at his pet and blinked. "Why, take him along. Dog won't bother anyone."

"He'll scare the ladies home faster than your lack of blunt will."

"He'll stay in my wing—they won't even know he is there." Andersen pulled playfully on the lion's ear. "Come you old curmudgeon—bedtime."

After settling Dog in his room for the night, the baron sought the quiet of his quarters. He found his bags already set beside the door, his traveling clothes for the morrow, hung on the clotheshorse. He could see that Fletcher had packed earlier in the day, wisely contemplating that he'd be too foxed by nightfall to render much assistance. At least the man tried to compensate for his shortcomings. Many men never admitted to theirs.

Andersen was glad to escape any more of Peter's interrogation. Often, the baron feared that the time would come when the mellowness of the wine and the mesmerizing warmth of the hearth would cause him to reveal more about his family than he cared to divulge.

He glanced at the gold and ruby band on his finger. Sir Percival Copley was presented the ring and commended by a grateful King William III for his valiant service to the crown in the Battle of Boyne. The king, running out of lands to award his knights, made Sir Percival a baron as well as presenting him with the two thousand acres of worthless rock and bogland in Devonshire, long since robbed of its tin, copper, and iron.

Regardless of other's opinions, the first baron held a high sense of his own worth, as Andersen thought he should. He married at the age of thirty, moved his new wife to his castle and embraced family life with a vengeance, fathering eleven children, ten of them girls.

From what Andersen had heard, Percival married for love, but it hadn't been that way for the following Copley heirs.

To the first baron's disappointment, his only son, heir to the Copley estate, proved to be a bounder and fast spender. Infuriated that he showed all the signs of remaining a bachelor, Percival issued the future second baron an ultimatum: to find a wife before he turned thirty or the old man would change his will and sell out the young jackanape's inheritance. True to his word, for he was a strict man, Percival wrote a settlement into his will, guaranteeing no heir for three generations could sell or trade any of the family holdings, only live off the income provided by the interest. His son married soon after.

The third Lord Copley followed in his father's footsteps, leading a notorious life. Within a hair's breath of his thirtieth birthday, he plucked the daughter of a duke off her horse while riding in Hyde Park and carried her over the border into Scotland. So compromised, she had to marry him, but she never forgave him. She bore him one son so she could be rid of him and then returned to London to live the gay life she loved, leaving her husband to pursue his mistresses or whatever pleased him.

Andersen's mother and father, the fourth baron, fared better in that he proposed in the conventional way. They rubbed well together, but both preferred the glittering life of le beau monde, and Andersen's upbringing as well as that of his younger brother Bertie, was left to servants. They spent most of their leading-string days caged like golden birds high in the third floor nursery.

At the age of seven, Andersen was sent away to school. He was certain that the solitary life that Bertie was forced to live for the next two years at home couldn't have been a very happy time for him.

The reputation that all Copley heirs were predestined to be rogues, wasn't taken lightly, and Andersen hadn't found it difficult to uphold the tradition. But when his father the fourth baron, realized that his son hadn't been spared the disposition to procrastinate in finding a bride, he felt duty bound to renew the restricted entail for another three generations.

Now, the family curse had Andersen by the throat. There was no choice but to find himself a wife.

After Andersen came into his title, his brother, who was always doing some outlandish derring-do to prove himself, badgered Andersen into buying him a commission in the army.

Thank God, his brother married happily. Soon after, Bertie's wife, Millicent, gave him a beautiful son, and sometimes, Andersen had envied his brother for that. If the truth be known, he was unduly fond of his little nephew. Upon Bertie's death in the Peninsula, Andersen settled an annuity on his sister-in-law from his own income to take care of her needs, and of course he planned on seeing to the education of his nephew when the time came for Rupert to attend Eton.

However, if Rupert inherited, what then? The baron was quite aware that it would be years before the child was capable of running his own affairs. Millicent was still young. If she remarried, an unscrupulous husband could rob her of the little they had. No, Andersen knew that he had to keep the entail in his hands, no matter what.

Melancholy threatened to overwhelm him, but Andersen refused to be downtrodden. His back stiffened. No, this was only a temporary setback. He would rebound. He always did.

The sun was only minutes away from rising over the Devon moors. From the depth of her warm bed, Sarah, fully awake, heard the soft knock and pulled her pillow over her head from where she could observe the door without being seen.

Nooney, one of the Proctors' nieces, elbowed her way into the room bearing a tray with a candlestick and the usual morning repast. She was a large girl, her face wearing a perpetual smile.

Without having to look, Sarah knew there would be hot chocolate, a steaming bowl of porridge and the usual plate heaped high with succulent cinnamon buns. Behind the serving girl would be a young boy named Cyril carrying a pitcher of hot water. It was his responsibility to rekindle the fire, while Nooney set her tray on the table by the window. Next, she'd take the candle and light the tapers in the wall sconces, and although it was still dark outside, pull open the heavy drapes from across the window, then quietly tiptoe from the room.

When there was no chance of her youthful face and slender figure being observed, Sarah would rise, wash and have her breakfast. Thank goodness, the real Miss Grimsley had had most of her enormous gowns cut to button down the front. Otherwise, Sarah could never have managed to dress herself. By the time she finished the complicated disguise that turned her into the chatelaine of Roxwealde Castle, the dawn would be peeking over the horizon.

From the moment Sarah decided to become Miss Grimsley, her new adventure had exceeded all expectations. Mrs.

Proctor took her on a tour of the castle, covering all four stories, except the baron's apartments and the old circular towers.

"Their steps are chipped and uneven, and the stones keep falling out of the walls. His lordship forbids anyone to use them," Mrs. Proctor admonished.

A pity, Sarah thought, for the view of the heath from the top must be one of great beauty. But, she soon forgot the towers, for excitement surged through her with every turn of a corridor, every new view from a window. The Great Hall, with its flagstone floor, immense hearth at the far end, was large enough to roast an ox in. The stairways in black oak on either side were dark wings spiraling to the floors above. Through tall doors on either side of the hall she discovered large and small saloons, a billiard room, and library. The morning room was obviously more used than the stately dining room, for the chandelier in the latter was wreathed in cobwebs and the chairs lay tilted toward the table.

Sarah's rooms were on the first floor of the West Wing directly under the baron's apartments. As far as she could see, the twenty-some-odd bedrooms along her corridor hadn't been used for years.

Mrs. Proctor pointed upward. "Ye need not concern yerself with his lordship's apartment," she'd said, "Mr. Proctor sees to that. Your rooms were always readied for the baron's special friend."

That explained the contrast to the other bedchambers, their shutters closed, the furniture under holland covers. But the baron's letter said that she was also to have his gentlemen friends usual bedrooms in the East Wing readied. She could see that there was a lot of work to do. Yet in no time at all, she'd tripled the staff—mostly with recruits from the Proctors' kin, and neighbors who were familiar with the castle and had worked there off and on. Not one to dillydally, Sarah made a schedule and set everyone to work. But she did wonder at the sideward glances thrown her way.

"Don't ye be minding the girls staring a wee bit. It be some time since we had a real lady in the house."

Sarah hadn't known what to make of that statement, for she'd been led to believe from the baron's letters that he planned to entertain quite frequently at Roxwealde Castle.

The maids seemed obliged to do her bidding, but she could see the men were going to be another thing altogether. They were undisciplined and inclined to let their hands take liberties with the female help. Whatever would the baron think if he knew how his staff behaved while he was gone? They were also most indifferent to their attire, their wigs askew, if they wore any at all, and their neckclothes turned sideways. It just would not do. Sarah determined that by the time the baron arrived, she'd have all things set to rights, the castle neat as a pin, and the servants schedules running like clockwork—or nearly.

The choice of stuffing for Sarah's corset was another problem. It had taken a good two weeks to become accustomed to carrying the large pillow in front of her without waddling or bumping into furniture. Sitting was a more difficult maneuver, accomplished with a flop, the pillow popping up to her chin, threatening to choke her. Getting up came more slowly and she'd often had to wait until a servant left the room before she dared try to rise.

After Mrs. Proctor had shown her the household, Mr. Proctor guided Sarah through several corridors leading to a small room where he kept the accounts. Indeed, there were so many twists and turns, Sarah wondered if the servants left clues to mark their way.

"The accounts don't amount to much," Mr. Proctor said. "The land ain't worth a ha'penny so the baron allows the crofters to graze their sheep on the upper heath. Lord Copley be quite heavy in the pockets, Miss Grimsley, and he told me I need not consult him when anything needs doing. He just has me put the bills on his desk in the book-room where he can go over them."

Sarah came to the conclusion that whatever Mr. Proctor had used the money for, it certainly hadn't been to tidy up the castle or see to proper uniforms for the servants.

In turn, Jacob took her around the outer buildings. In the stables an old, sway-backed dray horse stood, head down, snoring. Jacob grinned and whispered, "We use Ol' Hob to pull the wagon to Danbury Wells for supplies, but his lordship says not to overtax him. But that old horse don't seem to know when to quit."

In the next stall, a strange-looking, one-eyed donkey, half striped, half gray stuck his head over the gate.

"His name be Zee," Jacob said, scratching the animal between its ears.

A terrible scar ran across the left side of his head, making him appear quite wicked, but when Sarah reached out, he nuzzled her hand.

"The master always brings him a treat," Jacob said, his face turning red. "I forgot, this morning—escorting you around and all."

The animal snorted and tilted his head sideways to look at Sarah.

"Never you mind, Zee," Sarah said, letting him nibble on her glove. "It is my fault, not Jacob's, that you did not get your sweet. I shall steal some sugar from my tea tray this afternoon." Which she did later she had promised, taking some to Ol' Hob, too.

Sarah's charade filled her with enthusiasm. In three weeks she'd come to love the old castle, exploring every nook and corner, except for the baron's apartments and the towers, quite content with her decision to stay.

She wrote a letter to her parents telling them she was looking forward to the next five months. She didn't consider that to be a lie. At her request, Jacob sought out a tradesman in Danbury Falls traveling to London, and asked him to post the missive when he arrived in the city. She was certain that her parents would think she'd reached her destination and wouldn't expect her to write once she'd entered into the whirl of activities.

One afternoon, Sarah had taken a walk out onto the foggy moors, for she missed her treks into the hills around Elmsdale. She was surprised to find violets already coming up under the shelter of a tor, the strange rock formations that dotted the hills. A little farther on, she'd seen an odd-looking animal walking in the haze, but thinking the mist had caused her to imagine things which were not there, she made no mention of it to anyone. She did tell Jacob about the violets, though.

The man's eyes widened. "Oh, ma'am, his lordship don't allow anyone out of the Park. Too dangerous, he says. Even animals get caught in the bogs."

"Oh, fudge, Jacob. One has only to follow the sheep or pony paths to stay safe."

Jacob twisted his hat in his hands. "I'll get a right good setdown when the master finds out I let you go onto the moors by yerself."

Sarah pursed her lips and stared at the flustered man over the rims of her spectacles. "Then we just won't tell him, will we?"

The servant's face lit up with a grin. "Indeed not, Miss Grimsley. If you say so."

"Well, I do, Jacob. We will say no more about it."

Jacob seemed so relieved to drop the subject, Sarah never told him again when she took a walk.

Now, while she reviewed all that she'd accomplished, Sarah watched Nooney cross the room. The morning routine had become an accepted ritual and Sarah could count the number of steps and the minutes it would take for the servants to accomplish each procedure. Routine gave one such comfort, Sarah thought. It erased the chance of surprise, and her life had surely been full of surprises of late.

Sarah had picked the tall, pleasant-faced farm girl to serve her, because the good-natured Nooney, though of simple mind, was the most obliging of the new maids. If Miss Grimsley chose to dress herself, that was all right with Nooney. If she wished a plate stacked with enough cinnamon buns to feed a field of workers, who was she to question the habits of the Quality? This morning, however, the girl didn't follow the usual pattern. Instead, she turned at the doorway and stood, hands folded in her apron, and stared at the bed.

"Is there something you wished to say, Nooney?" Sarah asked, peering out from beneath her pillow.

The girl bobbed a curtsy. "Aye, mum. I am to tell you that his lordship come in the middle of the night. He says he wishes to see you in the library as soon as you finished your breakfast." With that the girl sped out into the corridor.

Sarah sat upright. "Lord Copley?" she called out. "What is he doing here?" But the maid had already disappeared. Was it the practice of rascals to always come and go in the middle of the night? She threw off the covers and clambered down the steps beside the bed.

What was the matter with her? Of course, he had a right to be here. After all, it was his home. She'd been so busy establishing an efficient and orderly pattern of behavior throughout the castle that she lost track of the fact that sometime in the future she must face the baron.

Sarah ran over to the tray, poured herself a cup of chocolate and took a big gulp, only to cough when the hot liquid nearly scalded her throat. Fanning her mouth, she hurried to the clothes press to find something appropriate to wear to meet his lordship.

As Sarah rifled through the dresses, she recalled the baron's letters. On the day that she'd awakened in this bedchamber and Mrs. Proctor mistook her for Miss Grimsley, Sarah had made it her first priority to read them through. They'd outlined what was expected of her. The first letter had begun:

My dear Miss Grimsley,

It is with great sorrow that we heard of the passing of the Duke of Warrick. With all due respect to your time of mourning for your late friend, may I place my plight before you. I own a large castle, in Devonshire, which I wish to make more pleasant for entertaining. Being a bachelor, I have no wife to act as hostess. Your reputation as a hostess, nonpareil, has come to my attention and it has occurred to me that you may be looking for a new place of residence.

Though I never had the pleasure of attending any of the duke's hunts in Cornwall, reports from my friends who have, said their praise could not do justice to your warm hospitality and many talents.

Roxwealde Castle has over one hundred rooms, but I shall need only a small portion of those opened for the intimate type of parties I have in mind. I do not believe I need to elaborate more. My staff is discreet and loyal. You will have carte blanche to effect any changes you deem necessary to make Roxwealde more comfortable. I assure you, expense is of little consequence.

If you have any interest in my offer, you may contact me at my London residence. I remain your most humble servant.

Lord Copley's signature was scribbled across the bottom of the page.

Of course, Miss Grimsley accepted the baron's offer, she'd told Sarah as much when they journeyed together.

In one missive, his lordship decreed that the ladies as

well as the gentlemen were to occupy their usual rooms on the second floor in the East Wing. This Sarah thought strange, for when her mother and father entertained, the single women and men slept in different sections of the house.

"I find it quite unusual, Mrs. Proctor, that the baron failed to mention what sort of entertainment he wished for me to arrange for his guests. Surely they will be bored if they have no activities planned."

For some reason, the good woman found this quite amusing, and it was some time before she stopped laughing. "No need ye worrying yerself about that, dear. His lordship's friends find no difficulty in entertaining theyselves."

Now, the baron had returned and wanted to interview her. Sarah stuffed the feather pillow under the cumbersome corset before struggling into a dress of brilliant blue velvet. A long swatch of the fabric sewn to one shoulder hung nearly to the floor. Since she'd never seen a fashion like it before except in an illustrated book on ancient Rome, Sarah ascertained that it was meant to be wrapped around her shoulders and draped over one arm like a palla. Perhaps Miss Grimsley had thought it made her look slimmer. Next, Sarah chose to make a demi-turban of blue muslin wrapped around her head and tied in a bow at the side.

She'd noticed Miss Grimsley's predilection for large pieces of jewelry, so she placed four large-stoned rings on her fingers, settled for several chains of gold around her neck and finished her costume with a deep, blue topaz in a gold clasp onto the front of the headpiece.

To her surprise, Sarah discovered the source of Miss Grimsley's cherry cheeks was in a little pot of creme. Sarah never used any sort of cosmetics in her life, but she knew if she were to play her roll with authenticity, she couldn't take the chance of looking a green country girl in front of the baron. Dipping her finger into the rouge, she made little pink circles under her eyes.

Sarah's anxiety had destroyed her appetite. Nevertheless, she popped a whole cinnamon bun into her mouth. She pushed it into one cheek, then forced another into the other side.

After that first day when she'd tried to blow out her cheeks to plump out her face, Sarah had found it not a practical practice. Her voice sounded like something between a goose and a frog, for she discovered it impossible to hold her breath, puff up her cheeks, and speak at the same time. She tried handkerchiefs wadded into balls, but they made her mouth dry and the lace tickled her tongue. It wasn't until she was chewing a cinnamon bun and chanced to glance into the mirror, that she realized she'd found the solution to making her face look fuller. From then on, she had Cook send up a platter of buns each morning, which lasted her all day.

With one last dab of powder, Sarah placed the spectacles on the tip of her nose and marched out the door to meet Lord Copley. Now, she'd find out how well she'd pleased his lordship.

Four

The corridors were empty when Sarah made her way down the wide staircase, across the flagstoned Great Hall and past the pillars which supported the upper balcony. She encountered nary a soul and arrived outside the library door to find it slightly ajar. No sound came from inside. Nevertheless, in case his lordship had arrived before her and was engaged in some weighty matter, she thought it best to knock before entering. She no sooner raised her hand than a string of shocking oaths colored the air.

Sarah inhaled so quickly that her feather pillow fell halfway to her knees before she caught it. Whoever was in Lord Copley's library needed to be confronted before the baron appeared. It had to be one of the newly-hired servants. After she'd chastised a footman in front of all the others for taking the Lord's name in vain, none of the former staff would dare speak in such a manner.

Stuffing the pillow into place, Sarah gingerly opened the door wide enough to slip inside. She glanced quickly about the room, but saw no one. Had the voice come from elsewhere in the castle? The vast rooms tended to throw the sound about in queer ways.

The morning light flowing in through the leaded-glass window was like a path of pale cotton gauze, dividing the room in half. Typical of a snowy day, but it was too late in the year for that surely, she thought.

There were rows of empty shelves. She had come to an

early conclusion that the library was seldom used for reading. She'd organized what few books there were into a coherent arrangement of sorts, for they had been scattered about as haphazardly as everything else in the room. There were some books on animals, a few collections of sonnets, and treatises in Old English script.

With dismay she had watched Mr. Proctor toss the castle bills helterskelter on the wide mahogany partner's-desk, the only piece of furniture of recent vintage that she'd found in the room. He was indeed a faithful retainer, but he proved to be as lackadaisical as the rest of the staff. He'd told her his lordship could well afford the expenses she was incurring, but she still looked with dismay as the pile of notices grew daily. Although Mr. Proctor insisted that they were no concern of hers, Sarah had taken it upon herself to stack the papers neatly, place the refilled ink pot in easy reach on the right side of the desk with the pens sharpened and laid in orderly formation near it. She didn't want the baron to think her negligent in her duties.

The gray morning light blanketed the desk at the other end of the room. Sarah squinted to adjust her eyes to the shadows and gasped. The ink pot lay on its side, its black contents leaking out across the leather-insert working surface, soaking into the papers she'd so carefully arranged the day before. A rustling sound came from behind the desk. There *was* someone in the room and whoever it was, was hiding. Whatever would the baron think of her if he found she'd brought a thief into his house?

A barely audible masculine growl emanating from the shadows sent a frisson of fear running down Sarah's spine. She grabbed the first weapon which came to hand, a small bronze statue of Mercury in flight, highly polished, of course, now that Sarah was in charge. Grasping the god by his neck, she raised him over her head and advanced across the room.

From the misty netherworld on the other side, a hand

reached up and plunked a crumpled sheet of paper on the desktop. A deep voice muttered unintelligible words, which Sarah was just as happy not to understand, if they were anything like the ones which had burned her ears a few seconds ago. Another fistful of papers materialized from nowhere and were dumped unceremoniously on top the others. Then a face appeared, golden hair slightly disheveled, eyes the shade of dark sapphires, a straight, aristocratic nose, and lips drawn in a taut line. One hand clutched his forehead. Even with the deep furrows creasing his brow, she recognized him.

"Lord Copley!" Sarah stood, arms frozen in an arch over her head. Mercury looked down on them.

The baron's startled expression mirrored hers. He rose quickly. He was in his shirtsleeves and vest, his neckcloth rumpled, but even in his disarray she could see the broad shoulders and narrow hips were as magnificently formed as his face.

He stared for a moment. "Miss Grimsley?" Then he glanced up at the metal object raised over her head, and the corner of his mouth twitched.

Sarah followed his amused upward gaze and for the first time realized why the housemaids had giggled when she told them to polish all the statues in the library. Except for his winged sandals and his jaunty hat, the little messenger had not a stitch of clothing on. Sarah wasn't quite sure when the realization occurred to her that the male before her was most likely modeled in a similar manner, but when it did, a shocking warmth spread throughout her body.

The baron quickly donned his coat which was draped over a nearby chair and ran his fingers through his hair. "I hope you do not intend to use that on me."

Trying desperately to keep her hands from shaking, Sarah placed the sculpture on the edge of the desk, turning the little god first one way then another to find the least embarrassing angle to present to Lord Copley. Oh, what must the baron think of her? But she decided she was not going to swoon. Hoping to divert his attention away from the embarrassing object, she stared him bravely in the eye. "You should take care, my lord. You could have been taken for a thief."

He laughed boldly. Then showing what Sarah took to be complacent disregard for the danger such foolishness could bring down upon him, Lord Copley reached over and slowly turned the idol in a complete circle. "I thank God that I left my home in such good hands, Miss Grimsley."

The glint she saw in his eyes nearly did her in. Oh, he was a rascal all right, just as the real Miss Grimsley had declared.

Andersen stared at the shimmering blue cloud across from him. He had never seen such an outlandish costume. The great topaz in her turban flashed at him like some omniscient eye. The Duke of Warrick had been known to be extravagant when it came to his own pleasures, but his reputation for being a nipcheese with his paramours had been equally well known. Anything so ostentatious had to be paste. But he had to admit, Miss Grimsley carried it off so well that it would take a true expert to tell that the stone wasn't genuine. But that was what he wanted, wasn't it? An original?

He straightened his neckcloth. "Your sense of style is legendary, madam. I am not usually this easily disconcerted, but some fool, excuse my language . . . put my pens on the right side of the desk." The papers he still held in his other hand, he pitched with no apparent thought of where they landed, making more havoc out of mayhem.

"Proctor knows that I am left-handed and always places my ink and pens on that side. Someone else was in here. That will never do."

"Left-handed?" As some of the cinnamon buns slipped down her throat, tears welled up in Sarah's eyes. Her voice croaked. "No one told me."

For some reason Miss Grimsley thought he was accusing her, and he couldn't understand why. He feared he was making a muddle of the situation, and he desperately needed her expertise if he was to pull off this escapade. He knew nothing about organizing a large country party. That was a woman's job. And as hostess for the Duke of Warrick. Miss Grimsley had entertained many people of wealth and high position.

Andersen took out a handkerchief and wiped his ink-blackened fingers. "I am sorry, I did not mean to take out my frustration on you, dear lady. Don't blame yourself for the blunder of a serving girl. I am certain she meant well. Most people do." He came around the desk and taking her hand bowed over it. "My only excuse is that I arrived quite late, last evening and have had little sleep. Please forgive me."

In no way was Sarah going to tell his lordship that she was the *fool* who rearranged his desk accessories. She glanced from the golden hair, now molded into a misleading halo, to the stained paper, to the soiled handkerchief on the floor. Oh, she saw right away that she was going to have to take the baron in hand, or the castle would soon be back in its original untidy state.

Then, Lord Copley raised his head and smiled—a beguiling smile which shot right into Sarah. She didn't know what happened only that at that moment, she would have forgiven him anything.

Sarah withdrew her hand and pretended to straighten the long shawl draped over her arm. What had he done to her? Nothing Mama had said had prepared her for such a man. Her face burned, and it was a certainty her brains had been put into a butter churn.

To hide her flaming face, Sarah began puttering about the desk, moving the pens to the left side and straightening up the ink pot. Thank goodness, all the ink hadn't run out. But, oh, the mess. The baron didn't seem the least concerned that he'd scrambled most of the papers which she'd so carefully stacked. Yes, his lordship was definitely going to be a challenge.

When she turned toward the window, Andersen saw Miss Grimsley more clearly. Her face was much more youthful than he'd expected. He couldn't see her eyes well behind the rims of her spectacles, but he'd say she was pretty in a plump way. She'd been one of the Warrick's favorites, hadn't she? If the stories were true, she'd been taken under the duke's protection when barely seventeen. That would mean she was even younger than he. A man was considered in his prime at the age of twenty and nine, but everyone knew a woman of that age who had never married was destined to be left on the shelf. However, he now had more challenging problems on his mind than contemplating how old his new hostess was. "Won't you be seated, Miss Grimsley?"

Sarah hesitated to sit down. What if she couldn't get up again? She cast about for an excuse that would permit her to remain standing. "Wouldn't you like for me to show you what improvements I have made in the castle, my lord?"

Andersen shook his head. "Later. I have come to discuss far more urgent matters, Miss Grimsley." When he saw her look of disappointment he added quickly, "Jacob answered the door for me last night. All I can say is that if you were able to make that big fustian look and act like a proper footman, your improvements are bordering on the miraculous."

When Sarah saw that the baron was not about to leave the library, she rounded the desk and eased herself into the heavy, medieval chair behind it. His lordship may be aggrieved that she took his seat, but it was the only one with a straight back and arms to give her support. If it bothered him that she usurped his position, he didn't press the point, for he continued to stand on the other side of the desk.

In the meantime, Andersen watched Miss Grimsley warily from the corner of his eye, contemplating how much he should reveal to her.

He couldn't very well pull off this charade without her help. How much should he tell her of his choice of guests? She, of course, must understand that none of the shenanigans which she permitted to transpire at the duke's hunting estate would be condoned here. His only choice was to confide that the true purpose for his party was to choose a wife.

Andersen rubbed his head. He'd cracked it on the underside of the desk, just before Miss Grimsley entered the room. He'd been trying to retrieve the fallen papers. It was about at that same point that he'd become aware of a very pleasant scent. The same sweet aroma which now pervaded the air. It was of short duration, but left him quite disoriented as if he'd been transported to another time and place.

Andersen cleared his throat. "Regarding the letters I wrote you, Miss Grimsley——"

Sarah relaxed. She was on more comfortable ground now. She'd tried her best to carry out every one of his directives. "I read them all, your lordship. Quite thoroughly."

"Well, I want you to disregard everything I told you."

Sarah blinked. "Disregard . . . everything?"

He turned and started to pace. "I have changed my plans. Instead of the little intimate rendezvous. I shall be hosting a large party. A very large party."

Confusion sent Sarah's thoughts somersaulting. Here she'd thought to start in a small way. Break in bit by bit to the ways of le beau monde.

Lord Copley swung around and winked. At least Sarah thought he winked. "This country party is to be an entirely different sort of festivity than that which you were planning."

"It is?"

Sarah didn't know if he was teasing her or not, for although her mother had a gay disposition and her father was not a gloomy man, they didn't banter with their daughter. "Are you bamming me, your lordship?"

Lord Copley pulled up a chair on the other side of the desk and sat down. There was that devastating smile again. "Heaven forbid I tease you, Miss Grimsley, this is altogether a very serious business."

His closeness unnerved her, and Sarah picked up a quill pen to keep her fingers from fidgeting. She didn't have the vaguest idea of how to respond to this game of verbal shuttlecock. Lord Copley denied that he was making fun of her, yet the gleam in his eye counteracted that declaration.

Not about to be intimidated, Sarah responded forcefully, "Explain yourself, my lord."

When Miss Grimsley spoke, Andersen had the most unbelievable sense of euphoria come over him. More a feeling of contentment than sensuality. A memory long hidden, but he couldn't quite put a finger on it. Just as he thought he'd remembered, it darted away before he could grasp it.

"Lord Copley?"

Andersen jumped.

"I thought I'd lost you. You were saying?"

Andersen sniffed the air, and his mouth began to water. "If I may be so bold as to ask, what is that scent you are wearing, Miss Grimsley?"

"Scent?" Sarah asked vacantly. She wasn't wearing any scent. The perfumes Miss Grimsley had in her bag were so heavy they made her sneeze.

"It is most pleasant."

Sarah blinked. "Thank you, my lord." For a moment she thought she saw admiration in his eyes, but she had to be mistaken.

The baron leaned closer. "Miss Grimsley, I believe I can confide in you. I am giving this party to choose a wife." He followed briefly with the tale of the Copley entail—that he must be married before his thirtieth birthday. He left out the minor details of his bankruptcy. That bit of information would remain between Peter and himself. He then told her of his other friends, Basil Ripple, Henry Smith, and the Marquis of Wetherby, who had all agreed to enter into the conspiracy.

"So you see, we will need more accommodations."

Sarah couldn't believe her ears. "You have made a complete list of your guests, of course."

"Why, no. Should I have?"

"Definitely, if you expect me to know the right number of rooms to ready. Sarah was beginning to suspect that it was a trait of all men to be impractical, not just her father. She pulled out a drawer and removed a clean sheet of foolscap. "Dictate the names and I shall write them down. Also, I will need a bit of information about each."

Andersen raised an eyebrow, his confusion showing.

Sarah resigned herself to be the one to set things in motion. "How much time shall you need with each young woman? Will half a day turnabout be satisfactory, or do you need a full day for a courtship?" Having never been pursued in the high style her mother spoke of so longingly, and only having her own experience of listening to the vicar rehearse his sermons on her, Sarah had no idea whatsoever as to the length of time it took for a man to successfully woo his lady. And what part did the female take in this game? It was a puzzle but she pursed her lips and tried to look knowledgeable about the subject.

"Is all this necessary, Miss Grimsley?"

"Yes, my lord, if one is to do a thing up brown, it must be done correctly."

He thought a bit. "I daresay, you are right. Well, I would say it depends upon the woman. If she is shy, a man must proceed slowly—give in to her sensibilities. If a man senses she is already attracted to him and eager to further the relationship, he can go all-out, neck or nothing, so to speak. It is understood that a true lady does not *have* to please the gentleman if she has better prospects. Is that the sort of thing you want to know?"

Sarah bent over the sheet of foolscap, writing furiously. "Oh, my, yes, of course," she said, wishing she knew what he was talking about.

As if he were conjuring up an image, the baron fixed his gaze on the far wall. "Lady Caroline is the most beautiful, and the daughter of an earl. She carries herself well, and speaks in well modulated tones. Prides herself in her impeccable dress—as a woman of her station should. I don't believe I have ever seen a hair on her head out of place."

Andersen heard a "Humph," and glanced down at the turbaned head, bobbing over the paper. "Is it necessary for you to write down everything I say, Miss Grimsley?"

She didn't look up. "It is important for me to keep a record of each lady, my lord. How else am I to plan your days?"

Andersen raised his brows, but continued, "Miss Anne Bennington will be accompanied by her parents. The Benningtons are landed gentry, an old, well-connected, aristocratic family. Their main seat is in Herefordshire with substantial farms in three other counties. High-ton. She is the eldest of seven daughters, so I know they are pressing her to marry—and marry well—for two of her sisters are making their come-out this year. They have one son who is in his first year at Oxford." Andersen laughed. "I hear Mr. Bennington does not enjoy the nonsense of the London Season and wishes to find husbands for all his daughters as soon as possible." Consequently he has offered more than substantial dowries, especially for his first born, he added under his breath.

Sarah scribbled faster.

"Miss Beverly Martin is coming with her aunt, Lady Martin, a widow."

Sarah didn't think that much to go on. "And since I am listing them, what are that young lady's attributes?"

Andersen pondered a moment, then laughed. "Well, Miss Martin tends to be a loose-screw. Never know what Bev is going to do next."

"And her appearance?"

"Very handsome, I would say. She was orphaned several years ago. More or less brought herself up."

"Oh, how sad," Sarah commiserated, thinking how lonely life would be without her parents. For a moment, homesickness threatened to overwhelm her, and she wiped a tear from her cheek. "It must have been hard for her."

Andersen guffawed. "Not with the special will her father had drawn up making her his sole heir. The lady is rolling in money and property. She is a bruising rider, breeds flying leapers for the hunt—which gives you an idea of her independent spirit." Andersen thought of his own blooded stallion, Hamilton, which Beverly had admired often. "It will take a husband with a strong hand and a love of bold cattle to rein in Miss Martin."

Sarah ran her finger down the names. "I thought you said you had invited four ladies."

"Oh, yes, Miss Edith Tremain. Miss Tremain is coming with her cousin Miss Glover, an elderly woman, I believe."

She wrote *elderly* beside Miss Glover's name.

"Miss Tremain and her companion will not be bringing any personal maids, so you will assign them someone from my staff."

Sarah made another note to appoint a footman to help the older woman up and down the stairs.

The baron looked down at his hands. "By-the-by, you need not arrange time for me to be alone with Miss Tremain. Assign a different one of my friends to escort her each day as you will the others."

"Why is that? Is something wrong with her?"

Andersen's conscience plunged. He couldn't very well tell Miss Grimsley that although Edith Tremain was as genteel a lady as he'd ever known, she possessed no dowry.

He'd placed her high on his list of acceptable brides when he thought he was heavy in the pockets. Now that he faced the threat of landing in debtor's prison, he had to eliminate her as a candidate.

"Let me say she is not suitable."

"She is ugly?"

"On the contrary, she is quite attractive."

"She has a mean disposition then."

"Nonsense. Everyone who is acquainted with Edith, that is Miss Tremain, knows she has the heart of an angel." Andersen snapped, shooting Miss Grimsley a dark look. "Miss Grimsley, you asked me to give you a portrayal of my guests. I am doing just that."

My, the baron was touchy over the subject of Miss Tremain. Sarah wondered why.

Thinking perhaps he'd spoken too abruptly, Andersen decided to show his concern for Edith. "You have the approximate number of attendants accompanying each family, and I will give Mr. Proctor orders to see that extra stalls in the stables are ready. I have arranged to have a mount available for Miss Tremain. She is the only one who does not own a riding horse". The baron paused a moment. "All, I should say, except for Mr. Ripple."

Sarah looked up. "You cannot bring a horse for him?"

"Won't do any good. Basil is petrified of horseflesh. Hasn't sat a horse since his pony threw him when he was five years old. Nearly have to blindfold him to get him into a carriage."

"Well, I am sure he can find other diversions to occupy his time."

Andersen grinned. "I'm certain you are right, Miss Grimsley."

She sat staring at the paper so long, Andersen began to feel uneasy. "Miss Grimsley? Is something amiss?"

Sarah jumped. "Oh, no, your lordship. I have just made the most amazing observation. The women's names are almost sequential to the alphabet. Anne becomes A, Beverly becomes B, and C for Caroline. We have to jump a letter and then there is E for Edith. It will be so much easier to make out a schedule for the men if they are able to follow the alphabet." She looked up questioningly.

The baron slapped this knee. It was amazing how she could restore his humor. "You are a card, Miss Grimsley. My friends attended Oxford or Cambridge. I think they learned the alphabet."

Tapping her chin with the end of the pen, Sarah nodded as if not quite certain of his appraisal of the situation. "Well, then, I reckon that is the most practical procedure to take," she said philosophically. "Hmm. You could not think of a 'D?' "

For some reason this amused Andersen even more. "If I had thought we would be going back to the schoolroom, madam, I undoubtedly could have come up with one."

She shot him a censorious look over the rims of her spectacles. "For someone who is backed up to the edge of a precipice, my lord, you don't seem to be taking this seriously enough."

Andersen couldn't envision any of the three ladies turning him down, even Lady Caroline, as long as they thought him to be heavy in the pockets. It was only a matter of his making his choice.

Sarah leaned forward and spoke forcefully. "However, it would have been better if the ladies had been perfectly sequential, but it cannot be helped now. I only hope your friends can keep the absence of the letter D in mind when I give them their assignments."

To stop his runaway laughter, Andersen inhaled deeply. No matter how strong her censure, there was something about Miss Grimsley . . . Placing his hands behind his head, Andersen relaxed back in his chair and shut his eyes.

Sarah couldn't imagine what she'd said to bring the pleasurable smile to his lordship's lips, but with his eyes closed she had time to observe him without his being aware of it. Had God ever made a more perfect specimen? She shook her head and prattled on, "Of course, more chambers will have to be readied."

Andersen opened his eyes. "Is that a problem, Miss Grimsley? Do you think Roxwealde Castle in danger of running out of rooms?" He was enjoying the lighthearted bantering with his hostess. She lifted his spirits inmeasurably.

Sarah waved her hand the way she had seen Miss Grimsley do so many times. "Oh, no, no, your lordship. La, the Prince Regent brought as many as twelve of his personal servants with him when he visited in Cornwall."

"Brava, Miss Grimsley. Then it is all settled."

"There is another thing, my lord."

"Yes."

"The additional guests will require more servants. I have quite run through all the Proctor kith and kin. It seems they have an overabundance of sons in their family. It is chambermaids I need. I could post a notice in Danbury Wells, but I fear time is too short to fill the positions and train the girls properly."

Andersen's eyes lit up. "Isn't that a coincidence, Miss Grimsley? I happened to hear only recently of three maids in London who happen to be hunting temporary employment. If that would help you. I could hire them and bring them along with me."

Hope rose in Sarah's heart. "Do they come well recommended?"

"Oh, definitely! They have been given excellent references by some of the highest members of the ton. I dare say they are only novices and have not reached the peak of their profession as you have, but they are always eager to please."

"Then I shall strive to teach them all I can," Sarah said,

remembering something the real Miss Grimsley had told her. "One is never too old, your lordship."

Andersen laughed until he had to cover his eyes with his hands to stop the tears. His spirits were rising already. "You are indeed a most generous woman."

Sarah wondered why a simple thing as instructing chambermaids should gain such praise from Lord Copley, but she basked in his approval nonetheless.

The cinnamon buns had by now completely melted in Sarah's mouth and she knew she must return to her room to get more. It wouldn't do for the baron to see that her face had thinned out considerably during their visit, so she tried to think of a way to get him to dismiss her. Keeping her head lowered, Sarah glanced up through her lashes. Taking advantage of his temporary distraction, she struggled up from her chair. Only then did she address him.

"Your lordship."

Andersen jerked up and seeing Miss Grimsley already standing, leaped from his chair. "I can only excuse my poor manners by my lack of sleep."

She wished she had her fan, but having none, Sarah waved her hand in front of her face to distract him. "I was only going to ask your permission to return to my room. There are some things that need to be taken care of."

"Most certainly, Miss Grimsley. I also have matters with my tenants to attend to this afternoon, and I must visit the vicar in Danbury Wells. I shall start back from there for London to return Friday week. My gentlemen friends will be accompanying me at that time. The other guests should arrive soon after."

As she circled the desk, she tried not to glance at Mercury standing quite shamelessly on the corner. When she reached the door, Lord Copley called, "I have great expectations that we will rub well together, Miss Grimsley."

She still heard his laughter long after she had left the room.

On her way up to her chambers, Sarah encountered a most astonishing character on his way down. The man was tall, not old, and distinguished himself by descending the stairs sideways—feeling out one step at a time and not proceeding until the other foot was securely beside the other. Both hands gripped the railing as if it were a lifeline.

When Sarah came parallel to him, she stopped and smiled. "I am Miss Grimsley. You must have come with Lord Copley."

The man tried to bow and still maintain his hold on the banister. "Fletcher, ma'am. His lardship's man. He wisht t'see me."

If it weren't but ten o'clock in the morning, Sarah would have sworn the man was tipsy. "I just this minute left him in the library."

"Thank you, ma'am."

Sarah watched the valet wander into the middle of the Great Hall and turn around in a complete circle. It was obvious the poor man had trouble keeping his balance. What strange creatures Lord Copley kept around him. After a slight hesitation, the man shuffled to the left. Seeing him headed in the right direction, Sarah shook her head and continued to her room. She must pick up more buns before she hurried belowstairs to find Mrs. Proctor. There was no time to spare if they were to set in motion the baron's new plans. Little more than a week remained to accomplish a miracle.

A shambles greeted Sarah the minute she opened the door. The silver tray lay on one side of the room, the broken china pot on the other. A scattered trail of crumbs were all that remained of the six cinnamon buns. This looked like a child's mischief. But who? Young Cyril could have all the pastries he wanted in the kitchen.

Sarah picked two handkerchiefs to stuff in her cheeks and pulled the bellcord to summon a maid. She had no time to unravel the mystery now.

Five

Nooney stood in the doorway wringing her hands. "Oh, Miss Grimsley, such a mess I never did see."

Sarah was convinced that the maid was as genuinely shocked as she had been when she first viewed the upturned tray and the broken pot. "You have no idea who could have done it?"

Nooney quickly began to pick up the shards of china from the floor. "No, ma'am. I cannot imagine. We have all we can eat in the kitchen. 'Tis just plain mischief, if you ask me."

Further inquiry of the servants gained no more insight into the incident. Jacob was nowhere to be seen all day, but Sarah blamed his absence on the added duties Lord Copley's visit had thrust upon him.

Sarah decided to dismiss the puzzle of the missing buns for there were a great deal more important matters to be tended to in little more than a week's time.

The following days at Roxwealde became a whirligig of activity, and like her twirling childhood toy, Sarah was never still. She hired more servants, opened additional rooms, ordered the carriage way weeded and leveled and the horse paths through the park encircling the castle, raked.

The gray skies showed no promise of changing. Sarah stood with Mr. Proctor on the stone steps at the entranceway to the castle, surveying the work as she did every day. In her opinion the view didn't bode well for attracting a bride.

But commitment to purpose wasn't to be denied because of inclement weather.

"It is reasonable to conclude, Mr. Proctor, that not much can be done with stone and dirt, nor flowers made to grow where there is no soil to nourish them. Even the ivy vines covering the walls of the castle look more like cobwebs than the luxuriant green-leafed plants that flourish in the village. But at least the windows and floors can be scrubbed and the furniture polished."

The steward squinted into the mist. "Aye, ma'am, looks the same today as it did yeste'day and the day before that, don't it?"

Surprisingly Sarah had found much of the old furniture in the castle in good condition, protected as it was all those years under holland covers. However many of the bedrooms were short of essential tables and chairs and a few had only shutters and no curtains on the windows. To remedy the latter, she'd bought out all the nicest fabrics at the draper's in Danbury Wells and set the maids who could sew a fine seam to making curtains and comforters. But far more was needed.

On the fourth day, Sarah was in the attic with Mrs. Proctor looking for suitable furniture to add to the comfort of the many rooms, when she opened an old trunk. Diverse amounts of velvet, silk and brocaded clothing tumbled out. Ladies' dresses and men's costumes of a long ago era, intricately embroidered and appliqued with fine threads and jewels. Among them she found hauberks, a coat of red silk, woolen tunics, and leather belts.

Sarah shook out a voluminous piece of velvet, embroidered around the edges. "This must have been a bedcover. The fabric is thin in spots, but still quite usable. Do you think Lord Copley would mind that we cut out what is good?"

"Law, his lordship asked us to rid the attics of all this old stuff long ago. He said his great-great grandfather, Per-

cival Copley, the first baron, was besotted with stories of
medieval knights." Her arm made a sweep of the dark room.
"The old baron collected all this armour and costumes and
liked to give parties in the old way. We meant to, but we
jest ain't got around to clearing it out. I don't think he
would mind that ye helped yerself."

Sarah held a beautiful silk dress up to the candlelight,
revealing the laced bodice. "Some of these costumes are in
remarkably good condition. The ladies, I am sure, would
find these barbettes and wimple headdresses of great interest."

Mrs. Proctor came closer. "My, ain't they dandy?" she
exclaimed, fingering a cloak with fur trim and jeweled collar. "Almost too fine to be sitting here in a trunk in the
attic."

A thought along those same lines struck Sarah, too. "Do
you think Mr. Proctor could find a carpenter to make us
clotheshorses to drape the costumes on? They would brighten
up the Great Hall considerably. We could line them up against
the walls."

Mrs. Proctor looked as if she wondered why Miss Grimsley
needed to ask such a question. "Indeed, Mr. Proctor does
have a cousin who is a carpenter, and I am certain he will
build you what you want."

During the next few days, Sarah made endless journeys
to the attics, digging into the old trunks, selecting what
relics she wanted brought down to a lower level.

The suits of armour were polished and set up around the
Great Hall like warriors standing their posts. The old
dresses cleaned and pressed stood picturesquely beside their
knights. Most of the men's costumes and the apparel of the
ladies of the court which were still good and not being used
in the Great Hall, were stored in an empty linen closet. The

maids cut up the tattered fabrics and placed them in the rag basket, to be reused in any way they could.

Sarah used the servants' stairway from the kitchen area to go to the attic, but each time she passed the doors to the second floor hallway, she wondered more and more about the baron. What sort of a man was he? Was his apartment decorated in priceless furnishings, or did he prefer simpler things? Only Mr. Proctor and Jacob were allowed to enter Lord Copley's chambers. Sarah didn't want to sound too inquisitive about her employer, but how was she to prepare the way for the baron to choose a wife, if she didn't have more knowledge on what type of man he was?

Oh, she knew he was the most handsome of men and he had a way of bursting into laughter even though he was faced with a serious dilemma, the same dilemma as hers had been, to choose a mate for life. But she didn't have the burden of carrying on the family name. She was sure her father had been quite disappointed in not having a son, for if he should die, the Greenwood properties would pass on to a third cousin on his grandfather's side.

In the meantime the weather turned nastier. The moors looked bleak and weary. The inside of the castle fared no better, for regardless of what Sarah did, the dark furniture, the gray and brown stone and the sunless days only over-shadowed all her efforts to make things look more cheerful.

Miserable thoughts weighed on Sarah's mind as she entered her bedchamber to find her maid adding a brilliant red rose to a bouquet of flowers in a vase on her bureau. The sight chased all gloomy images away.

"Oh, Nooney, they look lovely. Wherever did you find flowers this time of year?"

The maid turned as red as the rose she held. "They aren't real, ma'am. I made them from the swatches you put in the rag basket."

"I did not know you possessed such talents. How bright it makes the room look."

Now, her spirits much recovered, Sarah tapped her chin with her spectacles. contemplating new possibilities. "Do you think you could teach the other girls to make flowers? There are so many scraps of fabric left over."

"Oh, aye, ma'am. It is really quite simple." Nooney said, drawing a piece of string tightly around a swatch of fabric and giving it a twist. "And I am sure they would love making them after supper. There really isn't much to do of an eve once the chores are done. We could turn the castle into a blooming garden, we could."

"Then that is your new assignment, Nooney. With your help, we will bring springtime to Roxwealde."

In the days that followed the weather turned worse. Although it didn't rain, the mists swirled constantly. The wind often whistled plaintively and other times howled like a wild beast up the twisting towers and through the vast corridors of the castle.

For three nights Sarah heard strange noises emanating from above her room, which prompted her to ask, "Are there any ghosts in the castle, Mrs. Proctor?"

"I have never met one, dear. Not that I wouldn't ha' welcomed a bit of company these lonely days before ye come. Why d' ye ask?"

Sarah didn't know much about haunts or their habits. "It is just that most old houses in England liked to boast of a spirit or two, and I wondered about the noises I heard."

Mrs. Proctor bent over laughing and slapped her knee. "Every time a door be opened, the air whooshes in, twisting and turning up the towers and down the halls. Sounds like wild beasts, don't it?"

"That it does," Sarah said, feeling foolish. She knew that there were many entrances to the castle on all sides. All were quite accessible to anyone who wished to use them, except those leading to the baron's second floor apartments. The front stairway to the second floor wasn't used, except when Lord Copley was in residence.

This afternoon Sarah had returned to rest awhile after nuncheon. It was a windless day and yet above her room, she heard the eerie cries commence. Naughty thoughts niggled Sarah. She glanced at the ceiling and wondered if she dared go abovestairs. Hesitation didn't go hand in hand with Sarah's questions at that moment. In case she encountered a servant, she replenished the buns in her mouth, then quietly opened her door.

Call it curiosity, but Sarah thought it the only sensible decision. She climbed the stairs to the second floor to inspect Lord Copley's apartment. Surely, she needed to know as much about his lordship's character as she could if she were going to carry off this charade. What better way was there to know a man than to see the rooms where he spent a great deal of his time? A blush spread across her face as a picture of Mercury in flight passed through her mind. But nothing was going to divert Sarah from her purpose. She let herself into the first room she came to, its ornate portal leading her to believe it the master's bedchamber.

The hinges squeaked so loudly that she only partially closed the door behind her. The corridor had been dark, but there was light enough coming in the window to show her that the room was large, a hodgepodge of clutter. The baron's enormous bed was higher than her own, its linens askew, its comforter hanging over the side. It looked as if someone had been sleeping in it only recently. The rest of the room was a jumble of covered furniture and sealed crates. Shards of a broken vase lay scattered about the stones on the hearth. Sarah shook her head in disbelief. For a man so clearly attentive to his own appearance, the baron seemed wrecklessly nonchalant about his surroundings. She was beginning to have her doubts about his man, Fletcher, too. Wasn't it his duty to see that his master's rooms were tidied before they left?

Sarah was about to straighten the counterpane on the bed when she heard a grating sound behind her. She knew the door was being pushed open. Caught in the act! Guilt of her trespass spread over her like fire, and she turned slowly to face her accuser. Two large, black-rimmed, yellow eyes stared back. Sarah had only seen a lion once before in her life in London all those years ago, but wasn't difficult to identify this scraggly beast as one.

She watched the cat raise a paw and lower it to raise the other, advancing inches at a time. Her mouth was too dry to call for help. Quickly, she looked about the room for some means of escape. If she could only put the chair between herself and the lion before he devoured her. From the glint in his eyes, that was exactly what he had in mind.

But it was too late for action. The lion leaped and pinned Sarah to the floor. Still grasping the corner of the bedcover, Sarah found herself staring into the beast's open jaws. The last of the cinnamon buns disappeared down her throat. Sarah was certain her end had come, but instead of biting her head off, his long scratchy tongue licked her face. Then he removed his paw from her stomach and rubbed his head along the length of her body.

A voice called from the corridor, "Dog! You hairy scoundrel. Are you in there?"

Sarah raised her head to see a man silhouetted in the doorway. She took the cat's momentary distraction to try to rise, but the animal seemed intent on keeping her prisoner.

Jacob leaped forward. "Oh, my! Miss Grimsley. Are you all right? I have no idea how Dog got out. I distinctly heard the latch click when I turned the key in the lock. The master will have my hide."

Suddenly what the servant said hit Sarah. "Dog? This monster is Dog?"

The lion gave Sarah's face another lick.

"He does that when he likes somebody," Jacob said apologetically, pulling without success on the lion's collar.

Wriggling away from the lion, Sarah rose clumsily, to find that the pillow over her stomach had shifted to the left.

Pretending to brush off her skirt, she pulled the stuffing back into place before Jacob could notice her sudden disfigurement.

Sarah wasn't yet fully in control of her emotions to be generous. "How in the world is it that Lord Copley has a lion in the house?"

Jacob pushed the animal to the side and picked up the spectacles from where they'd fallen on the floor. "The master heard the beast was to be put down. He doesn't like for us to mention it, ma'am, but his lordship has a soft spot in his heart for poor creatures."

Dog sat down and licked his chops.

Sarah gave the lion a scathing look. "That explains the striped donkey in the stable?"

"Aye, ma'am. Zee's papa was a zebra. Escaped from a traveling show and took up with a crofter's donkey. When Zee was foaled, the man beat him all the time. Said he was the devil's spawn. The master saw him take a stick to the animal one day and bought him."

"And that funny-looking deer on the moor?"

Jacob's eye's widened. "That be a reindeer. How did you see him? He doesn't usually come near the house. A Scotsman brought a herd from Norway for his hunting friend's to have a new kind of trophy on their walls. But that one grew only one antler. Made him look like a lopsided mule and no one wanted him. Lord Copley's sentiments being what they are, he brought him to Roxwealde. He said it ain't anybody's fault they get borned different. You didn't spy anything else, did you?"

"No, I did not."

Sarah put her spectacles back on and adjusted her turban. She was seeing a side of the baron she hadn't suspected. Was this the jovial man who refused to take his own fate seriously? If so, she felt it her duty to inform him that it was dangerous having a wild beast in the castle.

Jacob shuffled one foot, then the other, while his gaze

flicked nervously from Dog to her. "Lord Copley trusts me to care for the wild ones, ma'am, and I be overcome with guilt if his lordship think me failing in m' duties."

A surge of sympathy for the servant's plight curbed Sarah's impulse to want to reprimand the baron for his irresponsibility. Besides, if she spoke to Lord Copley, he'd not only know about the servant's negligence, but in turn she'd be informing him of her own trespass into his bedchamber. She'd backed herself into a corner.

In the meantime, the object of their disapproval, Dog, showing no remorse for his abysmal manners, padded up the step stool onto the expansive bed and began pawing at the coverlet.

Sarah stared in amazement as the large cat burrowed under the quilt, until only a huge mound with a tail sticking out remained. "Whatever is he doing?"

Jacob held up his hands, an expression of helplessness on his face. "He misses his master. Sneaks in here whenever he can."

Having regained her composure, Sarah stepped forward and threw back the coverlet, exposing the animal. "Well, I never," she admonished, not being taken in for a moment by the woeful eyes staring back at her. "He certainly cannot stay here."

Jacob leaped forward. "Oh, no, ma'am," he said, taking hold of the lion's collar and giving a fruitless tug.

Now that she knew the beast wasn't going to make a meal of her, Sarah's sense of propriety returned, and stamping her foot, pointed to the floor. "Off!" she ordered.

Dog, his gaze never leaving hers, slid stiffly over the edge. Sarah pointed toward the door. "Now, out with you!"

Head hanging low, tail dragging, the lion padded into the hall.

"How did you do that? Jacob asked, following the lion. "That is remarkable."

"That is what my Mama is always saying," Sarah said.

"There is really nothing remarkable about it at all. Animals must learn discipline or they will become quite impossible." As she watched Jacob tug on the beast's collar, she sighed. If only people were as easily trained as animals. "You must speak with authority. Do not tug at him."

"Yes, ma'am," Jacob said, pulling again unsuccessfully. Dog braced his front feet and refused to move.

Sarah wrinkled her nose. "He smells."

"Can't very well give a lion a bath, ma'am."

"No, I reckon not. But you will have to take Lord Copley's sheets to Mrs. Proctor to have them washed. Surely something can be done to make that animal's odor more agreeable."

Eyes wide, Dog looked back and forth between his critics as if waiting to hear their decision.

Sarah shook her finger at the animal. "However, I believe your first concern is to get him back to his room. And Jacob—"

"Yes, ma'am?"

"I think the less said about our little adventure this afternoon the better."

With a look of relief, Jacob grinned and touched his forelock. "Oh, aye, Miss Grimsley. Mums the word."

Sarah said sternly, "Dog, go!" She watched the big animal pad softly down the corridor after the obliging man. Then she hurried back to the front stairway and down to her rooms.

Andersen had made it back to London in a record three days. Now that all was settled with Miss Grimsley, he threw himself wholeheartedly into wrapping up the loose ends before his party. Regardless of his financial status, he had to maintain the appearance that all was well. Thank God, his unsuspecting creditors still accepted his signature. The family coach was freshly painted, the Copley heraldic aims prominently displayed on its doors. He'd outfitted his coachmen in new liveries, and fine teams of four were posted at inns along the way to Devon. He'd hired a hack to carry Penny, Twist, and Genevieve, the three actresses. Fletcher was given the responsibility of seeing to his wardrobe. Most importantly, Andersen picked up the special license he'd applied for. On his way through Danbury Wells, he'd stopped and informed the vicar that there would be a wedding at the end of next month.

Peter Trummel had arrived that afternoon ready to accompany the baron to Devonshire in his own carriage. Now, he sat occupying his usual chair before the fireplace, listening to his friend's interpretation of his journey to Roxwealde Hall.

"We shall refer to the ladies as A, B, C, and E, for Anne, Beverly, Caroline and Edith. That way no one will hear a name and be able to cipher what we are doing."

"Haven't heard anything so preposterous in a long time." Then added, with a mischievous grin, "But you forgot D."

Andersen acted as if he didn't hear his friend's last remark. "Miss Grimsley was quite agreeable when I confided to her what I needed."

Peter frowned. "Do you think that was wise?"

Andersen laughed. "I believe she understands fully what has to be done and said we must have substitutes for their names. It is she who came up with the A, B, C, E succedaneum. Surely after living twelve years catering to one of the most devious rakes in England, Miss Grimsley knows exactly what to do to make my venture successful. Don't worry, Peter, she is quite a clever woman. Of course, I kept back the fact that I was empty in the pockets. I only told her that because of the entail, the purpose of my party is to find a wife."

"This is a dangerous game you are playing, Andy. What happens if you are found out?"

"Never fear, Trummel. Just because I have lost my fortune, does not mean that I have lost the art of charming a lady. Why, I even persuaded the incomparable Miss Grimsley into letting me hire the three actresses as chambermaids. She thanked me for being so helpful."

Peter shook his head. "Someday you will find you have stirred the pot once too many times. Then where will you be?"

Andersen chose to ignore the gibe and pulled the bell rope. Then absentmindedly reaching over the side of his chair, he stroked vacant air.

"Damned if I don't miss that old lion."

Peter's look of relief left no doubt as to his thinking on the subject.

When Fletcher entered the room, Andersen held his empty glass up to be refilled. "By-the-by, Fletcher. Did you remember to tell Cook that I wanted cinnamon buns for breakfast?"

"Yes, m'lord. I did. Same as yesterday and the day before."

Peter looked quizzically at the baron.

Andersen shrugged. "Strangest thing. I have suddenly developed a ferocious appetite for cinnamon buns. Haven't thought about them for years, but our cook at the house I was raised in used to make the most delicious breads. When Bertie and I managed to escape the scrutiny of our nurse, we'd sneak down the servants' stairs to the kitchen. Cook would let us sit at a long table and eat our fill until we culprits were discovered and returned to the nursery. Those were some of my warmest memories of childhood."

Peter gave a bark of laughter. "This is the great lover?"

"Cut line, Trummel. That is another matter altogether. And as to the subject at hand, I want you to remember that Lady Caroline is my main target."

While the Lord Copley and Peter Trummel were discussing their plans in London, Randolph Cavendish, the seventh

Earl of Favor sat behind his huge baronial desk in his impressive study at his country estate in Gloucestershire. His fingers drummed a tattoo on the desktop while his eyes stared at the doors as if commanding them to open.

Shelves of books lined the walls on three sides, though seldom was a volume removed from its place. Busts of Socrates, Plato, Aristotle and some forgotten Roman emperor sat on ornate marble pedestals, giving the impression that great thoughts emanated from this room. The word *study* was a misnomer, for the earl seldom contemplated anything in this room more serious than his next pleasure trip to London or the extent of his wine cellar.

When the doors finally opened, he leaned back, steepled his fingers and waited for his daughter to come to him.

"What took you so long?"

Lady Caroline, the plumes on her wide-brimmed hat bouncing up and down, swept into the room. Her short, fur-lined military jacket of Bishop's blue, topping her riding habit, suited her well. Impatiently she slapped her whip against the side of her skirt. "Father, you know it is inconvenient for me at this hour. My morning ride will be delayed."

"Don't be impertinent, daughter. I do not give a fig for your inconvenience." He pointed to a chair. "Sit down."

Pouting, Lady Caroline did as she was bid. One look at the scowl on her father's face and she decided it best not to challenge him.

The earl narrowed his eyes and scrutinized his only daughter as if she were a prize mare. Her blond mane curled and coiffed, her trim-waisted figure, bespoke the daughter of a peer. With eyes which revealed the hot blood roiling under the proud exterior, she made a prize for any man. That was what he was counting on.

Favor took the piece of paper he clutched in his hand and waved it toward her. "This is an invitation from the fifth baron, Lord Copley, to attend an early season, country gathering at his estate in Devonshire."

"What has that to do with me?"

"It is addressed to you."

"You have no right to open my letters."

"As long as you are under my roof, I have every right. When you marry—and you *will* marry soon—I leave it to your husband to rein you in."

Caroline raised her chin. "Of course, I shall say *no*. It is a terrible time of year to attend a party. Besides, I wish to go to London early to have a new wardrobe fitted for the coming Season."

"I already acknowledged it—a week ago."

She rose from her seat. "How dare you!"

"You have no say in the matter. For all purposes, you have accepted the baron's invitation."

"Lord Copley is devilishly charming and is reported to have more money than he knows what to do with, but I have decided I shall press the suit of Lord Wetherby. If I marry the marquis, I shall be a duchess someday. Do you expect me to step down to become the wife of a baron, Father? That is more than enough."

"Has Wetherby indicated he will offer for you?"

Caroline made a moue with her lips. "It will not take long to bring him to the altar, once I set my mind to it."

"And how pray tell do you expect to live if you marry the marquis? His father is only forty-eight years old, and in his present state of health will live to be eighty-eight. He keeps his son on a small annuity of five thousand pounds a year, and I hear Wetherby spends every last farthing of it. The duke makes him beg for anything above that. Do you think that you can wait another forty years before you become a duchess?"

Caroline thrust out her lower lip. "We shall live on my dowry."

"What dowry? I am broke. To be very blunt, daughter, I

do not have two pennies to rub together. This estate is mort-
gaged to the hilt. My Yorkshire holdings were sold to cover
my last gambling debts. You never wondered why I had to
rent a London townhouse last spring? It was because I no
longer owned one. I will lose this house, too, if I do not
acquire some ready funds."

The startled look on Caroline's face showed the earl he
had her attention. "Now, listen well, daughter. You will go
to the baron's party, and you will get him to propose to you
or there will be no Season for you this year or any year
thereafter. He is ripe for marriage. I can read the signs. If
you cannot get him to tie the knot, I shall be very disappointed in you. It is your responsibility to marry well and
get my creditors off my back."

Caroline tossed her head. The baron was looking more
the thing by the minute. "That should be no trouble at all."

The earl exhaled and smiled for the first time. "I don't
care how you do it, but I shall accompany you to make
certain that you do as you are bidden."

"Do you have no confidence in me?"

"I have all the confidence in the world in you, my dear,"
the earl said magnanimously. "After all, you are my daughter."

Six

Only one night remained before Sarah expected Lord Copley to arrive back at the castle. She stood in the Great Hall with Mrs. Proctor, watching the maids sprinkle sweet-smelling herbs into the vases of flowers and bracken fronds. A spicy aroma permeated the air. The room was truly a flower garden. Wood lay stacked along the wall, ready to fuel the fire which raged on the hearth.

"My, ain't it a wonder!" Mrs. Proctor exclaimed. "His lordship will be most impressed, Miss Grimsley."

Not only had the maids filled the ground floor rooms, but the bedchambers as well with bouquets. They teased some of the men into making blooms also. These were tied to the bare branches of furze bushes, which were used for stems. Even Mr. Proctor, scolded by his wife to quit gaping and try a twist or two, produced a large red poppy. Out of the leftover cloth the women sewed brilliant banners which now hung out over the room on poles attached to the banisters around the balcony.

"If only the outdoors did not look so stark," Sarah sighed.

"Well, that's up to the Good Lord, now ain't it?" the housekeeper said sagaciously. "Ye best get a restful night's sleep before everyone starts coming."

Sarah watched Mrs. Proctor shoo the maids from the room. It seemed to her that nothing perturbed the good-natured woman. Sarah wished she was as sure of the baron's response. Well, she could do no more now, she thought as she climbed the stairs to her room. She entered to find the ever solicitous Nooney had already filled her tub with steaming-hot water. A good bath should help her sleep.

Out of habit, she glanced over at the window table, half expecting to see bread scattered about the floor. Two days after her encounter with Dog, Sarah had returned to her bedchamber after lunch and unlocked the door to find the huge animal sitting complacently in the middle of her room, crumbs smeared all over his chops.

"You!" she cried. "How did you get in here?"

The lion had sunk down on his haunches with no intentions of answering her, of course. Sarah left the room, locked the door and went to find Jacob. When they returned, Dog was nowhere to be found.

A few minutes later, Jacob had reported. "Dog is back in his own room, Miss Grimsley, looking as innocent as you please. I scolded him good. Just as you said. I told him he wouldn't like it if someone came in and ate *his* food."

"Well, he has to be getting in some way besides the door," Sarah said. She hunted everywhere for an opening, pounded the walls, listening for hollow sounds and looked into the interior of the clothespress. The carpet covered no hidden trapdoor. It was a mystery.

Sarah was stern, but she had a kind heart, and the picture in her mind that night of the woeful eyes wouldn't leave her. She dreamed of a lost kitten meowing for its mother. The next afternoon before she took the sugar lumps to Zee and Hob, she gave Jacob a couple of buns to take up to Dog.

Her pastries remained untouched after that, but Sarah had the strangest feeling as she went about her chores that she was being followed. If she didn't see Dog, she smelled him. Once she spotted a pair of yellow eyes peering at her from around a heavy medieval armchair which sat at the end of the corridor down from her bedchamber. Before she traversed the length of the hallway, he was gone.

Another afternoon, she sensed something or someone spying on her from between the banisters on the balcony. By the time she could summon Jacob, the lion was back inside his room.

"Mayhaps it's a spirit, Miss Grimsley and can go through walls," Jacob had said hopefully.

"You are not talking to one of the hired help, Jacob. A spirit would not smell so badly, I am sure. You know as well as I, who the culprit is."

"I be afraid all the servants talk of hearing ghosts at night and only the Proctors and I—and you, of course—know it ain't so. The master says we daren't tell about Dog because he won't be able to find workers if they know there is a lion in the house."

"No, I dare say he could not, Jacob. But however do you keep it from them? The animal surely has to go outside."

"I take Dog out before daylight and at night by way of the tower staircase and through a back way. The old tower connects all the floors of the West Wing."

Since Dog didn't really bother her, Sarah left him to his wanderings, still wishing she could discover by what means he got into the rest of the house. Perhaps when the baron came, the animal would be content to stay on the second floor.

Midafternoon the next day, Lord Copley's coach entered the gates of Roxwealde Park. His mount and a pair of gentle mares for Miss Tremain and her companion were tied to the back of the coach. Fletcher sat prim and proper on the seat across from him. Andersen found that without a regular source of potation over the last three days, the man had been decently capable of performing his duties as a gentleman's gentleman. However, his valet was definitely not a chatterbox, and the baron had extracted few words from him.

It wasn't raining, neither was the sun showing any promise of shining through the cloud cover. Andersen hadn't looked, really looked, at the castle for many years. Now for the first time in ages, the structure in front of him registered on his consciousness. It appeared the same to him as it always had, its stone-blank face with eyes of glass staring out over the lifeless heath. He didn't know what he'd expected. Some sort of miracle perhaps? However, he did notice a difference in the smoother carriageway, for his teeth weren't set on edge before he got to the front door.

Andersen felt inside his heavy coat, as he had several times since he'd left London, to make certain the leather pouch containing the special license was still strapped under his arm. He checked his watch. He had less than three weeks—eighteen days, ten hours and eleven minutes to be exact—to have his prospective bride standing in front of the vicar in Danbury Wells.

It wasn't as if the young ladies he was about to woo were strangers. Miss Martin . . . no he must think of her as *B* for Beverly. He had known *B* since they were children. *E* was the sister of a school chum from Oxford. *A* and *C,* he'd come to know well during the last two Seasons. Of course, *E* wasn't a consideration now. Andersen gave a bark of laughter. A ludicrous thought suddenly registered. The fifth baron, Lord Copley, was being sacrificed on the marriage block to the highest bidder. What for? The dubious privilege of being able to hang onto the ownership of this pile of rock, and a stipend amount of interest from his ancestral estate.

His vehicle stopped, and as the baron alighted, he saw the hack with the actresses and Peter's carriage only seconds behind. Before Andersen reached the top step to the castle entrance, the high arched double doors were already open. Mr. Proctor stood all respectable in a black suit, his gray hair slicked down with some sort of oil.

"Lord Copley has arrived," he announced over his shoulder. "Good to see you, your lordship."

Behind him, resplendent in red and gold livery, white wig only slightly askew, Jacob proudly stepped out to meet him. "Welcome home to Roxwealde, my lord," he announced, in well articulated tones.

Although always warmly greeted, he'd never been heralded with such ceremony. Their performances had to be Miss Grimsley's doing, Andersen thought. He wondered how many times it had taken the men to rehearse their lines.

"Thank you, Proctor, Jacob. It is good to be here." From the corner of his eye, he saw Peter speak to the three young women before starting with them to the house.

Inside, the entire serving staff, triple what it had been before, was lined up on either side of the Great Hall to greet their lord and master, but his eyes scanned the crowd unsuccessfully for someone else. Disappointment spread over him. He'd thought to see Miss Grimsley there to greet him.

Then, Andersen looked up in time to see the woman he sought descending the stairs, her generous body enclosed in a flowing, bright orange gown. She was the picture of the garden marigold, a plant that often escaped from tamer environs and reseeded itself in the wilderness. Her head was wrapped in a golden length of gauze which continued around her neck and over one shoulder. A large ruby brooch decorated the headpiece and matched the two spots of scarlet on her cheeks. Andersen didn't know whether to laugh or cry. She was overpowering. All sense of foreboding left him. With such genius to guide his little charade, he knew success was his. As he stepped forward, he heard Peter's quick intake of breath behind him and one of the actresses exclaim, "Gawd! Did'jer ever see the like?"

With a grin on his face, Andersen bowed as his hostess reached the bottom step, and taking her gloved hand, said. "Miss Grimsley, may I say that you indeed look magnificent. Please let me present my best friend. Mr. Peter Trummel."

Peter's mouth dropped open, and for the first time in his memory, Andersen found his friend speechless. "Excuse Mr. Trummel, Miss Grimsley, I fear the trip here has tired him beyond words."

"Oh, I say, Copley. You do it up too brown. If I am knocked speechless, ma'am it is because of your . . . that is . . . the baron did not do justice to your person."

Sarah felt her face flush, and she was thankful when Mrs. Proctor came forward to claim the three new chambermaids and the attention switched back to Lord Copley.

"I'll take them to their rooms and tell them their duties, yer lordship," the housekeeper said.

Lord Copley raised a hand. "That will not be necessary, Mrs. Proctor. The chambermaids are very specialized in pleasing the best of the Quality, and I have assigned them to work the East Wing. They have already been instructed as to their specific duties, and I took it upon myself to have them fitted with uniforms in London."

"Now ain't that thoughtful, Miss Grimsley?" Mrs. Proctor said, turning to Sarah. "One more burden off yer shoulders."

Although she dared not look directly at the dazzling nobleman, lest she lose her nerve altogether, Sarah nodded in agreement.

"Miss Grimsley—"

Lord Copley spoke to her directly, and she had to turn to him.

"Miss Grimsley," the baron repeated, with a smile of devastating proportions, "I will be expecting my other three gentlemen friends within the next few hours. You did make provisions for them for dinner, did you not?"

Sarah tried to collect herself. "Why, of course, your lordship. Everything is in readiness, their schedules as well. I think the sooner I can go over them the better."

Peter looked at the baron and raised his eyebrows.

Andersen only gave Peter an amused grin. "Ah, yes, the schedules. I do believe that is wise, knowing my friends as I do. We shall see to your assignments as soon as dinner is over. Now, I think Mr. Trummel and I will retire to our rooms and change out of our traveling clothes. I shall greet the men when they arrive, for I wish a few words with them alone. I shall summon you when they are all assembled. You will excuse us, Miss Grimsley?"

Sarah observed that the noblemen's servants were already carrying their masters' trunks up the staircases. "Why certainly, Lord Copley."

After giving the staff their final instructions for dinner, she gratefully retired to her own room. A cool drink of water cleared her throat. Nerves all a tangle, she flopped on her bed for a few minutes rest.

All had gone well, Sarah thought. She hadn't stumbled or swallowed her cinnamon buns. Thank goodness, she hadn't had to say much. Mr. Peter Trummel appeared to be a delightful, well-mannered gentlemen. If his lordship's other friends were as bright and pleasant, she could see no reason why their plans shouldn't run smoothly. Lord Copley would be able to make his choice of a bride by the end of the party. Then when he and his fiancée returned to London to be married, perhaps he would let her stay on at Roxwealde until the end of the Season as chatelaine, the title Miss Grimsley preferred to give herself.

Strange though that his lordship hadn't made any mention of the festive decorations adorning the hall. A twinge of disappointment threatened Sarah's composure. Even if the baron didn't care for flowers and banners, the least he could have done was to have applauded her efforts.

It wasn't half an hour later that Sarah heard the clatter of hoofbeats and the clang of wheels on the gravel below and rose from her bed to observe a coach tooling neck or nothing up the carriageway, a magnificent roan gelding trailing behind. From the descriptions she had received from the baron, and the crest on the coach, she concluded the first to arrive was Ernest Lance, the Marquis of Wetherby. He rode, not inside the coach, but atop the driver's seat holding the ribbons. He leapt to the ground, tossing the reins to one of his attendants with the air of a man sure of his own consequence. Sarah concluded him to be a fine-looking young man from what she could see of his face beneath the tall, curly-brimmed beaver hat. But not nearly in a league with the baron. No man could top the unearthly beauty of the lord of the manor, Sarah thought, with a strange unsettling awareness in the pit of her stomach.

Mr. Smith and Mr. Ripple arrived soon after in their own vehicles. One was whipjack quick, bounding around the coach, giving orders then obviously changing them, for his men kept running back and forth in a disconcerted manner. The other gentleman had a rotund figure, short, slow, and quite satisfied it seemed, to leave everything to his valet. She wasn't certain which was Mr. Smith and which was Mr. Ripple, but she knew that she'd find out soon enough when the baron summoned her.

She waited an hour for the knock on the door. A footman announced, "His lordship wishes for you to come to the library, Miss Grimsley."

After thanking the man. Sarah again inspected her appearance in the mirror, only to wish she didn't have to be wrapped like a counterpane. There were only two buns left on the tray, so she broke one in half for now. The other she would leave to use at dinner. Then for the sixth time, she ran through her notes to make certain she had all the sheets of the schedules at hand. She didn't know when Lord Copley wanted her to go over the men's lists with them, but, whatever his wishes, she was going to be prepared.

Sarah was admitted to the library to find the gentlemen

enjoying a glass of wine, or three or four, she concluded for the ruddy hue of their cheeks and silly grins which all couldn't be contributed to the bracing weather alone. Immediately all five leapt to their feet.

"Ah, Miss Grimsley," the baron said, ushering her into the room with a flourish. "May I present my friends to you. Lord Wetherby, Mr. Ripple, and Mr. Smith. Gentlemen, my hostess for this occasion, the Honourable Stanhope Grimsley."

Sarah found out that the chubby fellow was Mr. Ripple and the sprightly one, Mr. Smith. The marquis turned out better-looking than he had appeared from her window, and quite aware of it, she could tell. They all did the pretty and stepped forward one by one to bow over her hand. Basil, his mouth open, kept staring until Mr. Smith punched him in the ribs with his elbow. Mr. Ripple blushed and closed his lips with a smack.

Watching her quizzically, Mr. Trummel too inclined his head.

"May I offer you a glass of wine, Miss Grimsley?" the baron asked.

Sarah looked helplessly down at the armful of papers. She never drank spirits during the day, and never had been asked to join men in their solitary pleasures.

"How unthinking of me. Here, let me take those papers. I shall place them here on the desk," he said. And without so much as a by-your-leave, he made a great issue of plunking them down—right beside the scandalous Mercury. For all the baron's act of innocence, the glint in his eyes gave him away.

The god had been removed deliberately from an obscure table and settled in all his male glory in plain view on the desk. Sarah knew, because she had hidden him in the corner herself after the baron's last visit. She clasped her hands together to keep them from trembling and chose to act as though she didn't see it. She wouldn't have him think her one of last year's turnips. With a wave of her hand, she replied, "That will be fine, my lord. Those are the schedules."

This satisfactorily distracted his lordship who turned to the men to explain. "Miss Grimsley has been so kind as to write a daily plan to guide you, so you don't come to blows over which lady you will escort every day."

Sarah looked at Andersen. "Oh, but I have one for you also, your lordship. I don't want you becoming confused and ruining the pattern."

Andersen choked on his drink.

"I say, old boy," Basil said, "that sounds only fair to me. Don't see why you should not have one too. Keep things on the up and up, so to speak."

"Yes, yes. I quite agree," Andersen said, grinning at Sarah. "We would not want anything to go wrong with the plans."

Sarah was glad to hear the baron agreed with her. "Thank you, your lordship. Do you want for me to go over them now?" she said, setting down her glass to pick up the papers.

"After dinner would be better."

Sarah gave Basil three sheets of paper. "I disagree, your lordship. There is nothing like the present to set things in motion."

The baron furrowed his brows. His wishes were never questioned in his house. However, Miss Grimsley was so intent on handing out the assignments, he realized that she'd completely missed his look of censure.

In the meantime, Basil turned his papers one way and then the other before squinting and holding them closer. "Dash it, Copley! This looks like a bloody document—" Turning a brilliant scarlet, Basil glanced at Sarah. "Excuse my language, ma'am. Didn't mean . . ."

Henry snorted. "You dunderhead. Y'know what Copley said. We don't have to worry about Miss Grimsley. I'm sure she is used to worse language after associating with Prinny's crowd." He gave Sarah a twisted grin. "Heh, what?"

Sarah felt the heat creeping up her neck and was certain she was about to give herself away when the baron spoke.

"I will have no talk like that, Ripple . . . Smith. As long as you are in my house, you will conduct yourself as. gentlemen. If this charade is to be played successfully, you will be as proper as you would be attending any social function of London's high society. To do otherwise will be detrimental to my cause." He turned to Henry. "Mr. Smith—"

Henry shot Andersen a sour look. "My most humble apologies, Miss Grimsley. I spoke out of turn."

"Same," stammered Basil. "M'apologies, ma'am."

Andersen thought it best to send his friends to their rooms before they did anything more to upset the goodwill which had been established thus far. "I believe you all are quite familiar with the East Wing. Mrs. Proctor has informed me that she has prepared the same rooms for you which you have occupied on your former visits."

Sarah watched him collect the papers back from the men and once more set them at the feet of the statue, an act which Sarah knew was deliberate. Determined not to let him see that he ruffled her, she marched to the door, then turned and glared back at him.

"I believe you are right, my lord. Perhaps after a respite and a good meal, *everyone* will be more disposed to discuss the arrangements. Dinner is to be served in two hours. You must be very tired from your journey and may want to lie down awhile before you change your clothes. There will be plenty of time later for you to collect your schedules."

After the men and his hostess left the room, Andersen closed the door and gave a whoop of laughter. Oh, Miss Grimsley was sharp. How quickly she had picked up on his joke about the statue—and thrown it back in his face. What a wit. Her look of embarrassment over the men's language had appeared so sincere that she almost had him believing she was shocked.

Or was he wrong? Had Basil's cant and Henry's coarse remark offended her? Was his estimation of her wrong or was she just being discreet in front of his friends? Of course, that was it. The perfect actress, playing her part to the hilt. He'd told her that this party must be conducted with strict adherence to the social amenities.

Andersen went back to the desk, picked up the statue, and carried it to the table by the window. Miss Grimsley had stuck to her role. It was he and his partners who had dropped their guard. If he expected his rapscallion friends to tow the line, he must be careful to do likewise. Those two, Henry and Basil, mimicked anything he did. From now on, he would pay closer attention to what he said and did in front of them. Wetherby followed the rules—when he wanted to, and of course, Peter could always be counted on.

Andersen stood looking out the window, when there was a knock.

"Enter."

Sarah stuck her head around the door, frowning. "May I have a moment, my lord?"

"Of course, Miss Grimsley."

He'd thought they'd come to have a sort of camaraderie between them, but she truly looked uncomfortable. Perhaps the freedom he'd felt to express himself when he was with her wasn't reciprocated.

"You did not comment on what we did to the Great Hall."

Andersen wondered what it was he was supposed to have seen. His lack of awareness to his immediate surroundings was forever getting him in deep water. All that came to mind was when he'd entered the castle, he'd been over-whelmed by the multitude of his staff lined up like an army at attention. Dozens of faces stared back at him, triple the usual among the domestics. Now she seemed to be wanting his approval for something that had been done. What did he dare say?

He leaned forward. "Miss Grimsley, I meant to tell you. I was so astonished that I was rendered speechless." He felt relieved when he saw her eyes light up.

"Oh, thank you, my lord. I shall pass on your compliment to the staff. They worked so hard."

As soon as the door closed again, Andersen let out a sigh of relief. He'd give her a minute to be on her way, and go take a look. Then, he could make a more appropriate compliment at dinner.

A few minutes later, Andersen truly *was* speechless. The entire entrance room was in bloom. Why hadn't he noticed it before? Flowers were coming out of the walls, they climbed the beams, they sprang from tall vases, and even sprouted from the railings around the balcony. It looked as if an army of medieval knights, noblemen, and their ladies stood encircling the entire room. How had she done it? No hothouse existed at Roxwealde. Andersen went over and fingered a large yellow flower. It was dry to the touch. Cloth. He touched another. How could he have missed this wonder? Then he saw them, banners, bright patterns of color hanging on long poles thrusting out from the balconies above. God! He'd engaged a genius.

Whistling, Andersen started the climb to his rooms, taking note along the way of the flowers lining the steps. He met Mr. Proctor on his way down, who when he saw the baron, stopped to cradle a large red bloom which stuck out of a bouquet of variegated blossoms.

"It is truly amazing, Proctor. I would never have believed it possible that this heap of granite could look so alive. The women have accomplished a remarkable feat."

The steward coughed and pulled out the red flower even farther. "It is not very good, I know," he said, "but . . . I tried m' best."

The realization of what he meant struck Andersen. "You? You made that?"

"Miss Grimsley insisted on putting it in the center of the arrangement. She said I showed a natural talent," he said proudly.

"You most certainly do, Proctor," the baron said, shaking his head in disbelief at what he'd just heard.

Continuing his way on up the stairs, Andersen wondered what surprises his hostess would come up with next?

Abovestairs in her room, Sarah decided to wear a saffron-yellow and pistachio-green, striped dress with long darker green sleeves and bows, which looked like butterflies sprinkled about the bodice. The outer gown was split up the sides to the knees to reveal the green underskirt which matched the darker hue of the trim. Although the neckline was high and quite modest for most of Miss Grimsley's costumes, the top was so overly large that Sarah had to stuff two silk stockings over her bosoms to keep the cascading fabric from sagging. The resulting silhouette she presented to the mirror was so astounding that she blushed. But what did she know of the fashions of the beau monde when she was nothing but a simple country girl from Devon? Yet hadn't she been hesitant to wear the orange dress this afternoon and the baron had claimed her to look magnificent? She only hoped that he was as pleased with this dress, because Miss Grimsley's fashions seemed strangely odd to her.

Sarah had started to reach for the last cinnamon bun when it suddenly occurred to her that she couldn't place the bread in her mouth and not expect to swallow it when she ate her dinner. So no matter how they annoyed her, she'd have to make do with two handkerchiefs to fill out her face and hope that she'd spaced her guests far enough apart at the long table to enable her to remove the pieces of linen without being observed.

After settling a yellow turban over her hair and rouging her cheeks, Sarah set out to host her first dinner as hostess of Roxwealde Castle.

Seven

Sarah felt miserable. She sat at dinner toying with the food on her plate. Lace tickled her tongue, stockings poofed out her bodice so she couldn't see her plate, and the pillow rode uncomfortably on her stomach. It was a mistake from the beginning to think that she could take out the handkerchiefs she'd stuffed into her cheeks without being observed. She made every effort to cut the lamb into smaller and smaller pieces, trying hopelessly to make the bits tiny enough to not have to chew them. How in the world, she wondered, did Miss Grimsley manage to get her arms around her big bosom to cut her food in the first place?

The long table which could easily have seated thirty people, now held only five men and herself. The baron sat such a distance away at the far end, she'd thought herself safe from his close inspection. But, alas, even the soft shadows cast by the flickering light of the candles didn't hide her every move from the watchful eye of the baron. So Sarah pretended to eat, hoping he couldn't see the large amount of food she left on her plate each time a servant removed it.

Adding to her confusion, Sarah couldn't fathom why Lord Copley raised his glass to her before every remove. Each time he did so, all the men imitated his salute and shouted.

"Here, here!"

"Brava!"

"Good show!"

Sarah was quite aware that the men were foxed before they came to the table, any muttonhead could see that. But for some reason they made her feel as if she were the fool. Acknowledging their boisterous attention with a weak smile, she brought her drink to her lips but did no more than taste the wine. Swallowing anything was impossible with the linen stuffed in her cheeks. While she watched enviously as the men ate course after course, her mouth became drier, her stomach emptier.

Lord Copley's friends, Mr. Smith and Mr. Ripple were seated on one side, and opposite them, Mr. Trummel and the marquis, Lord Wetherby. All were acting just as oddly as their host.

Now Sarah had never been one to consider herself a wit, but to her surprise they seemed to find everything she said amusing. To add to her confusion, she didn't understand half their responses.

Nonetheless, that was no excuse for lack of manners on her part, she decided, and she tried to steer the conversation to more understandable subjects. She had especially been eager to find out if they'd noticed the difference between the newly stuffed feather mattresses and the old straw-filled ones of their previous visits.

"Did you have a chance to try out your beds before dinner?"

Mr. Trummel only glanced at Lord Copley, but the others went into gales of laughter.

What the reason was for their merriment escaped Sarah, and she thought mayhaps they were too embarrassed to say they didn't understand her question. "Did you find comfort in your beds?"

All three silently raised their glasses to her.

Sarah frowned. Perhaps they weren't pleased after all. She glanced toward the end of the table, but his lordship was suddenly putting all his concentration into carving a

piece of beef. She could see he would be no help whatsoever in keeping the dialogue going.

Shrugging off the vagaries of men to refuse to admit
when they weren't finding things to their liking, Sarah
thought to assure them. "If you don't think you will be
warm enough tonight, you have only to call one of the
chambermaids."

Now why this simple statement should cause them to
double over, Sarah couldn't imagine, but after Mr. Ripple
choked on his food, Sarah ceased trying to make pleasant
conversation for the duration of the meal.

Finally, when they had finished their pudding, the baron
dropped his napkin on his plate. His voice boomed down
the table to her. "Miss Grimsley, I am certain you would
like to retire to your room for a few moments, while the
men have their port and cigars."

Giving a silent prayer of thanks, Sarah forced a smile.
"Thank you, my lord, I certainly would."

With a wave of his hand, the baron signaled to a footman.
"Then that is that," he said jovially.

Well, Sarah could see that his lordship's good humour
wasn't affected by the reprehensible behavior of his friends.

"Then shall we say in twenty minutes we will assemble
in the library, and you can go over their assignments with
them? Gentlemen," he said, addressing the four, "how goes
it? Are you not pleased with the way my hostess has arranged things for you? Would you say, so far so good?"

"Well done!" Mr. Smith said, placing his napkin over his
head as if it were a hat, then slithering down on his chair.

Mr. Ripple sniggered.

Sarah watched the marquis sitting wordlessly, observing
her through shuttered eyes. She didn't know if he was studying her or merely falling asleep. But then, she reminded
herself that all the men had had only a little respite before
dinner and had imbibed quite heavily. She only hoped they

still had some of their wits about them when she went over their calendars.

Mr. Trummel and the baron glanced at each other and shook their heads, which only reinforced Sarah's despair that not much would be accomplished this night.

The footman held her chair for her to rise, which somehow she managed to do without falling forward onto the table. Heaven help her! She was top heavy and her knees were stiff. As she made her way across to the door, it was all she could do to keep from waddling. It was the longest Sarah had sat through a meal since she'd come to Roxwealde. Once in the Great Hall, she removed the wads of linen from her mouth and hurried to her chambers.

Andersen watched Miss Grimsley make her way from the room. Only someone of her stature could get away with such outlandish costumes. They must have cost a fortune. He knew fine materials when he saw them, and the yards it had to take for each of her dresses would make three or four of the simple styles fashionable in London Society. No one could match her.

It didn't seem to him that she had eaten much at dinner, but then he'd been so far away from her that he couldn't really see for sure.

Basil picked a grape off the silver epergne in the center of the table and popped it in his mouth. "I say, Copley, I like the ol' gel. Makes quite a picture, doesn't she? Penny was quite impressed."

"Twist was too," Henry said, stopping first to blow a cloud from the cigar a footman lit for him. "I can see Miss Grimsley knows what keeps a man entertained. Ho! I nearly died when she asked as calm as you please. *"Did you find comfort in your beds?"* Twist won't know what's what when I call her *Comfort* tonight."

Andersen caught the looks two footmen gave each other.

He could see he would have to muzzle Smith and Ripple or his plans would be all over the servant's quarters before the night was over. He signaled the servants to remove the wine bottles. "Gentlemen, I believe it best if we wait until we are in the library to discuss arrangements for your entertainment."

Basil put his finger to his lips and made a shushing sound. "You talk too much, Smith. Can't keep a shee-cret."

Henry stuck out his lower lip. "Oh, cut line. Ripple. You wouldn't know a joke if it bit you."

Peter and the marquis had already approached the two quarrelers and each taking one by the elbow, propelled him toward the door.

Andersen gave them a grateful smile and followed.

Sarah thought she was early arriving belowstairs with the men's copies of their instructions, so she was a pleasantly surprised to find all the gentlemen assembled in the library when she got there. "I am glad to see you are eager as I to go over the schedules I made out for each of you," she said brightly.

With a grin, the baron stepped up to her and took the papers from her hand. "I think it best if you just give the men your plans and allow them to go over them in the morrow when they are feeling more the thing. I'm certain that they can follow a simple calendar. If not, there will be time at breakfast for you to answer any questions they may have."

Sarah peered over her spectacles, her face turning as pink as the spots on her cheeks. "If you say so, my lord."

The look on her face led him to believe she didn't agree with one word he'd said.

As for Sarah, she wasn't the least sleepy. When she'd gone to her room while the men enjoyed their port and cigars, she'd had a drink of water and two cinnamon buns. They did wonders to revive her spirits. She dismissed

Nooney for the night, then stuffed two more of the buns the girl brought her into her cheeks, leaving the rest for a snack before she went to bed.

. Now, Sarah took a good look around the library. She realized Mr. Smith was being held up by Mr. Trummel and Mr. Ripple was snoring on the couch by the hearth. Now that she saw the situation more clearly Sarah decided the baron was right. A meeting this late with the men would be worthless. She'd learned from experience with her father and his friends, that port and cigars seemed to curdle a man's reasoning powers. However, she had decided to give it a try—or a good *Heave ho!* as her father would say. Lord Copley seemed to be taking the setback quite stoically, though, for he was smiling. It would be well for her to try to follow his example.

Just watching the way the corner's of the baron's lips curved enchantingly upward mesmerized her. Giving herself a shake, Sarah managed to tear her gaze away from him and look at the others.

"How unthinking of me. Of course, you are all tired after your long journey today and wish to go to bed."

Mr. Ripple sat up. "Bed? Did someone say bed? This isn't my bed."

"Mr. Trummel and Lord Wetherby will see our guests to their rooms," Andersen said, handing a sheaf of papers to Peter. The disappointment on Miss Grimsley's face was quite evident to Andersen as the men left the room. "If you will give me a minute, there is something I wish to tell you," he said.

Sarah looked at him dubiously.

Andersen pointed to a chair. "I did not imbibe as much as my friends, Miss Grimsley. I assure you I am quite capable of holding a rational conversation."

Sarah allowed him to hold the chair for her. "As you say, my lord."

Andersen sniffed the air and closed his eyes. A pleasant

euphoria overtook his senses. He shook his head to clear the cobwebs from his brain and seated himself across the desk from Miss Grimsley. "May I extend my apologies for my cohorts. Their behavior was inexcusable."

Sarah pushed her spectacles farther down the tip of her nose to enable her to see him better. She had so wanted to get right down to the crux of the matter and show the men their lists, but she was sure that Miss Grimsley would have taken the disruption of her schedule in stride. Perhaps it was better in the long run to tell the baron about her overall scheme first.

"Well, I did want to have them straightened out on their programs, but it may be best to go over my plans with you."

Lord Copley raised his hand. "Before you do that, I want to say something about my reception this afternoon."

Sarah braced herself.

The baron gave a crooked grin. "I owe you an apology."

This threw Sarah off guard. "Whatever for?"

Andersen steepled his fingers and sat back to watch her reaction. "For not telling you, ma'am, that what you have done inside this castle is truly a miracle."

Sarah's mouth fell open. *He had noticed.* She brought her lips together quickly before the remainder of the pastry fell out.

Andersen was amused by her reaction to his pronouncement. He liked to watch the way she puckered her lips every time he startled her. "I had not comprehended the whole of it until Mr. Proctor informed me as to the extent of your embellishments. But the true miracle was how you managed to involve the servants in the process. Never before have I seen the enthusiasm or commitment to purpose that you have drawn from them."

Sarah felt her face burn. To cover her embarrassment, she reached for the papers on the corner of the desk. "Let me tell you some of the entertainments I have planned for your guests," she said hastily, not quite certain of where

she should begin. For she had organized activities from
breakfast onward for everyone. She even had a map drawn
showing the baron where he should take the women he
planned on wooing. "Here are suggestions of games to occupy your friends on the days they will not have a lady to
accompany," she said brightly, handing Andersen a paper.

She was certain the baron was quite impressed by the
way his eyes lit up when he looked at it.

Sarah made a sweeping motion of the room with her
hand. "You don't have many books to read, you know, but
I found several old games in the upstairs nursery and had
them dusted off. Spillikins and Pitch and Toss. There were
some decks of cards, and the billiard table is in surprisingly
good condition. I thought the old solar would provide a
cozy place for conversation."

Andersen was temporarily distracted as he watched the
little green butterflies on Miss Grimsley's bodice rise and
fall with each breath she took. He half expected to see them
fly into the air at any moment. Hoping he hadn't missed
much of what she'd said, he smiled abstractly. "I suggest
you leave the men to find their own diversions. They will
most likely stay in their rooms the major part of their free
days."

"I don't want them to be bored."

Andersen glanced about for Mercury and was amused to
see the little statue nearly hidden behind a tall vase. "They
are quite resourceful fellows, Miss Grimsley. Be assured
they will not be bored."

Sarah doubted that, for they appeared to be men who
were used to having their amusements provided for them.
Especially, Mr. Smith and Mr. Ripple. Now, Mr. Trummel,
she liked. He wasn't high in the instep like the others. The
marquis, Lord Wetherby seemed capable of taking care of
himself, too, but there was something underhanded about
the man. Of course, she had no intention of mentioning that

to the baron. One didn't downtalk one's friends to them. "As you say, my lord."

The baron had risen and walked to the tall mullioned window. The moon was out, but its light only emphasized the bleakness of the landscape.

"I only wish it were not so ugly out there. You may have produced a wonder with your decorations inside the castle, Miss Grimsley, but there never will be anything compelling about the Roxwealde moors."

Sarah forgot who she was supposed to be and without thinking, blurted out, "Oh, but my lord. The heath can be beautiful. There are already violets springing from the earth. I saw them coming up in the shelter of a tor on the top of a high rise to the west of here. And I do not think it long before we shall see—" The look on Lord Copley's face as he swung around, stopped her.

His eyes had changed to ebony. "You walked as far as that, Miss Grimsley? That will never do! Were you not told that no one is permitted out past the park?"

Sarah held her thumb and forefinger a couple inches apart "Well, yes—but I just went a tiny way."

"The tor you are speaking of is more than a tiny way. Miss Grimsley. You deliberately disobeyed my edicts."

She didn't like his frown. "Well, yes, if you put it that way, my lord. I did not think you would mind."

His fists were clenched at his sides. "I do mind. It is dangerous. A person unfamiliar with the terrain can fall into a bog and disappear in a matter of minutes."

It seemed to her he was making a greater fuss over her little gambol than was necessary. "Oh, but I am quite familiar with the moorlands, my lord. One has only to follow the tracks of the sheep and the wild ponies."

"Even sheep fall victim to the bog. I don't want you venturing out alone again. Is that understood?"

Sarah's eyes widened, and for a moment the real Sarah

forced through again. "Oh, but I love the moorlands, your lordship."

Andersen looked at her as if she had two heads. "How can anyone find anything of interest in rocks and swamps and brambles that tear at one's clothing?"

Sarah's face flushed. In an effort to cover her discomfort, she removed her spectacles and pretended to clean them with her handkerchief.

Andersen tried to control his annoyance. It would not do for him to upset Miss Grimsley. After all, he needed her. If she became angry and left him, he'd really be in a bind. "Do forgive me my outburst." Andersen saw the confusion in Miss Grimsley's eyes. He stared. He had never noticed before what lovely eyes she had. They were as gray as a swirling fog and flecked with gold. He shook his head to clear his brain of the thoughts mulling about in it and forced himself to smile.

"You really enjoy the moors?"

"Oh, yes, my lord."

"Most ladies find them forbidding."

"How can anyone say such a thing when they are so fascinating? Since I was a little girl I have kept a scrapbook of dried moorland flowers."

Somehow Andersen couldn't picture the plump Miss Grimsley trekking over the rocky hills or collecting wild-flowers to paste in scrapbooks.

Sarah saw the strange look he was giving her and quickly replaced her spectacles on her nose. "Is there anything more, your lordship?"

Whatever invisible connection had passed between them, Andersen realized now was broken. "No, that will be all, Miss Grimsley."

With a sigh of relief, Sarah escaped into the corridor. How odd the baron's response had been to her mention of going onto the moors. She could understand his upset at her having broken one of his rules, for after all, he was lord of the manor. But his reaction had been more than that. No matter how dangerous the moors could be, a man like Lord Copley couldn't be afraid of her simply having disobeyed one of his commands.

Well, she wasn't going to dwell on it now. Her thoughts went to her guests already established in the East Wing. Perhaps she had best check on their welfare before she retired for the night. On satin-slippered feet, Sarah crossed the stone floor of the Great Hall.

Making her way as quietly as she could so as not to disturb the sleeping guests, she climbed up to the second floor. Here and there she rearranged a flower in the bouquets along the staircase. Expecting to find only silence, it was a surprise to hear laughter coming from the men's chambers. Suddenly, she collided with one of the chambermaids coming from Mr. Smith's room, carrying a wooden bucket.

"Gor! Watch where ye're going," the girl said, until she looked up into her mistress's surprised face. "Oh, lawdy, ma'am. Beg your pardon. I didn't know 'twas you."

Sarah looked in amazement at the disheveled girl, her wet hair stuck to her forehead, and the big heavy pail. "Whatever are you doing up this late . . . Twist? That is your name isn't it?"

Before she could answer, Mr. Smith's voice called from inside the room. "Ho, Comfort, hurry with the water."

Sarah didn't know whether to be annoyed or not. "Do you mean he is asking you to work this late?"

Twist giggled. "Oh, 'tis no trouble, ma'am."

Sarah heard a second burst of male laughter from another room down the corridor, followed by a woman's squeal. Well, his lordship was right. The maid's he'd hired were most obliging, but then, he'd said they knew the way to go to please the Quality. Sarah felt she had a lot to learn.

"Well, if you say you don't mind, Twist. But if they overwork you, you let me know and I shall speak to them."

Sarah watched the girl head for the servant's staircase, then turned and descended once again to the Great Hall. It pleased her to know that her guests were happy with their accommodations. She only hoped the others would be as generous with their praise after they arrived tomorrow.

When Sarah entered her room, she had only to sniff the air to know that she had had an intruder. The tray on the table hadn't been disturbed, but it was licked clean. The old reprobate was getting quite good at leaving no evidence, but his behavior was not to be tolerated.

"Dog! If you are still in here, I shall find you and box your ears," Sarah called, looking behind her dressing screen. She picked up the candle stick that Nooney had left lit beside the bed and made a thorough search of the room before giving the bellrope a pull.

When a sleepy-eyed maid appeared a few minutes later, Sarah apologized and asked her to summon Jacob.

The doorman, breathing heavily, acted apologetic, but not the least bit surprised when he arrived a few minutes later, still buttoning his jacket.

"He has been at it again," Sarah said. "But I still cannot find where he is entering my room."

"The minute Nooney come to get me, I ran up to the beast's room and found him in the middle of his own bed, ma'am."

"Oh, thank goodness!" Sarah said. "I am afraid that his lordship is already quite disturbed about something I said this evening, and I didn't want anything more to put him in a worse mood before tomorrow."

"Tomorrow, Miss Grimsley?"

Sarah looked out the window and wrung her hands. "Lord Copley said that he expects all the remainder of his guests to arrive tomorrow. And, oh, Jacob, I must agree with him; the weather could not look more dismal."

* * *

After Miss Grimsley left the library, Andersen sat down once again at the desk and pulled over the stack of papers she'd left. Loosening his neckcloth, he settled down to run through her plans.

Disbelief ran through him. God! There was even a detailed map of the main rooms on the ground floor of the castle. No! They were of all the rooms in both wings—except those of his second floor apartment. Of course, she'd have no way of knowing what his chambers were like.

The rooms off the Great Hall were all named and lettered as to their purposes: Games, cards, eating, visiting, and some had strange little squiggles which looked like hearts. Andersen laughed aloud. No one he'd ever met before was like her. Miss Grimsley made all other Originals look ordinary.

A scratching on the door broke Andersen's concentration. "Enter."

Holding onto the frame for support, Fletcher stuck his bleary-eyed face around the door. " 'Tis late your lardssh-hip. Will you be wissh-hing to retire soon?"

"Ah, yes, Fletcher. It has been a long day, hasn't it? And tomorrow promises to be a more pressing one. I shall be up to my apartment shortly, as soon as I finish looking at these papers. Have a hot brick placed in my bed to warm it. I dare say we are in for a bone-chilling night."

The door hadn't been closed a minute before the baron tossed the papers carelessly onto the top of the desk and left the room.

Eight

It snowed.

"Oh, no!" Sarah moaned, looking out her bedroom window the next morning.

From where she stood, she saw nothing but swirling white powder. The iron entrance gates to the park, stark black sentinels on a clear day, weren't visible. The carriageway, the grounds, all had disappeared. Her fingers wiped a larger peephole on the damp glass. She couldn't even see the East Wing directly across the courtyard.

Disaster lay just around the corner, if she didn't move quickly.

Sarah once again chose her orange and yellow ensemble to greet the visitors. If the sun wasn't going to cooperate and shine, she'd substitute for it. She dressed swiftly, then rang for Nooney.

The maid appeared within a few minutes. "Wasn't the chocolate hot enough, ma'am? Cyril had a wicked time of it, lighting the fire. Did it go out?"

"The chocolate was fine, Nooney. The fire has taken. That is not why I called you. I would like for you to tell Mr. Proctor to notify the gentlemen in the East Wing that breakfast will be served promptly at nine o'clock."

The girl's eyes widened. "Oh, ma'am, I don't think Uncle Proctor will think it his duty to tell the Quality what they should do."

Sarah didn't feel she had time to argue. "You are right,

Nooney," Sarah said, deferring to the maid's sense of propriety. "Then tell him, I wish him to instruct Mr. Fletcher to inform the gentlemen's valets that Lord Copley insists their masters be ready and assembled at that time in the small dining room off the Great Hall."

A little humbuggery wouldn't hurt right now, she decided. If the baron wanted to waylay a catastrophe his soldiers must be ready at the front.

"Also tell Cook that I would like her to make *strong* coffee. I believe the gentlemen may have need of it."

The men had accepted the baron's invitation for this charade, Sarah thought, so like it or not, they'd have to cooperate. She didn't trust Mr. Smith or Mr. Ripple to follow instructions. From what she'd observed already, she feared those two men's characters sorely lacked discipline.

Now that she knew the maid was reluctant to pass on orders to her uncle, Sarah decided to try another tack. "Nooney—"

"Yes, ma'am?"

"Ask your aunt to make sure that Mr. Proctor informs Lord Copley's valet that it is imperative to have his lordship ready early also."

"Yes, ma'am," the girl said with more eagerness in her voice. She obviously was more at ease speaking by way of her aunt.

The minute Nooney was out of the room, Sarah gathered up the copy of her master plan. Desperate measures were needed. They couldn't risk a mishap now.

Sarah no sooner reached the Great Hall than she saw Mr. Proctor say something to Mr. Fletcher, which sent that man skittering up the stairs to the East Wing.

Before the steward got away, she called to him. "Mr. Proctor, please send servants to brush the carriageway immediately. Also have footmen posted at the park gates, or Lord Copley's guests will not be able to find the castle."

The housekeeper then caught her eye, hurrying from the

back of the house. "Mrs. Proctor, it is going to be a terribly chilly day. The fire here in the Great Hall cannot be allowed to go out. All bedchambers must be kept warm, too, because I want them cozy when the guests arrive."

Mrs. Proctor clucked encouragingly. "Now don't ye be worrying yerself, Miss Grimsley. Me and the Mister will tend to everything. Cook is fixing a hearty breakfast for the gentlemen. His lordship ordered lots of cinnamon buns. He seems to have as much a liking for them as ye do."

That was a surprise to Sarah. She should have been the one to ask the baron if he had any preferences for specific foods. She thanked Providence for such diligent servants. She mustn't fail his lordship now. He had so little time left to woo his bride.

That thought brought a stab of pain to Sarah's breast. It was not the first time that had happened. She didn't know its significance, only that a sudden feeling of sadness enveloped her. Perhaps it was fatigue or excitement. Well, she didn't have time to worry about it now. She had to check with Cook on the luncheon and dinner menus. The latter meal would be her first in the grand dining room.

The baron was already standing at the sideboard when she'd entered the breakfast room. Sarah couldn't tell by his expression whether or not he was still angry with her from the night before or only caught up in the tension of the impending activities facing them. Jacob, resplendent in red and gold livery, stepped forward and seated her at the round table while she still clutched the sheaves of foolscap to her bosom.

Lord Copley approached her with a dish of food. To avoid having him suspect what his presence did to her, she spoke instead to the servant. "You are looking fine, today, Jacob."

"Thank you, ma'am." the footman said, beaming proudly.

Sarah whispered. "Will you see that Zee and Ol' Hob get their sweets today? I am afraid I shall be too busy."

"Aye, ma'am. I be sorry to say Zee ain't been up to snuff of late."

"I am sad to hear that, Jacob."

"Oh, I daresay a sugar-treat will cheer him up."

By now Lord Copley had reached her side and placed a plate of steaming food in front of her. "Good morning, Miss Grimsley."

Sarah couldn't very well ignore him any longer. It took only one look into his steely expression for her to decide it inadvisable to begin a conversation with a comment on the snow—regardless of the fact that the dour weather was not something to be slacked off as unimportant today.

"I hope I have chosen what pleases you," the baron said, his voice polite but containing a certain edge.

Sarah had stared helplessly at the plate piled high with steak, eggs, bacon, all smothered under cream sauce. She nearly choked. The table already had baskets of steaming buns and toast, dishes of butter and a large selection of jams and preserves. "Thank you, your lordship. Your choices are exactly what I would have chosen for myself."

Andersen turned to go back to the buffet when she stopped him.

Sarah never was one to fret over trivialities like a walk on the moors, yet it took a few moments for her to gather courage to call to him. "Lord Copley—"

He glanced over his shoulder to find her holding out some sheets of paper to him. His eyes zeroed in on hers, and he crooked his eyebrows.

Sarah wasn't going to let the baron's sudden scrutiny unsettle her. Looking over her spectacles, she handed him several sheets of paper. "Here is a shortened version of your schedule. As soon as they arrive, I will give the other gentlemen theirs. You may be annoyed by my little abrogation of your rules; but I think we should put aside our personal differences and concentrate on the strategy for today."

Andersen couldn't remain angry with someone whose face looked like a dazzling sunburst. "Miss Grimsley, I agree, but I must warn you, that with my friends, it will undoubtedly be wiser to wait until all of them have their appetites satisfied before you approach anything of a cerebral nature."

He saw the pique in her tightly drawn mouth, and feared a confrontation, but was satisfied when she nodded and stacked the papers neatly beside her plate.

Peter Trummel and Lord Wetherby had entered at that moment, and did the pretty to their hostess before filling their plates and seating themselves.

Mr. Smith and Mr. Ripple were late to breakfast. When they finally stumbled into the morning room, Mr. Smith began to say something derogatory, Sarah was sure, but was cut short by the baron.

"If the rest of us can be here on time, Henry, I expect you to do likewise. I trust you had a good night."

Mr. Smith's expression registered somewhere between pain and pleasure, while Mr. Ripple had already forgotten his pique at being aroused from a sound slumber and was stacking his plate with food from the sideboard.

Sarah was glad she had started Mr. Ripple with A and Mr. Smith with B, for she feared anything more complicated was beyond their ken.

She gave them fifteen minutes to down some coffee and take a bite or two. What Sarah lacked in an understanding of inertia, she made up in enthusiasm, and she saw no reason not to attack the matter at hand.

"Gentlemen, you will agree that we are not attending a summer garden party." She was happy to see this brought all heads up and turned her way. "You brought your schedules with you, of course. I asked Mr. Fletcher to tell your valets to make certain that you did."

Sarah waited patiently while there was a mad scramble to produce the required documents.

Mr. Ripple, frantically searching through his jacket, finally extracted a somewhat rumpled paper from an inside pocket.

Sarah smiled at him. "I am certain you gave at least a minute's time to go over your schedule, last night." The blank expression that greeted her told her immediately that he hadn't. A little less patiently she tapped his copy with her finger. "You will note, I have asked you to escort Miss A to dinner this evening. That will give you an opportunity to set up your first assignment on the following day. Mr. Smith will escort Miss B and so forth."

Sarah riveted her attention on the baron. "You will be so busy today attending your duties as host, that I have assigned the Marquis and Mr. Trummel to C and E respectively. This evening, I have you escorting Mrs. Bennington to dinner."

Sarah didn't think much of the sudden discerning look the baron shot toward Lord Wetherby, until Mr. Trummel coughed.

"Is there anything wrong with that, my lord?" she asked.

"Oh, no, Miss Grimsley," Andersen said, a little too nonchalantly. "You undoubtedly did the right thing."

Watching the sudden tightening of his jaw, Sarah wasn't so sure.

Nonetheless, the baron spoke as if he were in perfect accord with her plans. "Miss Grimsley has made out a separate schedule for each of you. She has even marked the dates beside each entry. All you have to do for the next two weeks is follow down the list and entertain the lady identified by the A, B, C or E."

Basil squinted at the long sheet of foolscap. "Zounds, Copley! How am I supposed to remember what day it is?"

Andersen cast a look at the ceiling. "Didn't either of you go over your schedules last night? No, don't tell me. I shouldn't have asked. Give it to your man if you cannot remember, Basil."

"Will do that."

Mr. Smith looked more disgruntled than baffled. "I don't like lists. Always reminds me of Raxleigh, my headmaster at Eton."

Andersen gave an impatient shake of his head. "Just prop it on your chest of drawers, Henry."

The marquis studied his host through veiled eyes. "Come now Copley don't you think you have held us in suspense long enough. Who are the four lucky women you have chosen to vie for the honors of being Lady Copley?"

Mr. Smith banged the end of his knife on the table. "By George, he's right. You have kept us in the dark long enough. All this alphabet nonsense is for schoolboys. We are grown men here. Except for Miss Grimsley," he said, casting a quick look of apprehension toward the baron as if fearing another set down. "She's a lady, of course."

Andersen silenced Henry Smith with a dark look, then turned to Mr. Proctor. "Please have all the servants removed from the room. And see that we are not disturbed."

After the room was cleared, he continued. "Letter A refers to Miss Anne Bennington, B to Miss Beverly Martin."

Basil Ripple choked on a piece of toast. "Dash my wig, Copley! Not Bev. When I was no more than in leading strings, m'folks used to drag me up to their place in Yorkshire every summer. Haven't seen her in years, but always remembered she scared me to death."

Andersen laughed. "A man isn't put down by a strong woman, Ripple."

Basil bent over his plate and concentrated on slathering another piece of toast with butter.

Andersen avoided looking at Wetherby when he mentioned C for Lady Caroline. "E is Miss Edith Tremain."

Henry Smith chortled, trying his best to appear clever. "Where's D? Any fool knows you missed D."

Andersen glared. "If one more person asks me where D is, I shall throttle him."

Henry swallowed his grin, and Basil quickly returned his attention to emptying his plate.

Andersen's look challenged anyone else to interrupt. "From now on, gentlemen, as they appear on your calendars in code, the ladies will not be mentioned by name among yourselves or to your servants. Anything which pertains to our scheme we will refer to by their letter in the alphabet. Is that understood?"

The marquis pointed to the little squiggle beside certain dates. "What is this mark?"

Sarah leaned forward. "I placed a star beside the day you are free to do whatever you please. Lord Copley has insisted you are able to find your own entertainment."

"Righto!" Basil agreed.

Henry nodded, grinning. "I say, Miss Grimsley, you are a diamond of the first water in my book."

Sarah blushed at the compliment. If Mr. Smith was warming to her, she felt certain he'd be most pleased when she disclosed all the activities she'd thought up to help entertain him on his days off.

Wetherby continued to tap the spot with his finger with a look in his eye Sarah didn't comprehend, but which bothered her more than the audible expressions of the other two gentlemen. Only with Mr. Peter Trummel did she feel confident that her rules would be followed.

Sarah was getting hungrier and hungrier. She'd swallowed her cinnamon buns, but had replaced them in her cheeks with some of the toast from her plate. All the rest of the food lay untouched.

Nooney hadn't said a word when Sarah asked her to carry up a full tray of food this morning, even though she knew her mistress would be breaking fast with the gentlemen at an early hour. She wished she could return to her chambers to eat some of it.

Now Sarah was glad to see that the men had finished their meal, and as Andersen escorted Sarah from the room, she whispered. "The real reason I have you escorting Mrs. Bennington into dinner this evening, my lord, is because, I thought that it would be best if you did not show any partiality to any of the young women on their first night here. It might cause ill feelings among them and cast obstacles in the way of your goal."

With his stomach full and the men expressing enthusiasm over their parts in the coming charade, Andersen felt more benevolent. "Miss Grimsley, your decisions have been quite appropriate. But what are your plans for the next few weeks? I doubt I would look forward to listening to Mrs. Bennington every evening."

She gave him an accusing look. "You did not read your schedule last night either, did you?"

Andersen gave her a guilty grin. "It was quite late when I retired."

Sarah raised her nose in the air. "Then I suggest that you go read them immediately, your lordship."

He put his lips near her ear and said teasingly. "Don't you think it would save time if you tell me?"

Heaven help her! The rascal was impossible. Sarah took a step toward the stairs to the first floor. She wasn't about to tell him that she'd rotated his dinner partners every night. She felt her face flushing, and she didn't dare look at him. "However am I to help you, if you won't cooperate? Don't you realize your guests will be arriving shortly?"

Andersen didn't have time to reply, for Jacob called from the front of the Great Hall. "Your lordship, one of the footmen has just rid up to say that two coaches have passed through the entrance gates into the park."

Instantly, the entire castle became an efficient, whirling piece of machinery. Andersen swore that servants materialized out of the walls. As Miss Grimsley rang bells, footmen rushed forward, maids scurried up and down the stairs.

Jacob shooed boys out the door, telling them to direct the coachmen to the stables as soon as the guest's baggage was unloaded.

Mr. Proctor took his post at the great arched entrance doors ready to admit the guests.

The Benningtons arrived twenty minutes later in two coaches, with riding horses tethered to the rear, two outriders, liveried footmen and a gaggle of servants.

It wasn't until the great medieval doors swung open that Sarah saw the snow had stopped falling. The entire outdoors was as white as a sheet of bleached muslin. A whirl of capes and bonnets, tall beaver hats, mufflers, low masculine voices and feminine squeals of delight cascaded into the hall. Footmen carried in trunks, lady's maids scurried behind their mistresses, horses whinnied in the background, to the accompaniment of young boys, laughing.

Two fur-wrapped females entered. Farther behind, a portly, red-faced man, huffed and puffed his way up the steps, refusing any assistance from a younger, gangly youth beside him.

Lord Copley reached them first, his deep voice at its most elegant. "Mrs. Bennington," he said, making a leg, "and Miss Bennington. You do my humble home a singular honor."

He didn't pause for more than a curtsy from the ladies before speaking to the gentlemen. "Mr. Bennington. Welcome, sir." He looked quizzically at the young man, who stood uneasily shifting from one foot to the other.

"My son, your lordship. We . . ."

Mrs. Bennington interrupted him. "We hope you don't mind that we brought Elroy, your lordship. But of course you don't. What is one more at a party? He came home unexpectedly . . .

"Sent down from Oxford," finished Mr. Bennington.

The ball now jumped back to Mrs. Bennington. "And we

could not bear to be parted from him for one minute. Could we, dear?"

Without waiting for her husband to answer, the woman's curiosity turned to Sarah.

Andersen, made dizzy from looking back and forth between the pair, hurriedly made the introductions. "May I present Miss Stanhope Grimsley. Her father was the late Lord Grimsley of Kent. Perhaps you remember her mother, Lady Gwendolyn Flushing? Granddaughter of the Earl of Blessing? Miss Grimsley has been gracious enough to agree to be my hostess for this occasion. It is she who has made all the preparations. I could not have planned it without her *savoir faire.*"

As he watched for the Benningtons' reaction to his hostess, Andersen held his breath. Her acceptance or recognition could make or break his plans.

Mrs. Bennington frowned and glanced from her son to Sarah. "Is it any trouble—?"

". . . to put up our son?" Mr. Bennington said, raising his eyebrows.

Sarah was doing some quick ciphering. "Mr. Elroy Bennington," she said heartily, sending a quick blush up the young man's face. "You are indeed an answer to a prayer. It seems we are short one escort for our number of ladies. Who could have imagined that we would be presented with such a fine-looking gentleman at this late date? What good fortune that you brought your son," she said, smiling at Mrs. Bennington.

Elroy blinked. Andersen was certain the pink-faced, young man had not been long out of the classroom, and had yet to consider himself an adult.

Mrs. Bennington was about to add something when they heard a high-pitched squeal.

"Oh, Mother, look at this room!"

While they were all focusing their attention on the Bennington heir, young Miss Bennington had wandered off. She now stood pointing down the length of the Great Hall toward the roaring fire in the fireplace. "It's a faeryland!"

Immediately, Mrs. Bennington excused herself to join her daughter.

Mr. Bennington, his gaze still on Sarah, hooted. " 'Pon my soul! It finally came to me. I do remember Lady Gwendolyn. Quite a charmer, if I remember. The ladies called her an Original."

Sarah held her breath as Mr. Bennington looked her up and down quite thoroughly. His admiration showing in his eyes. "So you are Lady Gwendolyn's daughter. Well, well, don't that beat a hot pudding?"

Relief rushed through Andersen. So far so good, but before more memories were hatched up, he said, "I am sure you would all like to be shown to your rooms."

Andersen's eyes sent Miss Grimsley a silent message to act quickly before their guests had more time to contemplate her background. He was thankful to see that she had caught his meaning, for she immediately approached Mrs. Bennington.

Sarah wasn't certain what Lord Copley's frantic jerks of his head meant. She hoped he wasn't going to falter under the pressure of having guests for the next few weeks, but she supposed it was time for the family to settle in. She called Mrs. Proctor and asked her to take Mr. and Mrs. Bennington to their chambers in the East Wing, and to open up a room on the second floor for Mr. Elroy near the other bachelors.

"Miss Bennington," I shall escort you to your room in the West Wing," she said, "where all the single ladies will be staying."

Mrs. Bennington nodded her approval.

Miss Bennington was a pretty girl, not at all self-conscious or judgmental. Sarah decided that she liked this candidate for the next Lady Copley. The young lady expressed interest in everything around her, commented on the costumes in the

Great Hall, the colorful banners, and flowers. From the great number of trunks waiting in her room, Sarah wondered if Miss Bennington had come planning to stay for life. Two maids were already hanging up the dresses and arranging their mistress's accessories. Sarah thought of her own solitary trunk that she'd packed for her five months in London, and wondered how long her few dresses would have lasted.

After seeing to her guest's comfort, Sarah excused herself.

Once she was back in her own room, Sarah kicked off her slippers and sank gratefully into a chair before the hearth. She pictured Miss Bennington's trim little traveling outfit with its gold braid and fur collar. Plumes from some exotic bird embellished the stylish, broadbrimmed hat. Sarah stared down at her own bright orange dress and wondered if Miss Grimsley's gowns were terribly out of fashion. But hadn't Lord Copley admired her apparel? Confusion once more threatened to engulf her. She would just have to wait to see what the other women wore.

No more than ten minutes passed before there was a knock on her door.

It was Nooney. "Me aunt says to tell you more guests are coming, ma'am." She ran forward and picked up Sarah's slippers when she saw her having difficulty reaching them. "Do you want me to help you? Don't seem right, a lady like you, having to do for herself."

Accepting the shoes, Sarah gave the girl a smile that didn't expose her uneasiness. "Thank you, Nooney. You know, I prefer to do for myself."

Sarah waited for Nooney to leave before she struggled up from her seat. Adjusting her corset and giving her turban a twist, she hurried down to be ready to greet the next guests.

Half an hour later, Miss Edith Tremain and her companion, Miss Glover had no sooner been shown to their rooms, than Miss Beverly Martin arrived fast on their heels with her aunt, Lady Martin. Miss Tremain had come with only two small trunks, whereas Miss Martin's coach was piled high with baggage.

Miss Martin, looking fit as a fiddle, her cheeks ruddy from the chill, green eyes twinkling, had ridden the last eighteen miles on her gray stallion, Lightning.

"I left m'aunt and the silly maids to the safety of the vehicle," she said, with a hearty laugh.

No matter how much Sarah enjoyed the out-of-doors, to have ridden that far on a wintry day was beyond her comprehension.

"I say, Copley, d'you still have that prime bit of horseflesh you bought last year? My offer of eight hundred guineas still stands."

Andersen grinned at the tall woman before him and nodded. "I take it you are referring to Hamilton? He is not for sale."

Miss Martin cocked her head to one side. "From what I could see, you have a fair-sized park. While I'm here, we'll have to pair the two in a race. What say you to that? Perhaps a little bet on the side?"

Sarah watched Lord Copley throw back his head and laugh. The sound bounced off the walls, echoing throughout the room. Miss Martin made his lordship happy. That was a good basis for marriage, she was sure. Not as pretty as Miss Bennington, but there was no question that she was a handsome woman and healthy. Sarah could see a line of little Copleys, all seated on purebred horses, trailing behind their parents. That thought brought the little jolt to her heart again.

An hour later luncheon was served in the smaller room they'd used for breakfast. The two fireplaces warmed it well enough, and as everywhere else in the castle, the room was

filled with flowers. Pride filled Sarah when she thought of
what Nooney and the other serving maids had accomplished. Unless the guests looked out the tall, narrow window which faced a back courtyard, they would have thought
it the middle of summer.

Sarah had personal maids assigned to both Miss Tremain
and her companion, Miss Glover.

By now, Lord Copley's four friends had joined them.
With the exception of young Elroy Bennington, all the
younger members of the party seemed to have made each
other's acquaintance previously.

Sarah noted that the women had changed to high-waisted,
long-sleeved afternoon dresses. Either a sleeveless pelisse
or a beautiful shawl finished their costume. Only Miss Martin seemed oblivious to the cold and eschewed any garment
which provided additional warmth. Again, Sarah questioned
her own cumbersome attire, suddenly feeling fat and lonely.
Then during the meal, Lord Copley's discerning eyes found
her, and raising his glass to her from across the room, he
winked. What did he mean by his salute?

To hide her bewilderment, she looked about the room.
All were here now except the Earl of Favor and his daughter
Lady Caroline. It would be dark in a few more hours. If
they didn't arrive tonight, it would throw off her dinner
plans. If they arrived a day late, it would throw them off
more. She'd told Cook that the evening meal would be
served promptly at eight o'clock. Instead of meeting in the
solar, the smaller room off the main room, she'd planned
on having the guests assemble in front of the hearth in the
Great Hall. They'd expressed their preference for the large,
open fireplace.

She'd thought everyone would be so exhausted from their
journey that they would want to rest the remainder of the
afternoon, but instead their animated chatter electrified the
air.

An hour ticked by and Sarah despaired that they would

Take a Trip Back to the Romantic Regent Era of the Early 1800's with

4 FREE ZEBRA REGENCY ROMANCES!

(AN $18.49 VALUE!)

4 FREE BOOKS ARE YOURS

PLUS YOU'LL SAVE ALMOST $4.00 EVERY MONTH WITH CONVENIENT FREE HOME DELIVERY!

See Details Inside....

We'd Like to Invite You to Subscribe to Zebra's Regency Romance Book Club and Give You a Gift of 4 Free Books as Your Introduction! *(Worth $18.49!)*

If you're a Regency lover, imagine the joy of getting 4 FREE Zebra Regency Romances and then the chance to have these lovely stories delivered to your home each month at the lowest prices available! Well, that's our offer to you and here's how you benefit by becoming a Zebra Home Subscription Service subscriber:

- 4 FREE Introductory Regency Romances are delivered to your doorstep
- 4 BRAND NEW Regencies are then delivered each month (usually before they're available in bookstores)
- Subscribers save almost $4.00 every month
- Home delivery is always FREE
- You also receive a FREE monthly newsletter, *Zebra/ Pinnacle Romance News* which features author profiles, contests, subscriber benefits, book previews and more
- No risks or obligations...in other words you can cancel whenever you wish with no questions asked

Join the thousands of readers who enjoy the savings and convenience offered to Regency Romance subscribers. After your initial introductory shipment, you receive 4 brand-new Zebra Regency Romances each month to examine for 10 days. Then, if you decide to keep the books, you'll pay the preferred subscriber's price of just $3.65 per title. That's only $14.60 for all 4 books and there's never an extra charge for shipping and handling.

It's a no-lose proposition, so return the FREE BOOK CERTIFICATE today!

Say Yes to 4 Free Books!

COMPLETE AND RETURN THE ORDER CARD TO RECEIVE THIS $18.49 VALUE, ABSOLUTELY FREE!

(If the certificate is missing below, write to:
Zebra Home Subscription Service, Inc.,
120 Brighton Road, P.O. Box 5214, Clifton, New Jersey 07015-5214)

FREE BOOK CERTIFICATE

YES! Please rush me 4 Zebra Regency Romances without cost or obligation. I understand that each month thereafter I will be able to preview 4 brand-new Regency Romances FREE for 10 days. Then, if I should decide to keep them, I will pay the money-saving preferred subscriber's price of just $14.60 for all 4...that's a savings of almost $4 off the publisher's price with no additional charge for shipping and handling. I may return any shipment within 10 days and owe nothing, and I may cancel this subscription at any time. My 4 FREE books will be mine to keep in any case.

Name _____

Address _____ Apt. _____

City _____ State _____ Zip _____

Telephone (   ) _____

Signature _____
(If under 18, parent or guardian must sign.)

RF0396

Terms and prices subject to change. Orders subject to acceptance by Zebra Home Subscription Service, Inc.

ever go to their rooms. Her feet were aching, and she was
carrying so much unnatural weight on the front of her body
that her back was playing her up again. She'd eaten very
little. The truth of the matter was that although she was
having to pretend to be the rotund Miss Grimsley, Sarah
was losing weight. And no wonder, for she'd had no time
to eat a decent meal since his lordship had come back over
a week ago and announced that all her carefully laid plans
had been for naught. Recently, Sarah noticed she had to
lace her corset tighter to keep the pillow from falling out.

Finally everyone filed out of the room. With a sigh of
relief, Sarah told the servants to remove the remains of the
meal, then leaving most of the guests in the Great Hall, she
excused herself to go to her chambers.

Sarah only had to sniff the air to know that she'd had a
visitor again. She approached the silver tray on the table.
Not one bun was missing, not one item out of place. But
she knew Dog had been there. A quick look around the
room told her he'd already come and gone. What had the
beast wanted?

She stuffed two more cinnamon buns into her cheeks and
hurried out the door. There was no time to contemplate the
mystery. She'd reached the balcony when she heard Mr.
Proctor's voice below.

"Lord Favor and Lady Caroline have arrived, my lord."

Nine

Lady Caroline swept into the Great Hall. Her ermine-trimmed, bright green cape floated out behind her like great emerald wings. Close in her wake strutted a pompous man, wrapped in an enormous great coat with several capes, as impressive as the lady was beautiful.

"Darling," Lady Caroline exclaimed, extending both gloved hands toward Lord Copley, who had transversed the length of the hall to greet them.

Andersen walked quickly, but not too quickly to greet the earl and his daughter. It would not do to look too eager, he thought.

Sarah watched the pageantry from the balcony. She not only had an all encompassing view of all that transpired, but because of the peculiar acoustics, she heard every word spoken.

"Lady Caroline," Lord Copley said, giving her one of his charming smiles before bowing over her hand.

The nobleman beside her nodded his approval.

From the balcony above, Sarah watched, transfixed. Why didn't he just fling himself into her arms? she mused moodily.

The baron greeted his other guest. "Lord Favor, welcome to Roxwealde Castle."

So that was the Earl of Favor, Sarah thought, studying the man beside Lady Caroline. His jowls bounced each time he shook his head, and his body, once his coat and capes were removed, bespoke a man who took great pride in his appearance. His stance was erect, his grooming immaculate, but the immense girth showed all the signs of being constrained by a corset.

"It's Caroline, all right," Miss Martin's throaty whisper floated up to Sarah, "making her usual show."

"Oh, Bev, do be careful or she will hear you," Miss Bennington giggled.

"Don't care if she does," said the outspoken horsewoman.

"Well, I think anyone so beautiful cannot help but be a little vain," Miss Tremain said kindly.

"You are too generous in your evaluation, Edith," Beverly Martin replied. "Next thing you will be telling me I am the epitome of honesty."

Miss Tremain laughed softly. "You are too hard on yourself, Bev."

Afraid she'd be caught eavesdropping, Sarah hurried toward the stairs. It was her duty as Lord Copley's hostess to meet the new guests, not listen in on private conversations. She'd never approached anyone as high in the instep as the earl. A tiny frisson of fear ran down her spine. Fixing her gaze on a swag of purple morning glories festooned from the balcony across the hall, she took a deep breath, pulled back her shoulders and proceeded downward. She prayed for courage, reminding herself that the baron was depending on her to make his party a success.

Lady Caroline had already started toward the gathering of people silhouetted against the light of the fire on the monstrous hearth, motioning invitingly to the baron. "I am chilled to the bone," she crooned, as if imparting some intimate secret, but loudly enough for everyone to hear.

Andersen took her hand and tucked it over his arm. "While you are my guest, your comfort is my greatest concern, Lady Caroline."

Sarah's eyes narrowed.

The lady looked up adoringly at the baron. "I hope you mean that sincerely, my lord."

Lord Copley placed his hand protectively over hers. "Ah, but I do. Come, both of you," he said to the earl, "warm yourselves by the fire. I am certain you are acquainted with most of my other guests."

Lord Wetherby stepped out from where he'd been lounging against a pillar. "Lady Caroline," he said, making a low bow. "I can now say that my long journey has not been in vain."

Sarah wished with all her heart that the marquis would take the lady and depart immediately, but her hope plummeted when Lady Caroline cut him short.

"Why Lord Wetherby, I am afraid that if you count on my presence to be your sole source of entertainment, you will be sadly disappointed," she said, glancing up at the baron through long, thick lashes.

Wetherby accepted his defeat in gentlemanly fashion. Hiding any slight he might have felt under a mask of indifference, he bowed and engaged Lord Favor in conversation.

Copley grinned at Wetherby's abrupt putdown. It bode well for his own suit, but there was still the earl to win over. Would Favor agree to his only daughter marrying a baron? Of course, there were Miss Bennington and Miss Martin to consider also, and he was very much aware the two ladies were watching his every move.

Andersen didn't dare let Lady Caroline take up too much of his time. He needed Miss Grimsley. Where was she?

The earl who was still talking to the marquis stopped in midsentence and stared upward. "Gawd, Wetherby, who is that fine figure of a woman?"

Andersen knew only one person who could extract such an exclamation, and let his gaze follow that of the earl's. Thank God! Miss Grimsley had arrived. He stepped forward. "She, Lord Favor, is my hostess."

Lady Caroline stopped simpering. Andersen believed it the first time he'd ever seen her overshadowed. No one commanded the attention of an entire room as did the Duke of Warrick's former keeper-of-the-keys. No, Andersen thought proudly, she was his mistress-of-the-castle now.

The earl scrambled to take Sarah's hand. Then he turned around abruptly and barked. "Where are you, Copley? Introduce me to this angel."

The baron happily obliged.

"Lord Favor and Lady Caroline, may I present my hostess, the Honourable Stanhope Grimsley."

He wasn't quite sure he liked the way the earl was looking at Miss Grimsley, but he did want Favor to feel at home at Roxwealde, didn't he? Perhaps, his hostess was the key to winning the earl's approval for his daughter's hand in marriage. There could be no harm in it.

Caroline, clearly unhappy that the attention wasn't on her anymore, pouted prettily and tapped Andersen's sleeve. "I am feeling a chill, my lord. You promised me a place by the fire."

"Of course, my dear," he said, smiling at the beautiful woman on his arm. "Shall we join the others? I am sure you want to greet everyone."

Anxiety filled Sarah as she watched Lord Copley walk away from her. The earl, on the other hand, showed no inclination to leave her side. In fact, he moved closer.

"Ah, Miss Grimsley. I can see you don't recognize me, but I was a guest of the Duke of Warrick's in Cornwall five years ago. I can truthfully say, my dear lady, that the years have done you justice. You look younger now than you did then. Sometime you must tell me your secret."

The smirk on his face so added to Sarah's uneasiness that she blushed and was trying unsuccessfully to put some distance between them, when Mr. Trummel appeared.

After greeting the earl, he said, "Miss Grimsley, I believe Lord Copley would like you to see Lady Caroline to her room. And Lord Favor, Proctor is ready to see you to your quarters."

Sarah threw Mr. Trummel a grateful look. But it didn't stop the earl from whispering in her ear, "I do believe it's fate that brought me here, my dear. Now that Warrick has gone to his reward, and the baron, I am sure, will be thinking of starting his own nursery, you may be seeking another position in the near future."

"Miss Grimsley," Peter said, holding out his hand, "may I escort you to Lady Caroline?"

Sarah's heart was beating so fast she grabbed for Mr. Trummel's outstretched hand as if it were a lifeline. "Oh, thank you, that is most kind of you." She had no idea what the earl was talking about, only that he thought he recognized her. How well had he known the real Miss Grimsley? Was all to be in vain? She had to play the charade through for the baron. If she exposed herself, she exposed him. Oh, dear, she thought. She really was in a pickle now.

Mrs. Proctor intercepted her. "Miss Grimsley, as soon as you see Lady Caroline to her chambers, Cook wants to consult you on a matter concerning dinner."

Sarah looked about. Most of the guests had left the hall, and Lady Caroline stood impatiently tapping her foot at the base of the stairs. There was no time to commiserate on her own misfortunes. The plan must be carried out.

She was too tired to puff out her cheeks, so keeping her head down, she said, "Forgive me, Lady Caroline, if you will follow me, I shall show you to your chambers."

Lady Caroline didn't budge. "I am hungry. My father insisted we would be served when we arrived."

Sarah gritted her teeth. "It is past four o'clock, my lady."

"Why did you not wait for us?"

"The other guests had been here for several hours. But if you wish. I shall be pleased to have a light repast sent up to your room."

"I want an entire meal. Tell your chef that I like my meat very tender."

Sarah rolled her eyes and turned to motion to a footman. She didn't think Cook would be too happy to fix a luncheon when she was in the midst of preparations for tonight's banquet. "Now, this way if you please, my lady."

Gliding up the stairs, looking neither this way or that, Lady Caroline didn't make pretty comments about the decor as Miss Tremain and Miss Bennington had done. Even Miss Glover had given a hearty hoot when she'd reached the first floor landing and turned to observe the banners that festooned from the balcony.

Sarah had decorated Lady Caroline's room in shades of yellow. Caroline didn't even notice.

"Why are my clothes not hung up, Jessie?" she scolded her serving maid.

The small, dark-haired girl shrugged as if accustomed to being put down. "I was pressing the sarcenet gown you said you wished to wear this evening, my lady."

"You are a lazy girl, Jessie. You have not even sorted out my slippers. Pull the cord to summon Suzette. I want her to rub my forehead for me. And go find Damien and tell him I want him to start dressing my hair in another hour."

Before Jessie could follow all those instructions, Caroline threw herself onto the bed. "Pull off my boots. And be careful, you stupid girl. You nearly twisted my left ankle last night at the inn. Oh," she said to Sarah, "it is so hard to find competent servants anymore. Is it not, Miss Grimsley?"

Sarah wouldn't blame the girl if she had a mind to twist Lady Caroline's right foot this time. "I find a competent mistress has competent help," said Sarah. She realized that Lady Caroline missed the point altogether.

There was a tap on the door. Two servants entered carrying trays, one with covered dishes, the other with a tea set and biscuits. "We brung the lady's lunch, ma'am."

"Thank you," Sarah said.

"Put it on the table by the bed," Caroline ordered, bunching up a pillow behind her. "I am too exhausted to sit at a table. The day has been such a bore, driving for hours in that bumpy coach. Does the baron have a French chef, Miss Grimsley?"

"No, Cook is from a local family. I think you will find her cuisine quite satisfactory.

"Well, I suppose it will have to do."

Sarah set her teeth. "If you will excuse me, Lady Caroline, I have other duties that require my attention. Dinner will be served at eight o'clock. I have invited everyone to gather in front of the hearth in the Great Hall half an hour before."

Caroline dismissed Sarah with a wave of her hand, then took the cover off the first dish and wrinkled her nose.

With a snort, Sarah departed.

Everyone degreed dinner to be a resounding success. Lady Caroline even showed exemplary manners and exuded enthusiasm for every remove, at least as long as the baron was looking at her.

Sarah had chosen to wear a violet gauze dress over a deep purple, silk underslip. Her head was wrapped with the same shade of purple and secured with a large diamond brooch. The eye of a peacock feather was stuck in the pin. Sarah was glad to see that Lady Martin also wore a turban, although it wasn't quite as ostentatious as Miss Grimsley's creations. Lady Bennington was dressed modestly, but all her jewels bespoke her husband's wealth. Sarah wondered if Miss Glover wore only little brown dresses. The silk, brocaded shawl around her fragile shoulders told of better days.

It was the young women's dresses which Sarah envied most. Her own country dresses would have been quite out of style in London, and she was certain she'd have been a laughingstock if she'd worn them at the table this evening. These young women of the ton all had fashionable, high-waisted frocks made of the loveliest fabrics, long or puffed sleeves with evening gloves that came above the elbow. Ribbons and jewels decorated their hair and oh, such slender figures. Sarah wondered if the baron would gaze at her with such admiration if he saw how she really looked without her pillow.

Sarah watched all the young gentlemen admire and flirt with the ladies, even though they knew that Lord Copley had them here to make his choice of a wife. All except E, of course. Sarah couldn't see why he didn't consider Miss Tremain. She was more than pretty and had the sweetest disposition of any of them. It was a real puzzle.

The baron escorted Mrs. Bennington into dinner, much to that woman's delight. Sarah asked Mr. Elroy Bennington to be her escort, which turned the young man's face a permanent shade of red, that showed no signs of fading during the entire meal.

To Sarah's relief, Lord Copley's friends all remembered their assignments. The marquis was quite charming regardless that his partner, Lady Caroline, rudely turned her back to him and smiled mostly at the baron. The senior Benningtons continued to finish each other's sentences. Basil was not quite sure of how to divide his attention between his plate and A, Mr. Smith laughed more at his jokes than did B, Mr. Trummel and E kept up a quiet conversation just between themselves. Miss Glover didn't act the least bit *elderly,* and refused to let Sarah cut up her meat for her.

Lord Copley was too far away at the other end of the long table for Sarah to catch much of his conversation. She was glad that she'd seated Lord Favor next to his host, although, it still didn't seem to deter the earl's eyes from seeking her out and sending little messages that Sarah didn't know how to interpret.

Although the guests had been quite generous in their

praise of what she had done inside the castle, Sarah's despair had been that she could do nothing about the gray stones, the bare ground, and near dead ivy vines clutching the outer walls and fences. It would be terribly depressing if their guests wished to go outside. As Mr. Proctor had said in his practical way, *"Aye, looks the same today and yeste'day and the day before that."*

To Sarah's great surprise, it was through Miss Tremain's eyes and words that she saw her most trying problem dissolve.

"I cannot imagine why you haven't thought of throwing a party before, Lord Copley. When we drove up the carriageway this afternoon, I did not think I should ever see anything so beautiful. It was truly a wonderland."

"You are more than kind, Miss Tremain," Andersen said. "I had never heard this old . . . this home of mine called anything so fanciful."

"Some see and yet, don't see, my lord," she said.

Basil turned to his partner. "I didn't notice anything 'straordinary, did you?"

Miss Bennington in turn glanced at her mother. "Remember you said that you expected to see Rapunzel letting down her hair from one of the tower windows, Mama."

"Well, Mrs. Bennington," said her husband, looking at his wife with surprise, "I thought you got over such nonsense long ago."

"No woman gives up on romance, Mr. Bennington. It is only that it gets lost somewhere . . ."

"In the realities of life, Mrs. Bennington?"

Lady Caroline sniffed. "Well, I cannot imagine what you are all talking about. I saw nothing worth looking at when we drove up."

Miss Glover, who hadn't said one word all through the meal, spoke up. "I, for one, agree with Edith. Anyone who is not blind would have seen it was a sight to behold."

The baron was amused by the genuine rebuke given by

the little, brown sparrow of a woman. "Tell us what we missed, Miss Glover."

With obvious enjoyment, she nodded first at him and then at the others. "You know, you all remind me of the scholarly physicians who argued and argued about how many teeth a goat had. None of them could agree. Then a little boy came along and asked them why they just didn't go get a goat and open its mouth and count its teeth. They said they'd never thought of that. Now, I suggest that those of you who didn't have eyes in your heads today, take the little boy's advice and go see for yourselves what the these astute ladies are talking about."

The baron raised his glass in salute. "Well said, Miss Glover. Tomorrow we will do as you suggest. And now before the ladies retire to the Great Hall, I believe our hostess would like to tell every one what they can expect during the coming weeks."

Sarah blinked. The baron had tossed the entire package in her lap. She really wasn't sure of how to go about it, except to hand them all a copy of her calendar. But that would give away his lordship's scheme.

"A tour," Miss Glover said smartly. "I would like a tour of the castle tomorrow."

A low murmur went around the table.

Basil's face suddenly lit up. "By Jove! I have never seen the whole castle, Copley. How about you, Miss A? Would you like a tour of the castle? Tomorrow's my day with you. Whoops! I mean, Miss Bennington, I was going to ask you . . ." He frowned as if figuring out something quite profound.

Andersen had no time to reason, or to throttle Basil. He wanted Miss Grimsley to take over. He held up his hands and glancing down to the end of the table, threw Sarah a conspiratory grin. "Ladies and gentlemen, our hostess, I believe, has something to say."

Oh, he was a rascal, Sarah thought, thinking to escape

all responsibility for entertaining his guests. Well, he was in this game as well as she, and she was getting a wee bit tired of being the one on the teasing end. She smiled back at him before turning to the little lady seated next to her.

"What a wonderful suggestion, Miss Glover. Tomorrow morning as soon as breakfast is over, his lordship will take everyone on a tour of Roxwealde castle. I am certain he has many an interesting tale to tell about his ancestral home."

Sarah wasn't brave enough to look at Lord Copley and signaled for Jacob to hold her chair. Serves him right, she thought. "And now ladies, we shall retire to the Great Hall, while the gentlemen have their port and cigars."

It wasn't until she nearly reached the door before she turned. "Shall we say breakfast at nine o'clock tomorrow morning, my lord?" Sarah didn't wait for his answer. She was certain she'd hear his opinion soon enough, unless she could avoid being alone with him for the remainder of the evening.

Luck didn't smile on Sarah. Even though she tried to stay out of his sight, Lord Copley cornered her later in a back hallway, as she was going to talk to Cook about breakfast.

"Miss Grimsley, how dare you say that I would conduct a tour? And at that ungodly hour. Do you want me to be a laughingstock? Let me assure you, the remainder of the castle is nothing but a disgraceful ruin and bitterly cold."

Sarah could tell he wasn't too pleased with her, and she tried to pacify him. "But, my lord, Mr. and Mrs. Proctor showed me all through the castle—all except your apartment, of course. I thoroughly enjoyed their stories about your great-great-grandfather, Percival, the first baron. Besides," she said, turning her back to him. "I am sure that you can make it sound quite romantic—and that is what you want, is it not?"

His lordship now stood so close behind her, that Sarah felt his breath on the back of her neck. She was finding it very difficult to keep her mind on the subject. "Tomorrow the ladies will be escorted by your friends. It will give you an excellent opportunity to interact with all three women without having to spend all your time with one."

She could almost hear his mind working, but she wasn't sure in which direction.

"By Jupiter! You may be right. However, I doubt that many will be up that early. But we shall see. He gave her a hug. "Miss Grimsley, once again you have astounded me with your acuteness. And I must say to your credit, that when word gets back to London of the wonders which you have wrought in Roxwealde Castle, it will be the talk of the ton this Season. Carry on with whatever you were doing. I must go back to our guests."

With her back still to him, Sarah listened to Lord Copley walk away, whistling. He was gone, and yet, the warmth of his breath and the strength of his arms where he'd touched her still lingered. Sarah wrapped her arms around herself and squeezed, wishing she could feel that way forever. If his lordship was pleased with what she'd achieved in his favor tonight, just wait until he found out what she had in store for him on the morrow.

The next morning, a cacophony of strident sounds echoed through the halls at seven o'clock—and again at eight. Clasping her hands in satisfaction, Sarah was pleased to see that no one missed the tour.

After Lord Copley had left her in the hallway the night before, she thought long and hard on what he had said about their guests oversleeping.

For someone who always rose with the sun, it was difficult for Sarah to understand the desire anyone had to lay-a-bed. She didn't want the guests to be disappointed because they had overslept and missed the tour. Nor did she want Lord Copley to have his feelings hurt when no one turned up. So before she retired, she ordered several servants to march along all the corridors ringing bells and banging pan lids to announce the breakfast hour.

Miss Martin, Sarah found out, was the only one up before the wake-up call. She blew in from the outside, her face pink from the cold, slapping her leg with her riding crop. "Ho, Miss Grimsley, it's a jolly good day for a brisk canter around the park."

Sarah was impressed. "I am astounded to see you up so early."

Miss Martin guffawed. "Would not miss my morning ride for all the tea in China. I should have made a bet with someone last night, that I would be the first to follow Miss Glover's advice to take a good look about. She was right, you know. There are a thousand icicles handing on the trees and the roof looks as if it was tiled with white snow. Quite an impressive sight. Well, the first sleepyheads are coming down the stairs, so I shall change my clothes and see you shortly."

Sarah looked up to see the baron descending from the second floor and even in the dim light, she could tell his expression was not that of a happy man. She was certain she would have been in for a good tongue lashing if Miss Glover and Miss Bennington hadn't joined him on the first floor landing. Of a certainty, it was their lighthearted chatter that softened his heart, and by the time he reached the ground floor, he greeted her—if not cheerfully—at least with some restraint.

"Miss Grimsley, I am not sure whether I should strangle you now or wait until I have had my coffee."

Fortunately for Sarah, the guests arrived, some eagerly, some not so. Mrs. Bennington even dragged Mr. Bennington out of bed for the excursion.

Andersen advised everyone to put on their coats and

gloves, because most of the house wasn't heated. Surprised by his own eagerness, he soon warmed to the venture and even allowed the party to go up the tower on the East Wing.

"Careful everyone, the steps are chipped and stones fall off the walls."

When they climbed onto the parapet, the sun made a rare appearance. As they looked down over the landscape, silence fell upon the group. From the tower Andersen had a clear view of the West Wing, a large section of the park, the iron gates in the distance. The gray stone was tinged with golden light, and the once bare vines were necklaces of white-pearls climbing up the walls. Across the heath, the outcroppings rose above the thin blanket of snow.

Miss Tremain spoke first. "The rocks look like toy castles, don't they?" Several others agreed.

Over the heads of the others, Andersen searched the crowd for a glimpse of Miss Grimsley. Her scarlet turban was not hard to see. He waited until their eyes met, then he winked.

Relief once again warmed Sarah. Evidently his lordship wasn't put out with her anymore, and she was getting used to his flirting. But her eyes narrowed when she saw Lady Caroline sidle up to his lordship.

"I'm cold," Lady Caroline complained, breaking the faery spell.

Miss Martin harrumphed. "What you need is a little blood in your veins, Caro."

The marquis stepped forward quickly, and stripping himself quickly of his coat, he wrapped it around Lady Caroline's shoulders. "Here, take my coat," he said.

Caroline glared at him, but had to wear the garment, or look like a shrew, Sarah thought with a smile of satisfaction.

Miss Glover pushed forward. "Lord Copley, does the castle have any ghosts?"

Andersen tried to keep his amusement from showing. "I

am sorry to disappoint you, but Roxwealde has not been blessed with a haunt of any kind."

Lady Caroline tightened her hold on Copley's arm. "Well, I for one hope not."

"I think it a pity," the diminutive lady exclaimed, shaking her head. "A castle needs a ghost."

Sarah could see that there were more who agreed with Lady Caroline, and before the speculations could go any further, she announced gaily, "Shall we all go back inside, everyone? I have asked Mrs. Proctor to have some hot mulled cider ready for us by the fire before luncheon is served."

Later when everyone had retired to their rooms to freshen themselves, Sarah grabbed the opportunity to slip into her own chambers to replenish her cinnamon buns.

As the guests began to file back into the Great Hall the baron caught up with her. "You did it, Miss Grimsley—you've made them think my castle is beautiful. But," he looked at her quizzically, "there is something I must know."

Lord Copley was very close, but remembering how she'd felt when he'd hugged her last evening, Sarah was afraid to look at him.

"What, my lord?"

He laughed. "How did you ever get the sun to come out?"

She turned then and saw his face still ruddy from the cold air, his blond hair freshly combed. For a moment she couldn't speak. "I didn't . . . oh, you are bamming me, aren't you?" she said, giving him a tap on the arm.

"And I believe you are flirting with me, Miss Grimsley." Sarah blushed.

Andersen took a deep breath and leaned closer.

Sarah saw that strange otherworld look come into his

eyes, and for a moment, thought his mind had gone elsewhere again. Then just as quickly, he snapped back.

"It is going well, is it not, Miss Grimsley? C and B are
already beginning to act like rivals. Or should I say, B and
C to be correct."

Sarah realized his meaning. "Is that what you want?"

"Why of course. You should know as well as I, that once
I get them all reeled in, I have only to make my choice.
They are all fine-looking women. A man would be proud
to have anyone of them on his arm."

With a knowing grin he nodded and walked to a group
which included Mr. Smith and Mr. Ripple, who were performing all sorts of silly antics to entertain A and B. Lord
Copley bowed over each lady's hand and by their expressions, she knew he'd said something complimentary to each.
Mr. Ripple and Mr. Smith continued to act like clowns.
Sarah sighed. A man never made a fool of himself over her.

When Lord Wetherby came in with C, Sarah thought her
to be the most beautiful—and so slender. B was broadshoul-
dered, slender hipped, and straight as an arrow. Sarah could
see her with a string of healthy children, all riding thor-
oughbred horses. And A—she had an inquisitive mind. She
was pretty, and she was slender, too.

Suddenly Sarah had no desire to eat lunch. She looked
down at her dress made of yards and yards of lime-green
muslin, over her too big bosom to her protruding stomach.
She wanted to be treated graciously like the other young
ladies. No—she only wanted Lord Copley to treat her that
way. Oh, he was most polite, but his attitude when he addressed her was of the same voice he used when he spoke
to Mrs. Bennington or Lady Martin. No, heaven help her!
He jested with her more as he did when he addressed his
male friends.

Sarah studied the elegant gowns worn by the other
women. A bit of envy niggled her conscience. Well, she
couldn't do anything about her position as hostess of Rox-

wealde Castle, but she could do something about her size. Starting today she was going to put Miss Grimsley on a diet.

Ten

For the next several days, the guests seemed quite content with the activities which Sarah proposed. The gameroom became the most popular in the castle. Tables had been set up for cards, chess, and children's activities which Miss Grimsley had found in the nursery. At first Andersen had laughed at Miss Grimsley's exuberance over her schoolroom discoveries, never believing they'd be so popular.

Mr. Bennington challenged everyone who would play him to a round of spillikins, a skill of picking up little sticks one at a time without disturbing the others in the pile. The blustering gentleman smiled proudly as he beat his own son for the fourth time.

"Always whipped everybody in the nursery," he boasted.

"Well, I never," said his wife. "I haven't known Mr. Bennington to spend more than ten minutes at one time with Elroy since the day he was born."

A pitch and toss field was set up using wooden trenchers instead of holes in the ground to catch the coins. Lady Martin and Miss Glover found this exchange particularly to their liking.

The billiard room was nearly as popular a meeting place. Lord Favor asked Copley to teach his daughter the particulars of the game, and showed no objections, although it meant Andersen had to keep his arms around her in a most improper way. As for Lady Caroline's demeanor, the baron had never known her disposition to be so agreeable. Yes, all was going well with his courting.

Andersen's four friends had fallen into their schedules quite willingly, with the exception of the day Basil was scheduled to entertain B, Miss Martin.

Andersen and Lady Caroline had taken off for an early morning ride. Upon entering the stable yard, they encountered Miss Martin and a sputtering Basil. Although he was coated, caped, gloved and scarved to his ears, he flatly refused to go beyond the gate.

Taking in a lusty breath of morning air, B whacked Basil on the arm with her crop. "Oh, come now, Ripple. A brisk rip around the Park will get the blood bubbling and all that."

"M'blood will more likely freeze."

Not to be deterred, Miss Martin grabbed the ends of Basil's woolen scarf and pulled him toward the stables. "Nonsense, it's warm compared to yesterday." Noticing for the first time that they had company, she cheerfully added, "Morning, Copley, Caro."

It took one brief look of censure from Andersen to make Basil capitulate to the inevitable. For the next hour, the portly little fellow bounced along on his mount, reins held loosely, his hands grasping the horse's mane.

"The man has no bottom at all," Miss Martin declared to Andersen, as they cantered side by side.

"He's afraid of horses," Andersen told her.

"Nonsense! Just needs to get more practice."

After that, Miss Martin seemed to be of singular mind to teach Basil to ride, and he in turn did everything possible to avoid her. But since the other young ladies enjoyed a daily ride, poor Basil found himself obliged to follow.

Later that same day, Andersen made it a point to gloat about his own progress toward his matrimonial quest for a bride.

"Ah, Miss Grimsley, my plans are going much better than

expected. I feel I am making positive headway with all three women. Our C shows a great preference for getting me into the darkest rooms of the castle alone, and her father is not objecting. If I did not know better, I might think my greatest draw for Miss B, is my horse Hamilton," he said, laughing. "Miss A asked to see my library. I told her that though I had but few books to offer her, she had my permission to borrow any volumes she wished. She exclaimed the collection of ancient treatises to be quite interesting. I never particularly wanted to read Old English papers, but I told her I admired her mind to be able to do so. Nothing pleases a beautiful woman more than to be told she is intelligent," he said confidentially. "But alas, my dilemma is being surrounded by so many pretty ones. I must own it is much to your credit, Miss Grimsley, that everything has gone so well in my favor."

Sarah should have basked happily in his praise, but strangely she didn't.

In the evenings, Miss A entertained on the piano, which Sarah had had the foresight to have tuned before the party began. Miss E, who proved to have a lovely voice, accompanied her. The vicar of Danbury Wells had recommended a local tutor who not only was capable of tuning the piano, but was accomplished on the instrument himself. On a couple of occasions he brought two of his acquaintances who played the harp and violin and provided music for dancing.

However, it was the grand tour which continued to dominate everyone's mind, and the interest in the castle grew to the point that the baron finally gave his permission for his guests to explore wherever they pleased in all areas except the West Wing. Upon popular demand, he even agreed that those who wished could climb the eastern tower. "I only ask that you step carefully and don't go alone. It's better there are at least two of you to watch for falling stones."

Consequently, the guests spent hours happily exploring endless passageways, old rooms, even the dark cellars.

The costumes and armour, which were on display in the Great Hall escalated such an interest in medieval times to the point that one evening at dinner, Miss Glover asked, "Would it not be interesting to have a medieval dinner in the manner that your ancestor provided, Lord Copley?"

"What a splendid idea," Mrs. Bennington agreed.

Andersen, quite surprised by the enthusiastic response, held up his hand for silence. "My hostess will know if this can be accomplished. Miss Grimsley, what say you to Miss Glover's suggestion?"

Sarah, who had been seated beside Lord Favor for the meal, and had been quite engrossed in trying to remove his hand from her knee under the table, had not been following the conversation. Nonetheless, when she looked up to see the guests eagerly waiting for what she guessed was an affirmative answer, she smiled weakly. "Why, I agree, of course," she said, wondering what she'd agreed upon.

The baron looked at her with satisfaction. "Then, it is agreed. We shall have a medieval dinner in four days time."

The next day a quarrel erupted between Mr. Smith and Mr. Ripple that threatened to bring them to fisticuffs. The guests had no sooner filed into the Great Hall after lunch then the two men's angry voices echoed about the room. Andersen excused himself from speaking to Mr. Bennington and approached the bickering men.

Henry poked Basil's chest with a finger. "Ripple isn't sticking to the schedule."

Andersen, aware of all the eyes turned their way signaled to Jacob. "Find Lord Wetherby, Mr. Trummel, and Miss Grimsley and ask them to come to the library immediately," he said to the servant. Taking each squabbling man firmly by an arm, he directed them away from the other guests. "I suggest we go elsewhere to straighten out your differences."

Miss Grimsley and the marquis followed on their heels. Without waiting for Peter, Andersen turned on the two men.

"Now, why are you two fighting?"

"It isn't my fault," Basil complained. "Henry is mixed up."

"It's you who don't know your alphabet, you ignoramus," Henry retorted.

"Gentlemen," Andersen said. "This should not be difficult to straighten out. I know I am assigned to C today. And you, Wetherby?"

"It's my day off," the marquis said.

Henry rounded on Basil. "He says he's supposed to have Miss Martin, and I know I have B."

Basil hooted. "Any six year old knows that Bennington starts with a B. You are supposed to be with her."

Henry rolled his eyes upward. "Stoopid! Miss Bennington is A. Miss Martin is B."

Basil hurrumphed. "That doesn't make sense. Martin doesn't start with B. By-the-by, who has E?"

As they spoke, Peter hurried into the room.

Sarah's head was spinning from swiveling back and forth between the two men. "Oh, for heavens sake, Mr. Ripple, do go take another look at your schedule."

Basil stuck out is lower lip. "Can't. Someone ate it . . . or tried to."

"What in the world do you mean, *someone tried to eat it?*"

"I couldn't remember all the letters and days, so I carried it in m'vest pocket. A couple of days ago, Miss Martin said she wanted to see me on the balcony, and I took m'schedule out to check to see if I had to go with her. You know—was it her day and all? I must've dropped it. When I went back to find it, there were only wet bits and pieces. It looked as if someone had tried to make a meal of it. Had to throw it away."

An uneasy suspicion niggled at Sarah's stomach.

Henry sniggered. "Are you saying Miss Martin eats paper?"

Basil turned red. "Don't you be puttin' down a fine lady like Miss Martin now. Besides, I already asked her to play a game of billiards today. She wins all the time, but at least it keeps me from having to go riding."

Henry stuck his nose close to Basil's. "Why didn't you say so in the first place? Don't make no nevermind to me." With a look of indifference, Henry turned to look at the others. "Ripple is such a nodhead. Seeing he has asked the lady to do something, he can't well go back on his word, now, can he? Anyway, I already told Miss Bennington, that is A, that I would accompany her up the tower after lunch."

Peter cleared his throat and stepped forward. "I believe A was to have been my charge today, but I don't mind escorting E if it will smooth things over."

Andrew grasped his head with both hands. "It surely would, Trummel, thank you."

But Sarah was not willing to be so charitable. "Mr. Smith, perhaps if you show us your calendar, we can make certain that a mixup does not happen again."

Henry stood as tall as he could on his spindly legs and stuck out his chin defiantly. "My valet lost it."

Sarah threw up her hands. They were barely into the second week and Mr. Smith and Mr. Ripple had managed to make a complete hash of her schedule. "Don't blame others for your own shortcomings, Mr. Smith. Perhaps if you had made the effort to take the responsibility, you would not have lost it. There is nothing for it but for you to make another copy."

Sarah turned to the desk to look for paper when she spied her nemesis, Mercury, standing guard over the ink pot. Peeringly menacingly over her spectacles at the baron, she said, "May we see your master plan, Lord Copley?"

Andersen decided now was not the time to test Miss

Grimsley's humor. He rummaged around in his desk drawers until he located the outline.

Sarah indicated to both men that they were to be seated on either side of the partner's desk, then placed the papers on the surface between them. "You will both make another copy of your calendar."

Mr. Ripple complied meekly. Sarah saw that being told what to do didn't sit well with Mr. Smith, but she stared him down. Sarah knew that strength of character sometimes took longer to foster in some individuals than others. Mr. Smith sputtered awhile, but finally did as he was told.

Sarah nodded her approval. "Very good, Mr. Smith. Now, perhaps after you have made the effort to rewrite your schedule in your own hand, you will not be so careless again."

Peering over her spectacles, Sarah watched while they wrote. From her point of observation, she concluded quickly that penmanship hadn't been a subject which either Mr. Smith or Mr. Ripple had mastered in school. She only hoped they could read the end product when they finished.

The baron motioned for Peter and Wetherby to follow him out of the room.

Once in the corridor, the marquis put his hand on Andersen's shoulder. "Wait a moment, Copley. I would have a word with you on another matter."

Andersen wasn't in the mood to hear anymore complaints. Every moment was taking time away from Lady Caroline. "What is it, Wetherby?"

"There is a problem with our little friends from Drury Lane."

Wetherby seemed determined to annoy him. "Isn't it something Mrs. Proctor can deal with?"

"Afraid not, old chap. Seems the gels are disgruntled that they aren't getting enough attention. Penny and Twist are unhappy that Henry and Basil are spending too much of their time with the ladies and not enough with them. You had better come see to it yourself, or I am afraid the gels may become embarrassingly vocal in their complaints, and that wouldn't set well with your guests, now, would it?"

With resignation, Andersen motioned to the marquis to follow him down a back corridor to the servants' quarters. They found the three actresses in their room near the kitchen. A candle provided the only light. Genevieve sprawled contentedly on a cot, eating bon bons from a box. Penny and Twist were holding an animated conversation in a corner. When the men entered, the two women folded their arms over their chests and fixed Lord Copley with cold stares.

Penny spoke first, "You said we wud get to live like princesses on our time off, as long as we play-acted we was maids."

"I also said you would be paid handsomely," Andersen said. "And you will."

"Aw, come on ducks! All we been doing is working our 'eads off like scullery maids. At night we stay in this windowless cell and listen to the weird noises creaking a moaning about this dismal place. It's enuff to give a saint the chills. Either we gets some better taking care of or we leaves."

"And before we do," Twist put in, "we'll see that yer fancy friends get an earful. Oh, we know wat's going on. We ain't featherheads, you know."

Andersen pulled the marquis aside. "Can't you deal with this for me, Wetherby?"

The marquis grinned. "I'll see what I can do." Turning to the actresses, he said, "Come, my darlings. If you can show a little patience, I have a gift for each of you in my chambers."

As the marquis herded the girls down the corridor toward the servants' stairs, he called back, "Remember, you owe me, Copley."

"I think it may be the other way round, Wetherby," Andersen threw after him.

When Lord Copley summoned Sarah to the library to confront Mr. Ripple and Smith, she had been relieved to get away from Lord Favor. The odious man had been making a pest of himself since breakfast, suggesting they meet in the most improper of places, where he promised he'd show her delights she'd never experienced before. Sarah had little doubt that she didn't want to see whatever it was he had to show her.

Now that Mr. Ripple and Mr. Smith had finally rewritten their schedules, she returned to her bedroom. The restful heath beckoned to her out the window. Most of the guests had retired to their rooms for a nap. Sarah had no desire to spend the afternoon sequestered in her room, yet there was no guarantee that should she go down to the Great Hall, she wouldn't find the earl lurking behind a pillar waiting to pounce on her. A fast trek out-of-doors was what she really desired. She decided that if she took the servants' stairs at the end of the corridor, she could slip into the kitchen courtyard without being observed.

The day was overcast, but it would be a few hours before nightfall came. It was not likely anyone would venture out into such a fog.

Sarah took off her dress and corset, and replaced them with a dark woolen dress for warmth. By wrapping Miss Grimsley's large cape around her, she had no need to encumber herself with all the stuffing she was finding more and more distasteful. Lastly, she pulled on Miss Grimsley's leather riding boots which had already on previous occasions, proved quite worthy of the gravel paths.

Cinnamon buns were still left on the silver tray. Sarah stuffed two of them in the inner pocket of her wrap. She hadn't eaten much lunch, and she could munch on them during her walk.

Outside the castle, she pulled the hood farther down over her face, and keeping close to the stone wall, moved quickly to a back gate south of the horseyards. She was certain the stablemen would be in their quarters over the stalls, and it was not likely any of the servants could see her from the house. Once on the heath, Sarah straightened up and taking long strides, quickened her pace. It was a glorious feeling to be able to be herself—even if it would only be for little more than an hour or so.

The first part of her journey was over familiar ground. She had only to follow the sheep and rabbit droppings to keep on a safe track. She pinned her sights on the balancing rock of an ancient burial mound about a mile away. She planned to explore farther to the left, where she'd seen interestingly shaped granite formations and a hint of an oak copse. Such a place oft hid a stream and gave shelter to many small animals and birds.

When she reached the foot of the tor, she was undecided as to which way to go. The fog kept rolling about, clear here, dense there. At times, she saw faint forms leaping in and out of the mist. Sheep most likely, playing. Twice she thought she heard something on the path behind her, and a flutter of guilt at being found out, made Sarah clutch her cloak more tightly about her. But when she looked back she saw no one. With a sigh of relief she turned her attention to the question of which way she should go.

The path which nearly disappeared in and out of the broad rocks to the left of the tor looked more difficult. If she went to the right she'd be led to the top of a meadow, already dotted with yellow daffodils and shiny yellow celandine among the longer grasses. A black grouse rose suddenly from the tall grasses at her feet, startling her so that she laughed outloud.

Being of an adventurous spirit, Sarah chose to go to the

left. But she also was of a practical mind, and looking about the ground, she collected small, odd-colored pebbles to mark her way back to the tor.

Her choice of direction soon rewarded her. A rabbit jumped across in front of her and disappeared through what looked like a hedge, but further investigation showed it to be a thick scrub which hid a narrow passageway. When she removed the bush, she found herself at the top of an oak woods.

She'd seen the like on her father's estate. It was a magical place, full of ancient twisted trees, moss-covered rocks and caves carved into the cliffs. This one didn't disappoint her. With a bit of slipping and sliding, she managed to clamber down the irregular jumble of plant-covered granite. Even though they were now leafless, the oaks and ash retained a covering of greens and browns from their cloaks of numerous lichens, liverworts and ferns that thrived in the damp, dark world.

It was difficult to walk through the gnarled, twisted trunks that seemed to grow out of the rock, but the squishing sound of her boots on the damp earth made a not unpleasant rhythm. To Sarah, it was a relief from the constant babbling of voices over the last several weeks.

When she stopped for a moment to catch her breath, the scolding *churr* of a wren broke the silence. Sarah followed the sound and soon knew when she heard the harsh *tic tic tic,* that she was about to find where it was hiding. Behind a stand of flat rocks, the mouth of a cave opened up. Peering inside, she wished that she had brought a lantern with her. She sat down on one of the rocks and enjoying the spring-like air, drew out one of her cinnamon buns. The warmth from within the copse was misleading, for she knew it would be cold once she climbed back up to the top. Besides the dusk would end quickly, and she must be back at the castle before dark.

It was then that she heard the soft *sluck sluck* of footsteps in the damp earth, and a huge furry head appeared from behind a gnarled tree.

Sarah stared in amazement. "Dog! It was you following me."

The lion hung his head, his large yellow eyes never leaving the sweet in her hand.

"Oh, come here, you old fool," she said, holding out the bun to him. "I have two.

The beast swallowed the bread in one gulp and looked hungrily at the other as Sarah raised it to her mouth.

"No, you are not going to get mine," she said, chewing slowly. "You must learn to have some manners."

Dog sat down in front of her and licked his mouth, his eyes following the bun as it went up and down to her lips.

Finally, she held out the last bite to him. "I have no time to argue, you beggar. I must get you back to the castle before you are missed."

The animal turned and plunged up the rocky hillside. By the time Sarah reached the path, Dog was nowhere in sight.

She looked down at her torn and muddy clothes and exclaimed, "Oh, I am a mess." Pulling her hood down over her head, she hurried toward the castle.

In the library, the baron glanced out the window toward the southwest. The last week and a half had gone so quickly that he'd had little time to converse with Miss Grimsley. It seemed she was always too busy, taking care of this or that. He told himself that it was only because he wanted to find out what she thought of the three women, but truthfully, he found he missed their chats—their bantering.

Dusk was falling when he saw a raggedy stranger scurrying along the stone wall behind the stables. Squinting to see better, he watched the vagabond peek over the stone wall, look this way and that, then lower her head. Yes, he'd recognized the culprit. He couldn't believe his eyes. Miss Grimsley! Did the woman have no sense at all?

He gave the bellpull a yank. When a servant arrived, Andersen barked, "Who are you? Where is Jacob?"

The man, wringing his hands, said, "I be Helmsly, yer lordship. I saw Jacob hurrying out a rear door several minutes ago."

Andersen took a deep breath and spoke more calmly. "My manner was not called for, Helmsly. I have no quarrel with you, or Jacob. In a few minutes, Miss Grimsley will be coming in the side entrance from the kitchen yard. Will you meet her and tell her I wish to see her in the library immediately?"

"That I will, yer lordship."

The footman was about to exit the room, when Andersen stopped him. "No, wait! On second thought, I shall intercept her myself."

After the servant withdrew, Andersen ran down a back passageway and made a final turn just in time for the cloaked figure to plunge through the side door. She stopped short just before hitting him.

"Miss Grimsley!

Sarah didn't have an inkling of what she should say. So she kept looking at the top button on his waistcoat and remained silent.

The baron lowered his voice. "I cannot talk to you here, where we can be overheard. Follow me." With that he turned, then as if giving it another thought, reached back and taking her elbow firmly in his hand, propelled her along the corridor until they reached the library. Only after he'd closed the door did he speak. "Miss Grimsley, I thought I forbade you to go out upon the moors. Now explain why you blatantly disobeyed my orders."

If she had any doubts before about his lordship's mood, she had none now. He was put out with her. "I am sorry," she said. "I will not let it happen again."

Andersen was becoming quite annoyed with Miss Grimsley. Every time he tried to see her face, she pulled her hood down farther. "Perhaps, I have been harsh, Miss Grimsley."

Sarah glanced quickly in his direction.

Before she looked away, he noticed she didn't have her spectacles on. Her eyes as he had noticed before were quite nice, gray with speckles of gold.

Andersen looked Miss Grimsley up and down. Even wrapped in the shapeless cape, she didn't seem to be as round as she had been—or was he becoming used to her more generous figure?

"May I retire now, my lord? I really must dress for dinner."

The minute she spoke, Andersen had the greatest urge to kiss her, but he quickly quelled the impulse. Instead he indicated a chair and walked around the desk to the other side. "Please hear me out."

Sarah sat down and folded her hands in her lap.

Instead of taking a seat himself, the baron turned his back to her and placing a hand upon the carved back of the medieval chair, stared out onto the now blackened landscape. "When I was small, my parents used to come to Roxwealde in the summer and bring their friends for short weekend parties. My brother Bertie and I were always in the care of a nurse and she was forbidden to take us beyond the park. Of course, to little boys, this made the land beyond the gates quite irresistible, until Nurse filled us with all sorts of terrifying tales of people falling off cliffs or being lost forever in the bog. Her ghostly descriptions of the moors were all that it took to keep me from wanting to venture out beyond the front door.

"My little brother, however, was the adventurous one, and he said he was going out onto the moors whether I wanted to go or not. Late one afternoon he slipped away from the servants and of course, I followed. I was always

CHARADE OF HEARTS 161

looking out after him, but that afternoon we got into more trouble than we bargained for.

"Bertie saw a tall stand of rocks he wanted to explore and left the path to cut across the heath. Instead of a rocky surface, it was a mud bog and right before my eyes, my brother began to disappear. I could not reach him, for I would have met with the same fate. I screamed for him to get out, but the more he struggled, the deeper he sank. In desperation, I ran back to the castle, knowing on one hand that I would be in deep trouble, on the other, that it was the only way to save my brother. By the time the servants came with ropes and poles to rescue him, Bertie had been sucked down to his armpits. Because of my disobedience, I nearly lost my little brother."

Sarah realized he blamed himself. "But Bertie was the one—"

For an instant, Lord Copley turned his head just enough for her to glimpse the glazed look in his eyes, sweat dampening his forehead. "But I was the elder. I was responsible." He swung back around. "Miss Grimsley, if I frightened you, it is for a good reason. I don't like to think of any of my family or friends coming to harm. You may return to your chambers now, but after this, I expect my orders to be obeyed. Is that clear?"

"Yes, my lord." Sarah studied his back for a moment before leaving quietly, quite shaken by her knowledge of the pain her behavior had caused his lordship. But more than that was the realization of the hurt he'd caused her when he called her his *friend*. She wanted to be more than a friend.

Sarah understood what her maid Minnie had gone through when she had to leave Albert and suddenly the realization struck her. *Oh, my goodness! I am in love with Lord Copley.*

Eleven

The medieval dinner was about to begin. A long trestle table covered with white linen sheets was set up in front of the hearth, already laden with baskets of hot breads in easy reach of the revelers.

The Copley coat of arms, set between two colorful medieval shields atop crossed spears, was predominantly displayed over the huge fireplace.

A great boar turned slowly on the spit, the meat to be carved off as needed. Nearby a cauldron of stew bubbled. Trays of succulents: basted goose, hocks of mutton, trays of fruits and vegetables, were being brought in from the kitchen by a steady stream of servants.

Just as their host entered the room, the Earl of Favor pulled Lady Caroline aside. "You are not trying very hard to capture the baron, daughter. Copley spent yesterday with Miss Martin, and Wetherby has been too attentive to you. Are you going against my orders and encouraging the marquis?"

"I *am* trying to get Copley to offer for me!" snapped Caroline. "The fool insists on playing the gentleman. One day he is paying me the utmost attention, the next day that bookish Miss Bennington lures him into his library for a discussion on some treatise or other. Then Miss Martin makes a bet with him on a race, and they spend hours outside riding and comparing their stallions. I swear that woman is half horse. Once a man gets to discussing horse-flesh, nothing will tempt him away."

"You should know better than that, missy. There is always one other thing that erases everything from a man's mind. Women the world over have brought down kingdoms using it. Why did you not insist one of the men take you riding also?"

"It was raining, and I did not want to spoil my coiffure."

"Blast your hair! Time runs out. Only three more days remain of our visit. I want to see some action."

Caroline pouted. "Twice, I persuaded him to take me into the cellars. The last time I managed to fall behind the others and pretended to sprain my ankle. I collapsed into his arms. I thought to have him carry me out looking disheveled, but he called that pimply-faced Bennington boy to come help him."

"Think of something else."

"Tonight he has asked me to sit beside him at the banquet."

"Well, that is a good sign, but not good enough."

"What else can I do? I have done about everything I can think of to get the rogue to propose except throw myself into his bed."

"Then mayhaps you should begin to contemplate that, daughter. You will be a sorry sight when your father is in debtor's prison and you haven't a feather to fly with." With that, he left her scowling after him.

Mr. Proctor, dressed in parti-colored hose, one leg white and one black, and short jacket, called for the guests to be seated.

Lord Copley took his place at the head of the table, truly lord of the manor. Lady Caroline was on his left, Mrs. Bennington on his right. His guests sat on benches on either side of the table, dressed in ancient costumes. Wine flowed freely. Most of the victuals were handled with fingers. Conical trees of sweets were dotted up and down the table to be picked off as desired.

Dried furze had been collected from the moors and strewn about the floor. Logs and branches from the gorse bushes were tiered to assure plenty of fuel, while the aroma of mulled cider hung heavy on the air.

The music teacher from Danbury Wells had once again been called upon to supply the music, and he with his lute, a harp player, and a drummer rendered ancient tunes from the gallery above the Great Hall.

For three days there had been nothing on the minds of the women except their costumes for the ensuing banquet. Sarah showed them the storage room full of ancient dresses and told to choose what they wished.

The men, not as venturous as the ladies to forsake their modern attire, nonetheless added a few of the leather belts and lavish blouses to their own full-length trousers. Elroy Bennington was fascinated with the swords.

Only the earl and Mr. Bennington chose to dress resplendently in ancient costumes. Mr. Bennington looked quite comfortable in an open-sided tabard of the age of Henry the Sixth, with leather boots and a large fur hat. Whereas the earl tried to impress everyone with his youthful vigor by going to an earlier era. He wore a much too short, brocaded jacket with wide bagpipe sleeves, tight woolen hose on thick legs which only emphasized his protruding stomach. He proudly flaunted a decorated codpiece so distracting that Sarah had to make certain she kept her gaze from going below his belt.

Sarah reveled in the fuller dress of a bygone era. She was now using far less stuffing to fill out her contours, and could secure a smaller pillow with a belt under the full-skirted costume without having to suffer the torture of Miss Grimsley's full-corset. She found a deep-green velvet dress cut with fullness from the neckline and a headdress of similar hue which had a long veil in back. For decoration she chose a large pearl and ruby brooch. She decided to forego any stuffing in her mouth for the evening, thinking that as long as she kept her mouth full of food, her face would appear rounded enough.

No matter how she had tried to avoid him, the earl had managed to gain the seat to Sarah's left. Because of the riotous spirit of the occasion and the conviviality soon established by the free-flowing wine, no one seemed to take notice when he leaned toward her and covered her hand with his. He then picked a candied fruit from one of the conical displays and stuffed it into her mouth.

His lips were near her ear, but his gaze was on his daughter and Lord Copley. "My dear Miss Grimsley. I don't know how long you have been in the service of the baron, but if the wind is blowing in the direction that I believe it is, it may not be long before his lordship will not be needing your services."

Curiosity made Sarah look at Favor. Whatever he had in mind, she wasn't sure she wanted to hear it. She extracted her hand from under his and waved it casually. "La, my lord. I did not mean for my position here to be permanent."

He grabbed her hand and held it to his chest. "Indeed, madam. I am most happy to hear that. I must claim that my heart has been sorely bruised by your inattention of late, but I understand your predicament. If I could, I would get down on my knees this instant and claim my undying love for you."

Sarah hoped that no one heard his declaration. She couldn't imagine the earl asking her to marry him. "Your lordship! It is surely the wine talking."

"Alas, no, my dear Miss Grimsley. I only want to say that when my Caroline is affianced to Lord Copley, I know you will be without a place to live. You cannot remain with the baron. It would not be proper, and I know my daughter would not permit it. Allow me to become your protector."

His mistress! He wanted her to become his mistress, not

his wife. All Sarah could do was stare at the earl, open-mouthed.

He patted her hand. "I know it is beyond your imagination that I would ask you to become my lover," he whispered. "But I am that besotted with you—have been ever since I saw you at Warrick's place in Cornwall. I yearned for you then, and I yearn for you now."

At the other end of the table, Andersen sought out Miss Grimsley. He wanted to give her a nod of approval for what she'd done to make the evening a success, but he found her so enraptured by whatever the earl was saying to her that she didn't even look his way. His fingers tightened around his mug. She wasn't supposed to be having a good time. She was supposed to be paying attention to the needs of all of his guests, not just Lord Favor.

He looked about the table. His other friends were biding by the rules. Peter had proved to be a good sport and had escorted Miss Tremain throughout the festivities, so that she hadn't seemed to notice that Andersen spent most of his time with the other three young women.

Basil was distracting Bev Martin by playing the fool. She was laughing at him, but then, everyone laughed at Basil.

Henry was sitting stiff-lipped but stoic, sandwiched between Mrs. Bennington and her daughter Anne.

Andersen couldn't locate Wetherby, however, he never was sure what the marquis was about. As long as the three ladies were at the table, the baron didn't worry too much about the bounder's wherabouts.

Suddenly the music stopped. Mr. Proctor stood at the gallery railing and announced that the Marquis of Wetherby and Mr. Elroy Bennington were about to commence a duel to the death.

A drumroll grew in intensity, and two knights in shining armour stepped out of the shadows into the Great Hall.

Andersen laughed. "Count on Wetherby to think of the dramatic," he said to Lady Caroline. He felt her fingers tighten on his arm, but she did no more than raise an eyebrow upon the entrance of the warriors.

The taller of the two men, who had to be the young Mr. Bennington, threw down his gauntlet at the feet of the other knight. Although the marquis was known for his dueling skills, it was the young Mr. Bennington who became so carried away with the drama that he managed to cut his opponent's arm enough to draw blood.

Lady Caroline screamed and clung to Andersen, who took the opportunity to put his arm around her. With a little secret smile, she placed her head on his chest. After a few shrieks from the ladies, apologies by Elroy, and Wetherby's assurances that it was no more than a scratch, the banquet ended with everyone satiated with good food and wine.

Already some of the guests were saying their goodnights. Thankful for an excuse to leave, Sarah stood up. "Pardon me, Lord Favor, but I must give instructions that the musicians are fed." The fact that Mrs. Proctor was quite capable of taking care of these trivial duties was beside the point, and she stayed hidden in a back hallway until she was sure that the earl had retired. Only then did Sarah find her way to her own chambers.

She had told Nooney not to wait up for her, and too tired to do more than undress, she threw her gown over a chair, put on her nightdress and crawled into bed.

Sleep came almost the minute her head hit the pillow, so she had no idea how late it was when she was awakened by the sense of movement in her room. The sound was almost undetectable, but when her nose twitched, the odor left no doubt to who it was. A shadowy form glided silently in front of the dying embers in the fireplace. She rolled over and pulled the bellrope before sticking her feet over the side of the bed.

"Dog! You old reprobate, I shall skin you alive if you break anything."

There was a shuffling sound along the floor, then, nothing.

By the time a sleepy-eyed Nooney arrived. Sarah had lit a candle and was peering about the dark corners of the room.

"You called me, ma'am?"

"I'm sorry to disturb you this late, dear, but would you please ask Jacob to come to my room. Tell him it is a matter of importance."

The girl bit her lower lip. "Jacob ain't in the house, ma'am. He called his lordship to the stables over an hour ago. I heard him say the beast named Zee be sick."

Well, so be it. Sarah dismissed Nooney. There was no place so huge a creature could hide from her, but for good measure, she looked behind the tapestries, around the furniture, and felt the walls for triggers she may have missed previously which might open secret panels. However the lion snuck in, he was gone now.

She'd no sooner decided to forget the mystery and climb back into bed, when guilt caught Sarah halfway up the step-stool. Zee was ill, and she'd forgotten to take him his treat today—and yesterday. She had helped her father nurse sick animals on their farm, and perhaps she could help now.

Sarah pulled the warm velvet gown over her nightdress, and wriggled her feet into the heavy boots. Then wrapping herself in the heavy cape and hood, she went down the servants' stairs. On her way through the kitchen, she scooped up some sugar lumps and placed them in her pocket. She went out a back door and headed for the stables. There was just enough of a crescent moon to light her way.

The noise of wood splintering and low guttural voices came from the far rear of the stables. Zee's stall was lit only by the dim light of a lantern hanging from a hook. She heard Lord Copley's urgent command, "Jacob, go waken one of the stablehands, we cannot handle this alone."

As she passed the horse stalls, she saw Jacob hurrying toward the back of the building. The animal lay on his side in the straw, striking out with his hooves. The baron knelt beside him, trying to hold him down. For a moment he succeeded, but a violent spasm traveled the length of the beast's body and started him thrashing again.

Before the baron was aware of her presence, Sarah entered and spoke. "Is there anything I can do?"

Lord Copley's head jerked around to look at her. By the blank expression on his face, it was plain that the last sound he expected to hear was a woman's voice. "What the devil are you doing here?"

It wasn't the reception Sarah had expected, but under the circumstances, she excused his lordship's rude greeting. She scrambled around the flaying hooves and kneeling, slipped her hand underneath Zee's neck. It was then that Sarah noticed his lordship had placed his own cloak under the animal's head to elevate it. She stroked the velvety spot on Zee's nose. For a second the animal stopped his violent actions. But not for long, and as he threw his head, Sarah was knocked back into the straw, her hood falling down over her face.

"Miss Grimsley, this is no place for a lady. Go back to the house immediately."

"But, I want to help."

"I don't have time to argue."

Jacob arrived with a stable hand, just as a flying hoof knocked Lord Copley to the other side of the stall. It took all three men to subdue the animal.

The baron stood and dusted off his pants, his eyes blazing. Reaching for her arm, he pulled Sarah to her feet and led her out of the stall. "I am ordering you to return to the castle."

She could see her protestations would do her no good and perhaps even cause harm to one of the men. Reluctantly she turned to go, but not before she heard him say, "Jacob, you'd best fetch the pistol we use for killing rats. We may have need of it for more humane purposes before the night is ended."

With heavy heart. Sarah started back to the castle, but

she couldn't bring herself to go in. She stood debating whether or not to wait for him, when she heard the muffled shot. Now that it was all over, his lordship would have need of a friend. At least he'd said she was that.

In the stables, Andersen handed the smoking gun to Jacob. He thanked the stable hand, and when he had departed, said, "You go to bed now, too, Jacob. We will dispose of the carcass in the morning." Then as if talking to himself, asked, "I wonder what brought Miss Grimsley out here tonight?"

"She always brought Zee and Ol' Hob a treat every afternoon. Sometimes, a cherry tart. The old beggar really liked those tarts."

The baron looked at him in wonder. "She did that?"

"Aye," Jacob said. "Hardly missed a day. But she been so busy of late." He stooped and picked up two sugar lumps and handed them to his master. "I reckon she was bringing these to him."

Andersen looked at the sweets in his hand, then down at the silent animal. Shaking his head, he started back to the castle. "You take the lantern, Jacob. I know my way well enough without it."

The baron recognized the cloaked figure standing near the gate. "Miss Grimsley, you shouldn't have waited for me. It is cold. You will catch your death." When he heard her start to cry, he didn't know what else to do but take her in his arms. She didn't feel at all as big as he thought she would. But now that he thought about it, Miss Grimsley hadn't appeared as plump as she had when she first came to Roxwealde. "Have you not been well, Miss Grimsley?" he asked. "I hope the work I have assigned you has not been too much of a burden."

Sarah liked being held by Lord Copley, and was quite disappointed when he released her. Instead of heading for the kitchen entrance, he led her toward the door of the west tower. Reaching inside his cloak, he selected a key from a ring hooked to his belt and twisted it in the lock. The tower was much the same as the one on the opposite side of the castle.

"Jacob told me of your visits to the stables every afternoon."

Sarth sniffed. "I forgot to take Zee his treat today."

The baron ushered her inside where they were assaulted by the dank smells of a seldom aired structure. "You are the first person, besides my servants, who has shown any concern for my animals, Miss Grimsley."

Sarah was glad he couldn't see her tear-stained face in the dark. "What will you do with Zee? The ground all around is too rocky to dig a grave."

Taking her right hand, he placed it on the wall to steady her. Then gently gripping her left elbow, he guided her up the stairs. "Would you like to accompany my men and me in the morning? We will take the carcass out soon after sunrise."

"Yes, I think I would like that."

Suddenly he halted, and she heard a key turn. "This is the door to the first floor," he said. "You have only to follow the passageway and turn right at the corner. Once you enter the corridor, I am sure you can find your room."

"I'm certain I shall find my way." Sarah wasn't going to tell him she'd tried to get the thick tower door to open many times over the last few weeks. "Good night, my lord," she said.

"Good night, Miss Grimsley."

She heard the door shut, waited a few minutes to catch her breath, then felt her way down the narrow hallway to the main corridor which led to her bedchamber.

Sarah bundled up the next morning and joined the little procession out onto the moors. The carcass was already loaded in the back of the cart. Ol' Hob stood in the shafts, patiently waiting for the signal to go. Aside from the baron and Jacob, she was the only one who turned up for the funeral.

Jacob holding the bridle, tugged at his forelock, while Lord Copley acknowledged her with a slight inclination of his head. She'd made sure this morning to have her full costume on, pillow, spectacles and buns in her cheeks. She was aware of his lordship's inquiring look, but she kept her head lowered and her hood pulled down to her eyes. The men started out walking on either side of the cart. In silence, Sarah followed after them.

The first part of their journey took them over the same road Sarah had followed previously toward the oak copse, but about a quarter of a mile across the moors, Jacob directed Ol' Hob onto a narrow-rutted road. She would have never taken it herself, because she could see that there weren't droppings of any large animals, only those of rabbits.

The land slowly rose then dipped again, and about half an hour later they came to a cliff which dropped off so suddenly that if Sarah had been walking alone, she would have pitched off into nowhere. Below lay a bog marsh. Jacob turned the horse around and unharnessed him. Then the two men pushed the cart to the edge of the cliff and tilted it up until Zee slid over the edge of the cliff. Sarah was watching the poor tormented body of the half-donkey, half-zebra sink slowly into the soft dark mud below when she felt a hand rest lightly on her shoulder.

"It is time we go," the baron said hoarsely. "He's at peace now."

Jacob had already hitched Ol' Hob to the cart and had started back, when Lord Copley stated, a certain hesitancy in his voice, "You are not aware of it, Miss Grimsley, but I have acquired many exotic animals over the years and have set them free to roam my property."

Sarah looked at him wide-eyed, trying to feign ignorance of what he'd just told her.

"Many of my sporting friends have oft talked to me about turning my estate into a hunting park." Lord Copley kept his gaze on the horizon. "Truth of it is, Miss Grimsley I abhor the hunt. When I see an animal marred by disfigurement or age, I have an impulse to protect it. Many of my acquaintances who know of my sentiments, say it is quite unnatural for a man."

"Well, I don't think that an unnatural act at all, your lordship," Sarah said vehemently, too enraged to keep her silence any longer. "Oh, people think things in nature are all helter-skelter. Seedlings coming up where they drop, birds just happen to find a limb to their liking to build their nests—but it is much more than that. The seasons come quite well on schedule, and that is one thing men cannot change. The farmer does his planting, the animals give birth when there will be food aplenty to feed them. The sun tells us the time to get up and a time to lie down. If mankind were only so well organized, the world would be a better place, don't you think?"

He looked at her strangely, but said nothing.

Sarah searched her mind to think of something fanciful or amusing to say to him. She had the impression his lordship didn't know how to respond to her outburst. All she really wanted to do was to take him in her arms and comfort him, the way he'd held her last night; but she was glad she'd let her feelings be known. Sarah was not one to show missish character when it came to animals.

The sun was fully over the horizon, now. As they began to walk to the castle, Sarah saw that the heath was already beginning to bloom with wild daffodils, and she knew that it was going to be a beautiful day.

Sarah didn't think Lord Copley noticed. He looked straight ahead until they entered the park and a lone figure on a horse raced neck or nothing toward them along the riding path.

Drawing up abruptly, Miss Martin saluted them. "Copley! Miss Grimsley! Seems I'm not the only one up to see the sunrise this morning. What a bunch of slug-a-beds you invited to this romp, your lordship."

A smile creased the baron's face. "Bev. Should have known you wouldn't miss your morning ride."

"I say, Copley, whatever happened to that challenge you issued—that your beggar of a horse could beat mine? I will be here only a few more days. Not chicken-hearted, are you?"

Sarah watched with amazement as Andersen threw back his head and laughed. Yes, Miss Martin was good for his lordship. She never failed to bring a smile to his face.

"No one has ever accused me of avoiding a challenge, Bev."

Miss Martin pulled in the reins to control her nervous mount. "Well, what's the wager?"

The sudden unhappy thought that he didn't have two pennies to rub together caused Andersen to pause. "Blunt doesn't matter," he said, with feigned courage. "You name the prize."

"That is easy," Miss Martin said confidently. "Winner take all. Your horse or mine."

Hamilton had beaten the best at Newmarket and again at Winchester. That's why Andersen had paid seven hundred guineas to possess him. "Done! Shall we meet at four o'clock this afternoon? Two times around the park?"

"It's a go. Your old bag of bones won't last one time 'round against Lightning."

Twelve

With the sparkle back in his eyes, Lord Copley entered the castle whistling. Sarah only wished that she'd been the one to put it there.

They parted at the first floor landing. The baron continued on up to his own apartment, and Sarah returned to her room to remove her wraps and muddy boots.

It was nearly noon when she once more descended to the Grand Hall. Aside from Miss Martin, it seemed that all their guests had slept through breakfast and were now assembling in the small dining room for lunch.

Word of the horse race was already on every tongue and bets were being taken. Miss Glover volunteered to act as bookmaker.

After he'd eaten, Andersen excused himself to go to the stables, where he ordered a stablehand to exercise Hamilton.

A few minutes later, Andersen sat in the library, stroking his jaw. His party was down to the last three days. Tomorrow he'd decide as to which of the three women he'd ask to become his bride.

Miss Martin's challenge made her very appealing. Life with Bev would be an adventure. She was shockingly outspoken, but he'd never again have to worry about finances.

However, the beautiful and sophisticated Lady Caroline still topped his list. He'd be moving up in the ton. A great advantage in London. In the last two weeks she'd given every indication she was attracted to him. She was an accomplished flirt, but she could have no idea what effect she had on a man—especially the time she'd fallen into his arms in the cellar. It had been all he could do to remain a gentleman.

Then, there was Anne Bennington, intelligent, quiet, pleasant to be around. They would rub well together. Her family was amiable; her father generous. Marriage into the family wouldn't be all that exciting, but satisfying. He doubted she'd give him much of an argument if he wished to spend a great deal of his time in London.

Andersen wondered what Miss Grimsley would say to his assessment of his choices. She liked everything to be shipshape and orderly. He grinned. Perhaps she would think he should make out a time schedule for proposing, so that if one woman declined, he could go without delay to the next.

Contemplating Miss Grimsley made Andersen think about Mercury, and for the first time he realized the statue was not on his desk. She'd moved it again. He rose and navigated the room, searching for it. It was not on the table beside the door, nor behind the drapery.

Finally he located the errant statue, half hidden behind the large vase on the table by the window. But instead of his casual nakedness, Mercury wore a tailored pair of brown trousers, a long-sleeved white linen blouse, red silk vest and blue ascot, carefully tied. Andersen picked up the fashionable dandy and plunked him down on the corner of his desk. "Oh, Miss Grimsley, what am I going to do with you?"

Laughing aloud at the picture she made with her lips pursed and her eyes glaring at him over her wire-rimmed spectacles, he called to Fletcher to help him on with his coat.

It was time for the race. When he arrived at the stable-yard, Andersen was certain that not only was every guest standing at the ready for the event, but all of his staff as well. The air was brisk, a few clouds scudded across a blue-gray sky. The Park's riding path wound in and out of the ancient oak and rowan trees, giving way in places to walls of rock and brambles for over a mile before it zigzagged back to the castle.

Andersen mounted. Hamilton stamped and snorted, nostrils flaring. Neither Lightning, nor Miss Martin were anywhere to be seen, but the yelling and crashing sounds coming from within the stables relayed the message that all wasn't going well with his challenger. Finally, Miss Martin appeared, smiling, leading the great white stallion. On his back rode a pitiful character in black, his face bundled to his eyes, hatless.

Andersen couldn't believe his eyes. "My God. Bev! You don't intend for Basil to race me."

"Of course, I do, Copley. Best way for him to show what he's made of. Ripple, that is. I know what the horse is made of."

With his mouth swatched in wool, Basil couldn't speak, but the terror in his eyes was too much for the baron.

"Have pity, Bev," Andersen said, in a hoarse whisper. "The man is terrified."

"Nonsense!" She turned to Basil and shouted up at him. "You said you wanted to ride for me, didn't you, Ripple?"

The head on top of the great coat nodded stiffly.

"See, I told you he did." She looked upward again. "Just remember everything I taught you."

Andersen shook his head. Never would he have believed Bev Martin to have bats in her belfry. Lightning was his. "Twice around and winner takes all," he said, grinning.

Two stablemen led the horses to a white line drawn with flour across the riding path. Miss Glover, since she wasn't betting, was to call the start. She counted to three, yelled, "Go!" and the race began.

They were soon out of sight of the spectators, and the

only sounds were the hoofbeats on the gravel, leather creaking, and the hard breathing of both men and beasts. By the time they'd made the first turn, Basil had abandoned the reins and grasped the mane. By the second turn, his left foot had come free of the stirrup iron which flopped against Lightning's ribs. Andersen feared his friend was going to slide off onto the road, but somehow he miraculously righted himself and stayed on the horse.

As they galloped past the starting point and commenced their second round, Hamilton was four lengths ahead. By then Andersen knew he had the race in the bag, and with a shout of triumph, slapped Hamilton with his whip and let the stallion set his own pace.

Andersen was nearly to the last bend when he heard wild screams and pounding hoofbeats behind him. A quick glance over his shoulder showed him that Lightning was gaining. He leaned lower over Hamilton and urged him onward, but the hoofbeats came closer, the howling, louder.

Basil flew by on a white streak. Both legs were now completely free of the stirrup irons, banging against the sides of the run-a-muck horse. With every bounce, he rose a full foot off the saddle, first sliding dangerously to one side, then to the other, each shift of weight sending the horse into frenzied action. There was no way to tell who was screaming the loudest, man or the horse.

Andersen applied his crop. Immediately he felt the great horse's legs stretch to their limit. It was neck or nothing— but it was too late.

Hamilton lost.

It took two men and Miss Martin to catch Lightning and bring him to a halt. Basil slithered off the horse in a dead faint.

Miss Martin was first at his side, kneeling, cradling his head in the crook of her arm. "Come Ripple, wake up! I knew you could do it." When she got no response, she slapped his face until he opened his eyes, giving her a sick smile.

Andersen dismounted immediately to help Basil to his feet. His own loss was temporarily forgotten over his concern for his friend.

Basil stood on wobbly legs. "I won?"

Miss Martin nodded. "Of course you did. Told you, you would. And I'll keep my end of the bargain."

"Bargain?" the baron asked.

By now a sizeable crowd had gathered.

Basil tilted so dangerously to one side, he looked as if he were going to faint again. "Hurt my head," he said plaintifully. "I do believe, it needs bandaging."

At that, Miss Martin swooped the rotund, little man up in her arms and started for the castle. "Told him if he'd win the race for me, he got the horse and me as well," she called back, planting a loud kiss on Basil's happy face.

That evening after dinner, Sarah led the women into the Grand Hall to wait for the men to join them after they finished their port and cigars. Sarah had expected to see a despondent baron, but from the way his lordship laughed and joked at dinner, flirting inexcusably with all the ladies, one would never have known that he'd just lost one of his choices for a wife. She wondered if Lord Copley realized the seriousness of his situation.

They didn't have long to wait for the men to appear. It seemed that Mr. Ripple couldn't bear being separated from Miss Martin, and he followed close on her heels. The other men soon followed.

Lord Wetherby leaned close to the baron's ear. "I say, Copley, you seem to be in unusually high spirits. I thought to find you in the dismals after what happened today."

Andersen had prepared himself to field a great many such jests from his co-conspirators in this charade, but surprisingly, he found they bothered him far less than he expected. "You take life too seriously, Wetherby. Did you not see the daffodils blooming on the heath, this morning? It was a glorious sight. Everything has its time and place. Didn't you know that? If you were not such a slug-a-bed, you would discover there are a great many such splendors."

Andersen reminded himself that he'd also become the center of Lady Caroline's attention. Even now as he walked with Wetherby into the Great Hall, he saw her eyes watching him from under lowered lashes.

The marquis studied him with an amused grin. "How does it rub you to have lost not only your favorite mount, but one of your prospective brides to a cockalorum like Ripple?"

Andersen guffawed. "Probably the same as it does you to have gained the attentions of both doxies, Penny and Genevieve. I do believe that marriage to Miss Martin will be more a wrestling match than a honeymoon."

Wetherby laughed. "Mayhaps Ripple thinks nothing could be more difficult than the ride that stallion gave him this afternoon, but somehow I do believe Miss Martin will give him a good run for the money in that department as well."

"Now that Basil's doxie is without a benefactor, do you think you are up to consoling Penny without making Genevieve jealous?"

"I believe I can manage, Copley."

"I have no doubts that you will, Wetherby. Just make certain that you keep them so occupied they don't carry out their threats to disrupt my party. And speaking of enjoying myself, I see Lady Caroline sending glances my way."

"She could be looking at me as well."

"Aren't you supposed to be seeing to the welfare of Miss Bennington or Miss Tremain, this evening?"

The marquis nodded his head toward a group of the guests standing in the middle of the room.

"Trummel seems to be doing well with both of those ladies, but I see Smith over there in a corner, pouting. I am afraid our friend Ripple made such a muddle of the schedule over the last few days that it has been nigh to impossible to know who is supposed to be entertaining whom. Who knows which lady he was supposed to be with today?"

"Lady Caroline is beginning to look desperate."

The baron made a sweep of his hand. "Shall we go see which one of us the lady is signaling to rescue her?"

Andersen thought Caroline appeared extraordinarily lovely this evening, her golden hair piled into a crown, intertwined with pearls and flowers. The soft-blue India shawl about her shoulders didn't hide the wonders displayed by her lowcut gown. She outshone every woman in the room, except Miss Grimsley, of course. Her gown was more subdued than her usual costumes, but the dark green became her. Lord Favor stood close to her, too close for the baron's liking. His eyes narrowed. He'd taken notice of the earl's attentions to his hostess of late and it didn't sit well with him.

Once again, Andersen focused on Lady Caroline, her sweet smile welcoming him. His spirits rose. Tonight when all had retired he'd speak to Miss Grimsley and ask for her assistance in finding time for him to be alone with Lady Caroline sometime in the next day or two to ask for her hand in marriage.

He signaled a footman. "Tell Miss Grimsley that I wish to see her briefly in the library after all the guests have retired."

The marquis straightened his ascot. "Lady Caroline does seem quite bored with the conversation. I do believe one of us should brighten her life."

Andersen was beginning to enjoy himself. He stepped ahead of the marquis. "Then I suggest we join the party, and put to rest the question of which of us her ladyship is signaling."

Sarah, making another attempt to escape the unwanted attentions of the earl, was relieved when the servant said he had a message from Lord Copley. She stepped away to hear him. Lord Favor was still breathing heavily down her neck, but at least she didn't have to look at him. She glanced across the hall and saw the baron and Lord Wetherby heading toward the group.

When Lord Copley was behind her, Lady Caroline's voice became quite animated. "What is it you are talking about, Master Bennington? You must speak up. I cannot hear you."

The embarrassed young man stammered a few unintelligible words. Miss Bennington placed her hand on her brother's arm and patiently repeated the conversation. "Elroy was saying that Father's man related that one of the footmen told him that the coachman heard a shot last night in the stables. This morning he found out that the little striped creature had been put down."

Lady Caroline grimaced. "Are you speaking of that horrid animal I saw in one of the back stalls? It turned my stomach to look at it. Anything so grotesque should have been shot long ago."

Andersen blanched.

Lady Caroline fluttered her fan and smiled beguilingly. "I wish to have only what is perfect and beautiful around me." She then turned and held out her hand to the baron.

His expression still a mask, Andersen barely touched her fingertips. "You will have to excuse me." he said. looking from face to face. "It seems a matter has come up which has to have my immediate attention. Please continue without me." He then turned and motioned for Mr. Proctor to attend him. "Bring some brandy to the library. I will be up late tonight."

Mrs. Bennington shifted her gaze to her husband and raised her eyebrows. "Well, I must say, with all the excitement that has gone on today . . ."

"I think we should retire," finished Mr. Bennington, taking her arm.

Lady Martin looked over at her niece and Mr. Ripple sitting far too closely than was proper on the settle in front of the hearth. "I agree with you, Mrs. Bennington. It is time we all returned to our chambers. Beverly," she called, "you can see your fiancé in the morning."

Sarah said goodnight to the guests and with a worried look toward the library, wondered whether or not the baron still wished to see her, after his sudden withdrawal. Still, his summons couldn't be ignored, and as soon as she saw that Mr. and Mrs. Proctor had everything under control, she proceeded down the corridor toward the thick arched doorway.

Lord Copley slumped in the leather chair before the dying embers in the hearth. He took another drink from the glass in his hand, then stared into the clear amber liquid. He couldn't marry Caroline. He couldn't spend the rest of his life in shackles to a woman who saw only the outer surface of her world. Had he been so blinded by her beauty that he didn't recognize the shallowness of her soul? He reached over to grasp the pewter decanter and refilled his glass. Where was Miss Grimsley? He wanted her advice.

No sooner had these thoughts passed through his mind than he heard the soft scratching on the door.

"Enter," he bellowed, more gruffly than he'd intended. "What took you so long, Miss Grimsley?"

Sarah watched Lord Copley rise unsteadily from his chair. She couldn't imagine why his lordship was so angry with *her*. After all, she'd hurried in as soon as her duties allowed. He indicated a chair opposite his, so low and wide, that Sarah knew that once she sat in it, she'd never be able to rise. But seeing he gave her no other choice, she eased herself down.

Lord Copley held out his glass to her. "Drink, Miss Grimsley?"

"No, thank you, your lordship. David said you had a matter you wished to discuss with me."

"David?"

"The servant in the Great Hall. You must try to learn the names of your servants, my lord."

The baron nodded, staring straight ahead as if trying to gather his thoughts. "Oh, yes. I wanted to say that I believe that if we humans only had one eye, we wouldn't see so many flaws in others."

Sarah stared at him for a moment until she comprehended his meaning. "I take it you are referring to Zee. I agree, he couldn't be blamed for his appearance."

"You are very understanding, Miss Grimsley. Thank you." He didn't know why but having her there soothed him.

Sarah removed her spectacles to wipe a tear from her eye. "He was a sweet-natured beast."

"As was Bertie."

Sarah's head came up. "Bertie, my lord? Bertie was your brother."

Andersen ran his hand along the length of his jaw. He'd been told often enough that he'd been born with more beauty than was fair for a man to possess, but brother Bertie hadn't been so fortunate.

"My brother was born with a birthmark, Miss Grimsley. The whole right side of his face was covered with a strawberry-colored disfiguration which extended from his neck to his hairline." Now he had her attention.

"How sad. Couldn't it be covered with a scarf or hat?"

"There was no way to hide it. Creams only made it more noticeable. My mother was a very beautiful and vain woman, and she couldn't bear to look on anything that wasn't perfect. She dressed me in little velvet suits and paraded me in front of her acquaintances, while Bertie was left in the nursery. I used to tell him it was because he was too young, but as he grew older, he knew.

"As the first born and heir, I shudder to contemplate what would have been my fate had I been so unfortunate."

The baron held up his hand as if to stop her from saying anything. "I am well aware of how I look. It has opened doors and gained me favors, but I no longer count that a blessing. Even though I feel less than proud of myself for doing so, I still take advantage of people and situations because of it. Like Fletcher, I cannot help myself when the temptation is set before me."

The baron's knuckles turned white as they tightened around his glass. "When I was still very young, our coachman sometimes took shortcuts through the poorer sections of London, and I would see the squalor that existed: garbage everywhere; blind beggars with arms or legs missing; children running around without shoes; and poor skinny-ribbed curs slinking into alleys. Once I saw a horse down on its knees being beaten, because it did not have the energy to pull its master's load.

"I became paranoid that my mother planned to give my brother away—or heaven help him—throw him into that hell. I had nightmares in which I found myself on those terrible streets calling his name from the safety of our fine carriage, and not finding him. So I appointed myself Bertie's protector and kept him away from my mother as much as possible. I reasoned that if she did not see him, she would forget about him."

"And your father? Did he not chastise her?"

"My father enjoyed the social whirl in his own way as much as my mother. We seldom saw him. Occasionally he brought us sweets. I must say in all fairness, that he gave to us equally. He would draw from his pocket two peppermint sticks and hold them over our heads so that we had to jump and shout for them. We thought it a game, but now I sometimes think that he enjoyed watching us beg. Finally, he would give us our treats and leave the room, and we were so eager to devour our prizes that we didn't miss his going. Mother told us that he spoiled us.

"Most of the servants were kind, especially the cook. I would sneak Bertie down to the kitchen, and we'd play skittles on the stone floor with the gardener's children—and stuff ourselves on Cook's pastries.

"Then I was sent to Eton. What Bertie went through those next two years, it is hard for me to fathom. But he never complained. He read a lot and created a world all his own inhabited by brave knights and fair ladies. He told me of all the exotic places he would go, and the exciting adventures he planned to have.

Sarah asked softly, "Did he not go to Eton also?"

"Yes, but by then I was Head Boy and I didn't get to see much of him. It was impossible for me to protect him from the unmerciful teasing and bullying. So Bertie began to take chances—doing daring things to prove himself worthy of their friendship perhaps. He did make some good friends, male friends in high places, who recognized his merit.

"Then I left Eton to attend Oxford. I was just finishing when Father died, and I came into my title. Bertie begged me to buy him a commission in the army. He rose quickly in the ranks and for the first time in his life he seemed content. It was while his regiment was stationed in a small village in southern England that he met his wife, Millicent Huxley, on a picnic. She was the daughter of a local dignitary—a shy girl. Pretty. She was the first young lady who seemed not to notice his disfigurement."

Andersen had almost forgotten that he wasn't alone and seemed surprised to see Miss Grimsley still sitting across from him, her hands folded in her lap, a strange look in her eyes he couldn't quite interpret. "She is one of the only women I have met, except you, Miss Grimsley, who does not judge another by outward appearances. Millicent said that the war changed matters, and she insisted they be married after a short courtship. When his regiment was ordered to Portugal, Millicent would have followed the drum and gone with him, but they found her to be with child. Bertie forbade her to go. She returned to her parents' home in Sussex and Rupert was born there."

The little village of Herring's Cross had been so far removed from the war on the Continent that Sarah hadn't thought much about the families that were parted. "Couldn't your brother have left the army?"

The baron shook his head as if he too had a hard time comprehending his brother's decision. "He could have sold his commission, but Bertie had this sense of dedication—of purpose. He had trained for months with the men in his command, and felt he would be letting them down if he pulled out then. His commanding officer gave him leave to come home for Rupert's birth. They had the christening before he returned to the peninsula. I will never forget my brother's expression when he held his son in his arms. Rupert was perfect—flawless. If there is a God, I saw it in my brother's eyes at that moment. Bertie told me that he felt blessed. I believe it was the happiest year my brother ever had."

Suddenly the baron ran his hand across his eyes. He didn't look at Sarah, but rose and went to the window to stare into the darkness.

"Hah, Miss Grimsley! It is the wine in my speech, speaking. I am keeping you up late."

Sarah caught her breath. She realized she'd been so wrapped up in his tale, she'd forgotten to puff out her cheeks. Thank goodness, he hadn't glanced at her. "Didn't Miss Huxley's parents object to the marriage?"

"On the contrary. The Huxley's were extremely pleased with her choice, and loved Bertie as much as she. Wonderful people, not at all high in the instep. Prefer to live quiet lives in the country."

As she thought of her own dear parents, homesickness once again threatened to overcome Sarah and she sniffed.

He swung around. "Are you all right. Miss Grimsley? Am I keeping you up too late?"

"La, your lordship, it is seldom I get to bed before midnight. Please go on."

"It has been over four years now since Bertie died. Millicent is a pretty woman and it is conceivable that she will marry again. With her disposition to see only good in others, I am afraid of what would happen if she should marry an unscrupulous man. If Rupert comes into the entail before he is of age, a greedy stepfather could steal Rupert's inheritance, and I would be helpless to stop it. That is why, Miss Grimsley, it's imperative that I retain control of the principle of the Copley estate."

"So you must marry, and now that Miss Martin is out of the question, you must make your choice between Miss Bennington and Lady Caroline."

"Well, we do have another day to think about it, don't we?"

Sarah's heart was breaking enough, she didn't see why he had to put the burden on her shoulders. *"You* must think about it, my lord," she stated firmly, struggling to rise. "I am not going to be living with the lady for the rest of my life."

Andersen grimaced. Miss Grimsley didn't know that he already had grave doubts about Lady Caroline's character. That left only Miss Bennington. That shouldn't be difficult, for he knew that it would merely be a matter of asking Mr. Bennington for the hand of his daughter. But he did want a willing bride, and he'd thought of asking Miss Grimsley to set up an assignation the day after tomorrow with Miss Bennington. However, he could see that Miss Grimsley was too touchy to approach the subject now.

He hadn't meant to talk so much about his family matters, but once he'd started, he couldn't seem to stop. He'd told her things that he'd never told a living soul before. "You are right, Miss Grimsley. It is a matter that I must take care of myself."

The baron came back to help her out of her chair. "Good night, and thank you for listening. I hope I have not bored you with my family tale. It was the brandy speaking, I'm sure."

A sense of guilt washed over him when he said that. Quizzically, he looked into his full glass. Surely, if he was beginning to find Miss Grimsley attractive, it had to be that he'd had too much to drink. Only then, Andersen realized he'd not tasted a drop after she came into the room. Puzzled, he looked toward the door, but she'd already gone.

When Sarah came out of the library, two silent figures stood hidden in the shadows of the balcony. The Earl of Favor smacked his lips as he watched Miss Grimsley ascend, then turned to the disgruntled woman at his side. "Now you have done it, Caro. You have scared off the baron."

"Is that what you had my maid call me down here for?" she hissed.

"If you know what is good for you, you will learn to go along with what men want. I saw the look on his face when you made that stupid remark about the creature in the stables."

His daughter made a moue. "How was I to know it was his pet?"

"Whether or not you care for dumb animals is not the point. The baron does. You must apologize and make it right with him."

His daughter sniffed and started for the stairs. "He should apologize to me for humiliating me in front of everyone."

"Just do as I say."

Caroline threw back over her shoulder, "It will be simple. I shall have him eating out of my hand like a puppy."

"See that you do," he said, "or I shall marry you off to a wealthy cit."

Thirteen

The first thing next morning, Mr. Trummel confronted Andersen in the Great Hall. "Andy, I need to speak to you."

Lord Copley had enough to occupy his thoughts and didn't want to listen to the petty complaints of his friends. "Can't it wait, Peter? I have important matters on my mind today. Lady Caroline and Miss Bennington are coming down the stairs together right now, and I want to ask Miss Bennington something privately. Would you distract Lady Caroline so I can talk to Anne? Neither Wetherby or Smith are about. That's a good soldier," he said, giving the bewildered Peter a pat on the shoulder, pushing him toward the West Wing staircase. Before either man could traverse the width of the Great Hall, Henry Smith materialized from behind a pillar just below the balcony. Stepping up to the ladies, he offered an arm to both, then led them toward the breakfast room.

"Drat!" Andersen said. "I might have known that Smith would be punctual when it doesn't count."

Just then, Miss Glover and Edith Tremain descended the stairs. Both gentlemen made a leg. "Good morning, ladies," the baron said, giving Miss Glover his arm, while Peter extended the same courtesy to Edith Tremain. "May we escort you to breakfast?"

However, the minute Lady Caroline saw the baron, she deserted Mr. Smith and grasped Andersen's arm. "I must speak to you, your lordship," she said breathlessly.

Why everyone felt they *had* to speak to him today was beyond the baron's comprehension. "Lady Caroline—" Andersen began, when Peter interrupted.

"It sounds quite urgent, Copley," he said, extending his arm to Miss Glover. "My news can wait, and I don't mind taking two lovely ladies with me to breakfast."

Miss Glover gaily pranced off with Mr. Trummel and Edith, which left Andersen alone with Caroline." He turned to her coolly.

The lady's beautiful eyes, peered up through thick lashes. "Oh, Lord Copley, don't look at me like that. I spoke thoughtlessly last night. That poor little animal . . . I did not mean to sound so heartless. I only tried to speak lightly of the matter to ease your pain, not to cause more." A tear escaped and ran down one cheek.

She spoke so convincingly that Andersen was tempted to believe her. Mayhaps she did speak improvidently, not knowing how he felt toward mistreated animals.

More tears welled up in her eyes as she clung to his arm. "Please, forgive me."

As they entered the breakfast room, the baron removed her hand from his arm. "I hope you mean what you say. Caroline. Let us not speak any more of the matter."

Andersen continued to the sideboard, greeting his guests as he went. No matter how convincingly Caroline pleaded, his doubts about her sincerity remained. He looked about for Miss Bennington, just in time to see her hurrying out of the room. "Wait!" he called, starting for the door, but she was gone before he got there. "Smith," he said, "do you know where Miss Bennington was going?"

Henry stood looking with confusion first at the door, then at the plate piled high with food in his hand. "A servant just came to fetch Miss Bennington. He said Mrs. Bennington wants her to come to the East Wing. Her father has taken ill."

From the corner of his eye, Andersen saw Lady Caroline

motioning to him. Andersen frowned. "I shall go see if I need to call a doctor." He started out the door only to have Peter intercept him again.

"Please, Andy, I must talk to you."

The baron shook his head, "Not now. Mr. Bennington is sick."

"Sorry," said Peter. "I will catch you up later."

Andersen hurried to the Benningtons' rooms, only to find Mr. Bennington ill with a sore throat. But if all his hoarse protestations were any indication of how the wind blew, he was only going to make himself worse before he got better. The baron recognized a poor patient when he saw one, and knew it wouldn't be a propitious time to approach the man for the hand of his daughter in marriage.

Mrs. Bennington tried to assure Lord Copley that all would be well, that her husband had done nothing more than yell too loudly at the horse race the day before, but just to be on the safe side, Andersen insisted that he summon Dr. Gibbons, the physician in Danbury Wells. Until he came, Miss Bennington said she'd stay with her father.

Cursing all his ancestors, the entail, and entire system of British law, Andersen retreated to his library to study his options. For all Lady Caroline's pleas for forgiveness, Copley knew that there was no way that he could marry her. She was selfish and utterly spoiled.

Now that Bev Martin was out of the running, Miss Bennington was his only hope. But he couldn't very well ask her to marry him if she remained cloistered with her parents in their apartment. Time was running out. For a moment, the baron faced a humbling thought. What if Miss Bennington turned down his suit? Mr. Bennington seemed very friendly toward him, and he had let it be known that he wanted his daughter married. Would he insist that Anne accept his suit, regardless of how she felt? No, Copley decided that no matter how desperate his own circumstance, he didn't want a woman who was forced into marriage.

Well, there was always Miss Tremain. He could still satisfy the entail and build his fortune again. It would just take a little longer to do so. Edith was an angel. She was lovely. Yes, if Miss Bennington turned him off, then he'd ask Miss Tremain to be his wife. Though that thought should have brought the baron some sense of relief, it didn't. What was the matter with him?

Andersen had been ruminating in the library for over an hour when Mr. Proctor came to say, "Dr. Gibbons has arrived, your lordship. He has been directed to Mr. Bennington's bedchamber."

"Thank you, Proctor. I shall go up immediately. I fear I have been a neglectful host. Where is Miss Grimsley?"

"Oh, you need not worry about anything, my lord. Miss Grimsley has seen to everything."

Scowling, the baron rose from his chair. Seen to everything had she? Then why had she let Miss Martin slip through the net? He hadn't brought Miss Grimsley to Roxwealde to wheedle out of him tales of his family, and yet, that was what she'd done. Over the last two weeks, he'd exposed more of his innermost thoughts than he had to any other person in his life. The baron didn't like feeling vulnerable. Setting aside his personal concerns Lord Copley went out to greet the doctor, who was coming down the staircase from the East Wing.

" 'Tis no more than a case of exposing his throat to the chill air," Dr. Gibbons said, snapping shut the lock on his bag. "Bad thing this time of year. I left him some syrup and ordered him to eat only hot broth for a day. If Mr. Bennington will refrain from speaking for the next couple of days, that should take care of the problem."

The baron gave a sigh of relief. All he needed to complete this fiasco was to have an epidemic strike his guests. "Thank you for coming, Doctor. You have relieved Mrs. Bennington's family, I am sure. Proctor will see you out."

By evening, Mr. Bennington was feeling more the thing

and insisted on coming down to table. He nodded his approval when he saw his daughter seated beside their host, and smiled continually at everything Lord Copley said. However, since Mr. Bennington couldn't speak, his wife had to complete all her own sentences, a circumstance which she seemed to find quite pleasant. And except for the time she took to taste her food. Mrs. Bennington spoke nonstop throughout the meal.

Andersen exchanged amused glances with Miss Bennington. Her eyes seemed more than unusually bright this evening, and she looked very pretty in a simple, yet elegant peach-colored gown. Whereas her mother was swatched in jewels, a single strand of rare pink pearls appropriate to a young debutante, complimented Anne's good taste in fashion. Yes, tomorrow he'd ask Mr. Bennington for permission to marry his daughter. The baron saw nothing that could possibly stand in the way of his decision. Within thirty-six hours, the Copley entail would be safe.

Out of habit, he sought Miss Grimsley's approval. To his annoyance, she wasn't even acknowledging his triumph, because she was listening to the earl whisper something in her ear. Her face turned scarlet. Anger boiled up in Andersen. The man was a bounder. Regardless of what Miss Grimsley had been to the duke, she was a kindhearted woman. Favor had no right. 'Twas against all principles of the ton to make advances to her in his host's residence. The baron decided to put an end to the earl's tricks, and tried to signal to her that it was time for the ladies to withdraw.

Sarah was trying desperately to move away from Lord Favor. Tomorrow was the day that Lord Copley had to propose to either Lady Caroline or Miss Bennington. But if his latest behavior of running hither and thither was any indication of his sense of purpose, the rascal seemed destined to do neither. No matter how hard she'd tried to bring some organization into the baron's life, he seemed bent on casting aside that virtue, as did his friends. She'd wrestled with the idea of telling his lordship the truth about herself, that she was just the daughter of a simple country squire. However, she reasoned that if she did, surely he would send her home immediately, and she couldn't bear that. Of course, she knew that once he took a wife, she'd have to leave. But until that time came, Sarah wanted to stay near him.

She was about at wit's end with the earl, when she caught Lord Copley's directions from the far end of the table. With a sigh of relief, she motioned for a footman to hold her chair. "Ladies, shall we retire to the Great Hall?"

Immediately after the women were gone, Peter moved to the baron's side. "Andy, please. I really need to speak to you."

Andersen decided he'd better hear his friend's complaint. It was probably another quibble with Basil or Henry. "Say away," he said.

"Not here. I must see you, alone. Later, perhaps in the library?"

Warmed by a combination of good wine and the friendly Bennington family, Andersen was feeling quite charitable. "If you insist, make it after everyone has gone to their rooms. If I don't get there by one o'clock, we can talk about it tomorrow."

"All right, Andy. I'll wait."

No sooner had Peter left him than Lord Favor settled himself into the chair beside Andersen and started an irritating babble. He didn't hear a word the earl said, but the picture of those big lips brushing Miss Grimsley's hand and the blush creeping into her cheeks, soured his previous mood. Was there something between them? The thought made his blood turn hot.

Glaring at the earl, Andersen shot out of his chair. "Gentlemen, shall we join the ladies?"

* * *

Later in the Great Hall, the Earl of Favor searched out Lady Caroline and pulled her into a corner. "My life is going to ruin because of you, daughter. The baron has just cut me short, and it is all your fault. I told you to apologize for your remarks."

Caroline pulled away. "I did. I even cried."

"Well, it was not enough. You must do something to force the situation. You saw the way Copley was watching Miss Bennington this evening. If you are not careful, you will miss the prize altogether. You are going to have to do something—and quickly. You are not without your wiles, so don't give me that innocent look." He glared at her. "Why are you stalling?"

She stuck her nose in the air. "I have to think out a plan."

"Don't think. Act! Tonight! It must be tonight."

"What else can I do?"

The earl's eyes narrowed. "Listen to me, and do as I tell you. Retire early. As soon as I see Copley leave the Great Hall, I shall send a serving girl to your room with a red flower. Wait an hour. By then the baron should have retired. It should be easy for you to sneak up to the second floor without being seen. I shall be belowstairs, listening for your scream. Make sure the whole house hears you. And for God's sake, make it look as though you have been seduced."

Several hours later, Lady Caroline opened her door when she heard a knock, and grabbed the red silk poppy from the startled servant. "Now get belowstairs immediately, if you know what is good for you, you silly girl."

As a little chill of excitement ran through Caroline, she clasped the flower to her chest. She was still a virgin, but she looked forward to crawling into bed with the baron tonight. Even if nothing happened, he'd have to marry her.

He might be only a baron, but there was no argument that he was the best-looking bachelor on the London scene, as well as one of the richest men in the kingdom.

Caroline wrapped her robe around her filmy nightdress and opened the door. How stupid her father had been to lose all his money. But when she married the very rich Lord Copley, she wouldn't have to worry anymore about being empty in the pockets. She'd become even more a pattern card than she was now, and order the most lavish trousseau any bride ever had.

She crept up the stairway leading to the second floor. An occasional taper in the sconces along the medieval corridors, still burned. In their eerie yellow fingers of light, Caroline made her way along the hallway. She stopped at an impressive, brass-studded, oaken door. The coat of arms in the sculpture above on the stone arch designated it as the master's bedchamber. The door wasn't altogether closed, and placing her eye to the crack, Caroline peeked into the room. The fire on the hearth threw waves of gold upon a huge, four-postered bed. The drapes weren't fully pulled, and the mound in the coverlet molded itself to the body of its occupant. She caught her breath when the door hinges squeaked, but the baron's slumber didn't seem disturbed. After waiting a moment, she squeezed through the opening.

Caroline hurried across the floor in her bare feet, her flimsy clothing little defense against the cold air. She dropped her robe at the side of the bed. Although she'd followed her father's instructions and had torn the left shoulder of her lacy shift, she now gave it an extra rip.

Cautiously, she mounted the stepstool and lifted the edge of the comforter. It's feathery warmth welcomed her. Slipping underneath, she quickly rolled to the center of the bed and threw her arm over the body next to her.

No one would ever know how long it took Caroline to come to the startling conclusion that it wasn't Lord Copley who wore the fur coat to bed, nor how long it took Dog to realize the sweet-smelling morsel beside him wasn't his master. But both reared up at the same time. Lady Caroline screamed. The lion roared and made a flying leap off the bed.

Below Lord Favor waited for what he felt was an eternity. When the screams finally came they echoed throughout the entire castle from attic to the cellar, exceeding his every expectation. "Magnificent, Caroline!" Who would have ever believed that his little girl could roar with such volume? Although it strained his patience, the earl tarried. When he was certain there were others behind him, he charged up the steps, his silk dressing gown flapping, a sword he'd removed from the wall earlier, raised over his head.

"Where is the scoundrel?" he bellowed, as any irate father might. "You are all witnesses. Lord Copley has compromised my daughter."

When the earl arrived at the baron's bedroom, he found a malaise of women and servants from the West Wing already crowded around Lady Caroline.

"Let me through!" he shouted. "I demand satisfaction! Show yourself, you scoundrel." The earl twirled about, looking helplessly into the crowd. His daughter sat in the huge bed, screaming. Miss Grimsley, covered by a voluminous purple robe, her brown hair curling around her shoulder, stood nearby trying to calm the girl. On the other side, hovered Caroline's lady's maid, Miss Glover and Miss Martin. The guests from the East Wing were now packing the portal.

Although he couldn't see the baron, the assembly made a perfect audience for the earl's theatrics

"You see the proof that Lord Copley has maliciously taken advantage of my sweet, innocent daughter."

A deep voice cut through the hysteria. "Who has compromised your daughter, Favor?"

"Why, you have, you rogue," the earl said righteously, turning to the door to find himself face to face with the baron. "And you, my lord, will pay for what you have done."

Andersen stood in the doorway, still dressed in his dinner clothes, Mr. Trummel behind him.

"How could I have done what you say I have, when I've obviously just arrived. Mr. Trummel will attest to that. We have been in the library since the ladies retired."

Above the din, Lady Caroline continued to howl.

The earl shouted, "Oh, do stifle it, Caroline! Enough is enough!"

But the lady wouldn't be stifled and continued to stretch her vocal chords, pointing to the empty spot on the bed next to her. "Beast! Monster! I was attacked by a vampire."

"Come now, there are no vampires at Roxwealde," Andersen said, stepping forward and extending his hand to the distraught woman.

Caroline grasped the blanket up around her neck. "Don't touch me! I saw his teeth!"

The baron stepped back, frowning. This was one situation he'd not anticipated.

The earl, his face now broken out with red splotches, wasn't making matters any easier. "She's had a nightmare," he said, glaring at the baron as if it was his fault. "All this talk about ghosts and weird noises in the night would make anybody walk in their sleep."

Sarah picked Lady Caroline's robe up off the floor and stepped toward the bed. Sniffing the air she glanced quickly at Lord Copley. She could read nothing in his expression that implied he wasn't totally caught up in the matters at hand. "If all you ladies and gentlemen will go back to your rooms, I believe Lord Favor will see that his daughter is escorted safely back to hers," she said. "I am certain the earl is right. Lady Caroline has had nothing more than a bad nightmare."

Andersen watched as Miss Grimsley quickly and efficiently cleared the room of the onlookers. Not more than an hour ago, Peter Trummel, whom he'd thought to be his best and most loyal friend, had just informed him that he and Miss Tremain were going to be married. Andersen had no idea they were courting.

"I want you to be the first to know," Peter had said. *"We, of course, won't announce the engagement until I have a chance to speak to her parents. We plan to leave first thing day after tomorrow. I wouldn't think of missing your wedding, old chap."*

"Lord," Andersen swore. What was happening to him? Was he becoming that selfish? Of course, he was pleased for Peter and for Edith, and he'd told him, *"I wish you happy."*

"After all, it isn't as if I stole one of your prospective brides out from under your nose as Ripple did," Peter had jested.

He was right, of course. There was no way his friend could have known that just last night, the baron had considered Miss Tremain as a substitute in case Miss Bennington cried off, or that Caroline was off his list.

Andersen blamed the earl for this fiasco. Caroline might be selfish and spoiled, but a plot to compromise him had all the earmarks of a flimflam that only a scoundrel like Favor could hatch up.

A knock on the door, interrupted his thoughts. Miss Grimsley stood in the portal. He had never seen her before with her hair down, or her spectacles off. In the harsher reality of daylight, she might have looked differently, but here in the soft illumination of the fire, she appeared quite young—and very pretty.

"Do you want me to help you search for him?"

The shock of what she'd asked, brought Andersen back

to the present. He answered her with a question. "Him? Surely you don't believe in vampires and ghosts, Miss Grimsley?"

"I mean the lion, your lordship. I have known about Dog from the beginning."

The baron looked unbelieving. "And how may I ask did you come upon that knowledge, Miss Grimsley? The second floor of this entire wing is forbidden to everyone except Jacob, Proctor . . . and Fletcher."

Sarah jumped at the chance to take the conversation down another path. "By the way, your lordship, where is your valet? Shouldn't he have been in your room to discourage any intruders?"

Andersen spotted the empty bottle on the table. "I believe we will find him asleep in my dressing room," he said, opening the door to that facility. "If I am any later than midnight, Fletcher cannot be depended upon to be awake when I come to bed." True to what he'd said, there lay the aforementioned servant curled up on the floor, snoring loudly. Andersen eased the door shut. "Now before I ask you more questions, it may be wisest if we *do* look around for the beast, first."

"I doubt you will find him in here," she said. "He is most likely in his own room down the hall. He goes there after every one of his wanderings."

"That means Jacob has been remiss in executing his responsibilities. I shall have to take him to task for that. He has instructions to see that Dog is securely locked in his room at all times."

"Your servant is loyal and trustworthy, your lordship. He has always followed your instructions to the letter."

"Then there seems to be more to this than I know. Would you please explain that statement?"

Sarah brushed her curls back from her face. "He appears in rooms and corridors all over the castle, then disappears before we can find how or where he enters or exits. It's a mystery."

She could tell he was having a hard time believing her, for he said, "I suggest we go to Dog's room and see if what you say is true. We cannot have him roaming around the castle at night."

Quickly they traversed the corridors to the lion's chambers. The door was locked and barred from the outside. Andersen took down the key and inserted it into the lock.

Just as she had said, there on the big canopied bed lay his pet. The light from the fireplace made a golden outline around his body. Andersen would have guessed him to be asleep if he hadn't seen one eye watching him warily.

Sarah called out, not unkindly, "There you are you renegade."

Dog crept to the edge of the bed and yawned.

Lord Copley's day had left him in a dark mood. "Do not placate him, Miss Grimsley. I will not tolerate such behavior. My guests will be here only two more days. Tomorrow, I shall instruct Jacob to put a twenty-four hour watch on Dog. He and Fletcher will have to take turns staying with him."

The lion rolled over to have his belly scratched, but the baron didn't go near him.

"Don't look to me for sympathy," Sarah said, shaking her finger at the animal. "You have been naughty, and Lord Copley says you are to be punished." The lion looked so pitiful, that she reached out a hand to pat him.

"Leave him be, Miss Grimsley. I suggest we both go to our chambers."

Reluctantly, Sarah did as the baron told her, glancing back once more to see the lion's sorrowful gaze following them.

A few minutes later, the baron watched his hostess from his doorway. He wondered if Miss Grimsley had made such a cock-up of the duke's parties. She'd no sooner reached the staircase than he called out, "Miss Grimsley, tomorrow I must propose to my bride. Would you please try to see that things run more smoothly?"

With a little quiver of anticipation, Sarah paused, expecting the baron to recall her. Was it her allusion that for a moment he'd looked upon her with a different eye? The hard sound of a door banging shut gave her the answer. The man was impossible. She held her tongue until she reached her room, then gave vent to a myriad of less than ladylike vows.

She tried to reason out why his lordship should be so put out with her. Did he blame her for Miss Martin's defection, or Lady Caroline's nightmare? She hadn't been the one to let Dog wander about.

Sarah climbed the stepstool and flopped onto her bed. No, she had to admit, 'twas none of those matters which was upsetting her. It was his words which wounded her most. *Tomorrow I must propose to my bride.* Would he choose the intelligent, biddable Miss Bennington or the frightened, delicate Lady Caroline?

Her ladyship had looked so vulnerable and lovely in her disarray. Helplessness in females seemed to draw men. She surmised, it added to their own consequence to appear cavalier. Very sincerely did Sarah wish that she'd had more sense than to forget that wisdom, for with no sign of fear or without a by-your-leave, she'd reached right out to pat the lion.

She punched her pillow into a ball and buried her face in its softness. "You are a fool, Sarah Greenwood, to let yourself fall in love with a rascal like Lord Copley."

Fourteen

Andersen yawned and stretched, only to find he'd slept later than he wanted. His valet stood looking down on him.

"Why didn't you waken me, Fletcher? A second look at his disheveled servant standing over him still dressed in the same black suit of the night before, was a sure sign that the valet had been up no more than a few minutes himself.

Fletcher struggled to brush away some of the wrinkles from his rumpled coat. "You came in late last night, milord."

Andersen threw off the comforter and sat up. "Yes, I did."

"I waited. Must've fallen asleep," the man said, casting a guilty look toward the empty bottle.

"I cannot fault you for that, Fletcher. The human body can only take so much before it demands rest. I was delayed in the library. Now, help me to shave and dress. I have a busy day ahead of me."

Half hour later, Andersen descended to the Great Hall, only to find himself manuevering among boxes and trunks stacked helter-skelter over the flagstoned floor. Ignoring Proctor, who was trying to direct his footmen to carry out the baggage, the Earl of Favor rushed about barking his own orders.

Lord Copley tried to hide his smile. "What is this, Favor? Are you leaving us already? The party is not yet over."

The earl busied himself inspecting a lock on one of the trunks. "Copley. Circumstances, you know. Have to get back to Gloucestershire. Cannot be away too long."

Andersen surveyed the hall. "Where is Lady Caroline?"

The earl coughed. "She's already in her coach. Sudden attack of megrim. Causes these nightmares. Sends her regrets."

Andersen bowed. "Please deliver my condolences to Lady Caroline. I wish her well."

Sarah, standing on the balcony, saw the last of the luggage being carried out the front door and descended to the Great Hall. As she approached the two men, she saw a gleam come into the earl's eyes.

"You are leaving us so early, Lord Favor."

He made a leg. "Ah, Miss Grimsley. You have been the brightest jewel in this whole affair. Regretfully, my daughter has developed a terrible headache."

I don't doubt it, after last night, Sarah thought. "We are sorry to see you leave, your lordship."

Before she could stop him, the earl grasped one of her hands. "Truly, Miss Grimsley?" Then he leaned closer, breathing heavily, "My offer still stands, you know."

Andersen watched the little scene and frowned. There *was* something between them. "Miss Grimsley," he said gruffly. "I do believe that Mrs. Proctor needs you."

Sarah saw no signs of the housekeeper, but thankful for the excuse to escape the earl's unwanted attentions, she said her goodbyes and left the two men to enter the morning room. If everyone didn't arise soon, it would be lunch instead of breakfast.

The earl had no sooner been seen out the door, than the baron turned to Proctor. "Have you seen Miss Bennington yet?"

"No, m'lord. None of the Benningtons have come down. All the excitement kept everyone up late last night."

"Yes, yes, I reckon it did. Well, I shall be in the library. Inform me the minute she appears."

"I will, m'lord," the servant said, turning to go into the breakfast room.

At that moment, Lord Wetherby came whistling down the stairs from the East Wing.

Elroy Bennington. dressed in the most brilliant pink waistcoat Copley had seen him wear since his arrival, followed a few paces behind. He paused for a moment to dramatically adjust his neckcloth.

Andersen watched with amusement as the young man pulled back his shoulders, and descended with exaggerated arrogance to the Great Hall, surveying everything as if it were the first time he'd seen it.

"Morning, Copley," the marquis quipped, a distinct hint of humor in his voice.

"And to you, Wetherby." Andersen said, not taking his gaze from the young cock approaching him. "Good morning, Elroy. Hope you slept well after all the disturbance, last night."

Young Mr. Bennington giggled, then, lowering his voice several decibels, he stammered some nonsensical jibberish, which the baron couldn't understand. Finally, Elroy swaggered into the breakfast room.

Andersen looked quizzically at the marquis.

Wetherby shrugged, with mock innocence. "Our little actresses refused to stay in their room belowstairs, last night. Said nothing was going to make them sleep down there with ghosts and vampires wandering about. My bed would only accommodate two of them, so I introduced Twist to Elroy. Hope you don't mind."

Andersen laughed. "I don't mind, Wetherby, but I suggest you don't mention young Bennington's charitable gesture to his mother. Was Smith too foxed to give his little doxie some solace?"

"Lost track of him when Caroline started her theatrics," the marquis said. "He'll probably be angry this morning when he finds out young Bennington has stepped into his shoes."

"Poor Henry, nobody wants him."

"Who can blame them?" Wetherby chuckled. "By-the-by, where were Favor and Caroline going?"

"They had a sudden desire to see Gloucester."

"A pity. I thought I would have my chance to console her today. However for your information, I heard voices from the Benningtons' apartment as I passed their door. They should be down shortly."

Andersen straightened his neckcloth. "Thank you, Wetherby. With all the competition out of the way. I can now concentrate on paying court to their daughter."

"I surmise that means I am free to follow my own interests today?"

Before the baron could reply Miss Glover and Miss Tremain came down the stairs from the West Wing. With the odd way his life was going of late, he wasn't surprised to see Peter miraculously appear and offer an arm to both ladies, before either he or Wetherby could make a move. Good old Peter, always there when he was needed. Now, Andersen had time to consult with Miss Grimsley before Miss Bennington made her appearance.

"Why don't you go ahead and eat, Wetherby? It seems everybody is occupied for now. I want to consult with my hostess before Miss Bennington makes her appearance."

Copley looked into the morning room and signaled his steward. "Where is Miss Grimsley, Proctor? I saw her come in earlier."

"She said she and Jacob had to go search for something, my lord, but I believe she's coming across the hall this very minute. See, she's waving to you."

Both he and the marquis turned to watch Miss Grimsley's approach.

Andersen was puzzled. His hostess looked different lately. He couldn't quite put his finger on it. She'd labored so hard to make his party a success, he didn't want her suffering some malady just when his campaign was coming to an end.

Andersen was annoyed that Wetherby insisted on remaining at his side. He wanted to speak to Miss Grimsley alone.

Sarah called before she'd crossed the wide hall, "Lord Copley!"

He bowed. Miss Grimsley was a golden flower again this morning. But now he also had the knowledge that underneath those swirls of gauze around her head, were long, brown curls that fell halfway to her waist. A certain sense of comradeship came over him as if they shared a secret.

Lord Wetherby, not to be outdone. spoke first. "Ah, my dear Miss Grimsley. If our Royal Princess is a sonnet, you are an entire symphony."

Andersen impaled Wetherby with a pointed glare. Aye, he agreed that she was an exceptional woman, but he didn't like the inflection in the marquis's voice when he said it.

Miss Grimsley seemed to have her thoughts clearly on other matters than the two men's verbal jousting. Wringing her hands, she said, "I need to speak to you alone, your lordship."

With a look of satisfaction, Copley turned to Wetherby.

The marquis good-naturedly touched his hand to his forehead, bowed and left.

Sarah turned worried eyes to the baron. "Dog is missing!"

In those three electric words. Andersen sensed a note of doom.

"Have the castle searched while the guests are having breakfast."

Sarah spoke in a hushed voice. "Jacob and I have looked in every one of his favorite haunts."

"You use your words well, Miss Grimsley. If Dog had been kept in his room, we would not have these Banbury tales flying about of ghosts and vampires."

She gave him a withering look. "You do not understand, my lord. I think he has run away."

Andersen frowned. "Dog cannot get out of the castle unless Jacob opens the door."

Sarah stared down at her hands. "He has done it before."

Between clenched teeth, Andersen said, "I am not going to ask you how you know that, Miss Grimsley. I only have a day and a half to complete my mission. Miss Bennington will be down shortly, and I must press my suit. Dog will have to wait."

"Animals have hearts, too, my lord, and you broke his last night. Dog is old. I believe he left because you scolded him. You said yourself that he has rheumatism."

A sense of guilt washed over Andersen. "I think you sometimes hear more than is good for you, Miss Grimsley."

She brushed aside his rebuke. "I believe I know where he has gone."

"You do?

She spoke more hopefully. "It is out on the moors, a long way from the castle. I believe I can find him."

"You know my rules regarding that. I forbid you to even think of it. You saw the swamp where we took Zee, so you know how dangerous it is."

Sarah's voice was firm. "For a lion as well as for me, my lord."

Andersen glanced up to see Miss Bennington coming down the stairs from the West Wing.

"Miss Grimsley," he said, smiling as one would at a child. "When Dog has gone off before, has he not found his way back to the castle?"

Sarah blinked. "Yes."

"There, you see. It's likely that Dog is in his room at this very moment, and you will find that all your fretting has been for naught."

Sarah settled her gaze on his lips, gently upturned at the corners, and capitulated. "You probably have the right of it, my lord."

"After everything has settled down, we will make a thorough search of the castle to find out how the rascal is getting out of his room—"

"—and into the other chambers."

The baron threw back his head and laughed.

Sarah pursed her lips. "What is so humorous, my lord?"

"I was just thinking that we sound like Mr. and Mrs. Bennington—finishing each other's sentences. Oh, you are a quiz, Miss Grimsley."

Sarah didn't find that so out of the ordinary. Her mother and father did the same thing. She reckoned living together year after year, people get to know what the other is going to say before they say it.

"Miss Grimsley, you do give me hope. I believe that in time, Miss Bennington and I will achieve that same closeness which her parents have." He motioned with a nod of his head toward the West Wing staircase. "I see the lady is nearly down. You must have many duties calling you."

Sarah suddenly found herself in a brown study. "You are right, my lord," she said sharply. "It's near noon already. I shall instruct Cook to prepare some luncheon dishes for the sideboard. By the time everyone finishes their repast, it will be late into the day."

"As usual, you are right, Miss Grimsley." Lord Copley bowed gallantly and said, "Now, if you will excuse me, I shall take A into the breakfast room. It seems that the beginning of the alphabet is to be the ending for me as well." With a wink he was gone.

Sarah folded her arms across her chest. He called Dog a rascal. Well, as far as she was concerned, no one could outdo the baron in that area.

The circumstances surrounding the sudden departure of the earl occupied much of the conversation of Mrs. Bennington, Miss Glover, and Lady Martin. After they had eaten, they sat on the settles in front of the hearth in the

Great Hall. Sarah stopped for a moment to see if anyone would like one of the maids to bring them some hot cider.

"Oh, no, dear. I am quite satisfied." Mrs. Bennington looked up toward the high vaulted ceiling and sighed. "I cannot believe we have but a day and a half before we will be leaving, Miss Grimsley. I wonder if Mr. Bennington will allow me to turn our drawing room into a medieval solar." She tapped her chin with her finger. "No, he probably will not, since I just had it done over. We visited Brighton last year, you see, and I redecorated the room in an Oriental theme as soon as we returned home in August."

Sarah nodded absently. The activity on the other side of the hall drew her attention away from the ladies. Lord Copley walked with Miss Bennington toward her father and brother. From where Sarah sat, she couldn't see Miss Bennington's expression, but Mr. Bennington's smile nearly split his face in half. She wondered if his lordship planned to ask him soon for his daughter's hand in marriage.

Mrs. Bennington looked over at Sarah. "I have not been to such an interesting do for ever so long, Miss Grimsley. So romantic with all the flowers and armoured knights . . ."

"Don't forget the ghosts," added Miss Glover, smiling.

Mrs. Bennington gave a little shiver. "Well—that, too. The subject seems to thrill some people. Now mind you, the times we explored the castle," she said, looking toward Sarah, "there were so many people, I felt quite safe."

Lady Martin glanced up from her stitchery. "The medieval banquet will stand out in my mind: the harp music, the old costumes, eating from trenchers with our fingers."

"Oh, my, yes." Miss Glover said. "It's too bad more people cannot experience it. Many would pay a tidy sum to be able to spend a few nights pretending to be a knight or lady, don't you think?"

Sarah blinked. Her mind had wandered, and she but caught half of what was being said . . . something about how much they'd enjoyed staying in the castle.

Miss Glover sighed. "But, I did so wish to see a ghost. What a shame that Lady Caroline was the only one who claimed to do so."

"Lord Favor insisted it was a bad dream," Lady Martin said, laying her needlework in her lap. "Now my niece was quite taken with the riding paths. Of course, her youthful enthusiasm could have been swayed by having won both a stallion and a fiancé all in one day. But then Beverly never was one to do thing by halves."

"My Edith liked climbing up to the parapet atop the tower to look out over the moors," Miss Glover said. "She told me that Mr. Trummel was so nice to accompany her," Miss Glover added. "Such a polite young man. She told me she met your Anne up there quite often, too, with Mr. Smith or Lord Wetherby."

"It does seem strange, does it not," Mrs. Bennington mused, "that whenever Lord Copley entertained one of the gels, he stayed inside, sitting quietly, talking. But when any of the other young men asked them about, they explored the castle or went out riding. Do you think that perhaps his reputation as a rake may have been unduly exaggerated?" Mrs. Bennington didn't seem the least interested in receiving a reply, for she continued on, smiling knowingly. "I see my daughter now going toward the library with her father and Lord Copley. Anne does loves to read, but I never knew Mr. Bennington to be interested in anything but the latest livestock prices."

Sarah became more and more uncomfortable listening to the conversation. Time was running out for her at Roxwealde. As busy as she had been the last several weeks, she'd had little time to think about her future plans. What was she to do when the baron married? She steeled her thoughts against that inevitability.

At that moment, a very distressed-looking Jacob made his appearance. "May I speak to you, ma'am?"

"Excuse me, ladies," she said, going to meet him. "Yes, Jacob, what is it?"

"Dog has not come back."

"That worries me, Jacob. It is getting on in the day."

"I don't like it, either, Miss Grimsley. It's getting colder by the minute. I be afraid that we are in for a frost tonight."

Sarah glanced about the hall, looking for the baron, but she caught no sight of him. "Dog will not survive a night in this weather, Jacob. I am going after him."

"You dasn't do that, Miss Grimsley. His lordship forbids anyone to go out on the moors."

"I don't expect you to jeopardize your livelihood, Jacob. I think I know where he is. I shall be there and back before dark."

Before Jacob could protest, Sarah headed up the stairs. She needed to change to walking boots and a wrap. There was no time to remove her light-corset. However, she now used such a small pillow for stuffing, that she wasn't as encumbered as she had been when she first made up her disguise. She removed the spectacles, but left on her turban for extra warmth.

One look out the window at the swirling fog, and Sarah decided to cover her woolen coat with a hooded cape. Then as a last thought, she stuffed the four remaining cinnamon buns into the pocket of her coat. If Dog proved reluctant to return surely the sweet buns would entice him to follow her.

Caution thrown to the wind, Sarah moved quickly through the twisting corridors, down the rear stairway . . . only to be stopped at the door. Strong hands clamped on her shoulders.

Andersen couldn't see her well in the dim hallway, but it didn't take much imagination to know whom he held. "Miss Grimsley!"

"Lord Copley?"

He set her away from him, but kept his hands clamped

on her arms. "Jacob told me what you planned on doing. How dare you disobey my orders?"

Determination punctuated her every word. "No matter what you say, Lord Copley, I am going after Dog."

She couldn't tell if his answer was an agreement or a grumble. "Miss Grimsley, do you have any idea what your actions interrupted?"

"I did not interrupt anything, your lordship."

"Well, Jacob did. I was in the library having a very significant conversation with Mr. Bennington."

"You can always continue a conversation, my lord. But Dog, in danger of freezing to death, is another matter altogether."

He realized that she didn't see the entire picture. "You still don't understand the import of what I am saying."

Deciding to give him the benefit of the doubt, Sarah pursed her lips and waited to hear his explanation.

"Miss Bennington was also present at the meeting. I did not come right out with what I had in mind, but I detected no adverse reaction to my suggestion that I wanted to speak to her father alone."

"What objection could she have, your lordship?"

"Exactly what I was thinking," Copley replied. "But that is when Jacob interrupted. Ordinarily, I would not have tolerated a servant acting so bold. But, he was obviously more concerned for your safety than he was on retaining his employment here at Roxwealde. I admired that."

Sarah caressed her arm where he'd held it. "He was also worried about Dog. That is more than I can say for you. It is your fault he is out there, you know."

"I *am* concerned!" Andersen ran his hand across his forehead. "The renegade will catch the chills if he stays out all night. That is why I postponed my appointment with Mr. Bennington to later this evening after dinner."

Sarah looked at him, unbelieving. "You are coming with me?"

"Aye."

"What excuse were you able to give to Mr. Bennington?"

"I concocted a tarradiddle about having to visit a very ill widow of one of my former tenants."

"Oh, that was very good, your lordship. I can see making it a widow was more likely to gain sympathy from Mr. Bennington."

"I thought so, too. Now, you say you know where Dog is likely to have gone?"

"I am certain of it. There is an oak woods to the left of the old ruins at the grand tor."

"Good God! That is farther than I have ever been. If I come with you, Miss Grimsley, do you think you can find your way to the copse?"

Sarah Greenwood knew it was not a time to act mishish. "Of course, I can."

"If he is where you say, is it possible to get him back here by dinnertime?"

"I am certain of it. I only have to follow my markers."

One eyebrow shot up. "What markers?"

"Pebbles. My father showed me how to collect colorful stones and drop them to leave a trail."

"Miss Grimsley, you are—"

"Yes," she finished, giving a snort. "I know. I am remarkable. But we must go quickly, and you cannot go attired like that."

Andersen looked down at his immaculate super-fine jacket, tan trousers and his highly polished Wellington boots. "I don't have time to worry about my apparel, but I must fetch a coat and gloves. Wait here for me. We will also need a lantern and tinder box in case it turns dark. March is a fickle month, and the fog can turn day into night in a matter of minutes. But first, I shall tell Fletcher to deliver a message to Mr. Smith. He has been sulking all day. If he is not otherwise occupied for the afternoon, I shall ask him to attend Miss Bennington until I return. That should get him out and cheer him up a bit. Then we shall go after that errant lion and fetch him back to the castle before dinner. I still have some serious courting to do this evening, Miss Grimsley."

When Lord Copley and Sarah left the Park boundary, the baron insisted on leading the way. They had gone no more than a mile from the castle when the fog closed in on them completely.

Andersen looked at her with admiration. "You chose the stones well, Miss Grimsley. They are clearly visible, even in the mist."

Warmed by his praise, Sarah raised her hood to look about. It was impossible to see more than a few feet ahead of them. No tors, no ruins, no landmarks to go by. Only the tiny, colorful pebbles.

Andersen was startled for a moment. "Miss Grimsley, you did not bring your spectacles. Can you see?"

Sarah winced. She'd forgotten that he wasn't used to seeing her without them. "Don't worry, my lord. I only need them for close work."

"Nevertheless, let me take your hand. I don't want you to stumble."

Sarah pulled her hood back down over her face and plodded on, warmed by the feel of her gloved hand in his.

The temperature began to drop. By the time they found the copse, dusk was upon them. Sarah recognized the tangle of brush which she'd replaced over the opening to the narrow passageway. "I know the way from here, my lord. It may be best if I lead," she said, tugging at the dry, scratchy branches.

Lord Copley looking as though he questioned both her sanity and the advisability of her suggestion, stepped up and easily lifted away the obstruction. A few minutes later, he looked down into the depths of the ancient oaken woods.

"Miss Grimsley, do you mean to tell me you went down into that hell hole all by yourself?"

Sarah slid into the narrow opening between the rocks and started her downward trek. "It's not very far down, now."

She heard a clanking sound behind her, followed by a plop and a string of oaths.

Sarah didn't dare turn around. "Do you want me to take the lantern, my lord?"

"I am quite capable of handling it, Miss Grimsley."

The voice hadn't sounded happy. Sarah sighed. It was plain as a pikestaff that his lordship wasn't a person who was going to find any pleasure in the squishing sounds of his boots on soggy ground or receive solace from hearing the soft rhythm of water dripping onto mossy rocks.

By the time she'd reached the bottom of the dell, Sarah's cape had a hole ripped in it, and her turban hung on a branch somewhere up the hill. She dared not think what was happening to the baron, but by his continued use of his Lord's name, she at least knew that he hadn't deserted her.

"The cave is this way," she called up, stumbling over the protruding roots of the oak trees.

Sarah shouted into the dark opening, but received no response.

Andersen caught up to her. He was hatless and Sarah didn't think it wise to ask what had happened to his beaver. He lit the lantern and peered inside.

It took a while to locate Dog, but they found him right where Sarah said they would, inside the cave. At first, he lay so still, they feared the beast was dead. Then Sarah spoke his name, and Dog raised his head slightly. When she knelt beside him and stroked his nose, he licked her hand, but ignored Andersen.

No matter where the baron shifted, Dog rolled his eyes and refused to meet his master's gaze. Remorse over his treatment of the animal shattered Andersen. He ran his hands over Dog's body. "Let's see if we can get him to stand," he said.

For several minutes, Sarah and the baron shoved and lifted one end of the lion, then the other. But Dog wouldn't even sit up.

Sarah fell back on her heels and stared at the animal, then up at Lord Copley. "My goodness! Whatever are we going to do, my lord?"

Fifteen

Andersen glanced at the giant beast lying prone on the floor. Only an ear twitched now and then to show that life still remained in the tired body. "It's a fact that we cannot move the lion by ourselves. I'll go back to the castle for help." He held up his hand to stop her protest. "One of us must stay here with Dog. I can cover the distance much faster than you can encumbered by a skirt."

Sarah couldn't deny that.

The baron held the light high and looked around the cave. "I will need to take the lantern with me. It's not dark yet, but it will be by the time I get there. I'll build you a fire before I leave." He scraped together some dry rushes and lit them with the lantern. "Collect what kindling you can find in here. Everything in the dell is soaking wet. I'll climb back up the cliff to gather the branches and dried brush that concealed the path." He then wrapped his woolen scarf tighter around his neck and left.

Sarah searched as far back into the cave as she could see. She swore she heard some movement in the dark and saw bright little eyes staring at her. But since she neither had the lantern to light her way, or the time to explore, she left the inhabitants to conjecture. She piled up the sticks and leaves she found, and had a good blaze going by the time the baron returned.

She heard his grumbling before she saw him. It was plain that his lordship wasn't in the gayest of spirits.

Lord Copley came into the cave with his hair sticking straight out as if he were still walking with the wind behind him.

Her eyes widened. "Is it raining?"

"It's neither raining or snowing," he chattered, through gritted teeth. "In fact, although there is still some light on the western horizon, the stars are coming out."

"After so many misty nights, that must have been a sight to see," she said cheerily.

"My purpose of climbing that cliff was not to go star-gazing," he snapped, before dumping his armload of branches on the cold granite floor. "The temperature has also dropped down so low, Miss Grimsley, that I am certain that they will be begging for blankets in Hades tonight."

Sarah pursed her lips and turning away from the baron, started breaking up the wood into shorter pieces, placing each stick on one of three piles, thick, thin, and very thin. "I am only trying to make the best of a unfortunate situation, my lord."

He rewound his scarf around his ears and started back toward the entrance of the cave.

Sarah scrambled after him. "Are you leaving already?"

The anxiety in her voice made Andersen chastise himself for his surliness. She must be frightened to death. He spoke, more gently. "It will be warm enough if you keep the fire burning throughout the night. For you to do that, I must fetch more wood."

"Oh," she said, a little embarrassed at her outburst. She knew he hated the moors, but like most men, he didn't want a weakness mentioned.

When the bear-faced Lord Copley returned several minutes later, he tossed the thin branches onto her tidy piles of kindling.

Sarah stared at the pitiful offering.

Andersen shrugged. "That is all I could find." Why was he apologizing? She was the one who had propelled them into this mess. In another two hours he would have been engaged to Miss Bennington, accepting the congratulations of his friends, and making preparations for his marriage on the morrow.

Sarah glanced at him sideways from under her hood. She could see that the fresh air hadn't improved his lordship's disposition. "Will you be leaving now?"

"Miss Grimsley," he said, "the wind drives sideways from the north, away from the castle, and will sweep every living creature thither, whether they wish to go in that direction or not. If I climb to the top of the cliff one more time, I shall be swept across the entire peninsula to Exeter by morning. Neither of us will be leaving the cave tonight."

He then slapped his gloved hands together so hard, splinters of wood flew every which way.

Sarah thought it best not to argue and began rearranging the sticks properly again. "You are tired, my lord. I am certain we have enough kindling. Why don't you take the lantern over by the wall and rest?"

Contrary to her suggestion, Lord Copley extinguished the lamp, throwing the cave into near total darkness, except for the tiny faery-ring of firelight. Then kneeling beside her, he began to help her break up the branches. "I'm afraid we will have to ration our fuel tonight," he said, glancing at Dog. "Has he made any effort to get up?"

"None," Sarah said, looking over just in time to see a big golden ear twitch. "At least, he is alive."

Only when all the sticks were piled, did the baron settle down against the wall of the cave and stretched his feet out in front of him. "I am sorry, Miss Grimsley. There is no excuse for my reprehensible manners. We will not be going anywhere for several hours."

Sarah checked Dog one more time, and when he didn't move, she found a level place to settle, a few feet away from Lord Copley.

The baron's heartrending sigh broke Sarah's revelry. "My lord?"

Her inquiry brought a laugh. "I was only contemplating the dinner that I am missing at the castle."

Sarah winced. She was trying to think of some witticism to take his lordship's mind off his empty stomach, when of a sudden, she remembered—"The buns!"

Copley jerked his head around to stare at her. "The what?"

Sarah rifled through her pockets. "I forgot the buns," she said, pulling out one of the pastries.

Andersen looked at the flattened piece of dough in her hand. She smiled so proudly, that he hadn't the heart to show his disillusionment. Then, he sniffed and grinned. "Miss Grimsley, is that a—"

"Cinnamon bun," she said holding out the morsel. "I forgot that I had put them in my pocket before I left the castle. I thought they might help persuade Dog if he proved difficult."

The baron took her offering and held it to his nose. Breathing in deeply, he said, "Miss Grimsley, you are—"

"Amazing, your lordship?" Sarah felt a peculiar warmth flow through her.

The baron grinned and was just about to put the sweet-smelling bread into his mouth, when they heard a stirring on the other side of the fire.

The lion raised his head from the dirt and made a weak whimpering sound.

Sarah hurried to his side. "Cinnamon buns are one of Dog's favorite treats," she said. "He must have smelled it."

Andersen looked down at the mouth-watering pastry, then held it out to her. "Here, give it to him."

The bun disappeared in one gulp. The beast licked his chops, closed his eyes, and lay his head back upon the earth.

With a look of resignation, Andersen said. "It's a good sign when an animal eats."

Sarah didn't miss the disappointment in the baron's voice. "Oh, but I have more, my lord," she said fishing around in her pockets until she found the other three buns. She handed one to Lord Copley, relishing the sparkle it brought to his eyes.

Andersen had no more than reached for the sweet, when once again, Dog raised his head. The baron watched two more buns disappear into the mouth of the lion.

Sarah glanced at Lord Copley, then back at Dog. "No more," she said, stroking the animal's cheek. "Your master needs sustenance, too." She walked back to the baron and handed him the last cinnamon bun.

"You must have something," Copley said, refusing to take it.

"Nonsense," Sarah replied, breaking the bread in two. "The practical thing is to each take a half." She gave a portion to the baron.

Andersen noticed immediately that his was a much larger piece, and realizing that the woman standing before him would have it no other way, he accepted the offering.

They ate in silence, savoring every bite. Unless Miss Grimsley produced another miracle, Andersen knew that it would be the only food they'd have until morning.

Farther back in the cave, the temperature would be warmer, but since they couldn't move the lion, Lord Copley and Sarah remained near the entrance, also.

Copley kept watch throughout the night. He knew he dare not let the fire go out, yet neither could he make it larger, for fear they'd run out of fuel before daybreak.

The wind sounded like banshees howling through the treetops. Miss Grimsley had curled up on the floor beside him, her hood covering much of her face. He was glad she'd fallen asleep. Not once had she complained about their disagreeable conditions. In fact, her only regard had been solely for his comfort and that of the lion.

On the other side of the fire, Dog lay sleeping, but it

was a labored sleep. The temperature continued to drop, and with each breath Dog took, his great body shivered. Quietly, the baron rose and circled the fire. Removing his coat, he spread it over the lion.

"Whatever are you doing?"

Andersen jumped as if he'd been caught committing some dastardly act. "Miss Grimsley. I didn't know you were awake. I saw Dog shaking." He returned to his place by the wall, and hugging his arms around himself, he once more stretched his feet toward the fire.

"And, you think it's better that you catch your death, so that I shall have two sick creatures on my hands tomorrow?"

He could tell by the tone of her voice that she didn't appreciate his sacrifice.

Giving him an exasperated look, Sarah sat upright and began to unwrap her enormous cape.

"I will not take your cloak, Miss Grimsley."

It astonished Sarah that men thought themselves immune to every ill if they didn't order it themselves. When her father refused to wear his scarf and ended in bed with a cold, he blamed everyone and everything, but himself. "I have my woolen pelisse."

Andersen looked at the blue fabric peaking from beneath the cape. "It is not thick enough to withstand the cold. Unless—"

Sarah jerked her head up. "Unless what, my lord?"

His voice came in crisp staccato notes. "Y-your wrap does seem to be quite commodious, and u-under the peculiar circumstances which we find ourselves, perhaps you could share a corner of it with me?"

Sarah inspected the voluminous robe. "Of course, my lord, a very sensible idea," she said, holding one side open for him.

Andersen found that once he'd moved closer to Miss Grimsley, the voluminous cape did indeed accommodate

them both. Even more so when he moved his arm up under
the garment and around the back of her shoulders. With a
few adjustments, he lay his head back against the wall,
closed his eyes, and relaxed. Contrarywise, he felt a slight
rigidity in her body. He couldn't resist the temptation to
tease. Without opening his eyes, he said, "I assure you I
shan't bite, Miss Grimsley."

Sarah felt the flush come into her face. "On, no, your
lordship. I wasn't thinking anything of the sort."

Andersen grinned wickedly. He was certain that was exactly what she'd been thinking. "Then why are you so
tense?"

Sarah searched her brain to give him a reason. "I . . . I
saw eyes staring at me back in the cave. They were about
two feet off the ground. They frightened me."

She didn't seem the least bit frightened, at least of the
unknown noises. For some time now, Andersen had been
hearing the soft rustling sounds from the interior of the
cave. He suspected she was afraid of him and for some
reason was trying to change the subject. But he decided to
go along with her flummery and speak of other matters.
"You know by now that I harbor many odd animals at Roxwealde."

"Jacob told me as much, my lord."

Andersen noticed her body settle more comfortably
against his side. "What you saw are probably the three ga-
zelles I brought from Sussex. A collector of exotic species
died, and his estate was bought by an acquaintance of mine
who raises hunting dogs. I knew the little antelopes
wouldn't have long to live if they were left unprotected."

She lay her head back against his shoulder. "What do
they look like?"

The baron pulled the cloak tighter around them. "They
are brown with white underparts and a dark band running
along their sides, swift and graceful."

"I wish I could see them, but the poor little creatures are probably scared to death of us," she said sadly.

Strange, when he'd first ask her to come to Roxwealde to organize a party for him, Andersen had thought that after twelve years of indulgence by one of England's most shameless aristocrats, Miss Grimsley would be more uppish and demanding. Instead he'd found her amusing, much younger-looking than he'd pictured her, and to his surprise, the thing he'd least expected, to find her so kind.

Lord Copley leaned back, his amused gaze never leaving her face.

As the light played across his near-perfect features, Sarah wondered if she could ever get enough of looking at him. "You didn't tell me exactly when your birthday was, my lord. Only that it was soon and you wished to find a woman to marry before you turned thirty."

"Day after tomorrow—which means that by midnight tomorrow night, I must have a wife or I lose the entail to the Copley estate."

It took a second for his statement to register in Sarah's mind. She looked at him incredulously. "Tomorrow? I didn't dream it was so soon, my lord."

"Aye, Miss Grimsley. I have to be married before the clock rings twelve in little more than four and twenty hours."

"But that is impossible! You need to post banns . . . to make arrangements for the church and the reception—"

"I purchased a special license before leaving London, and the vicar in Danbury Wells was notified to be prepared to perform a wedding ceremony during this week."

"Why ever did you wait so long to choose a wife?"

"I believed I was a year younger than I was."

"I cannot believe you didn't even know how old you were."

"My solicitor keeps the family documents. It was he who

informed me that my thirtieth birthday was this April. Before this, I've never given it much thought."

"It is understandable, since you don't have a mother to remember those things."

"I have a mother, Miss Grimsley."

"My goodness, where is she?"

"My mother is in Europe, somewhere. After the war was over in France, she left for a tour of the Continent, and decided the warmer climes of the Mediterranean were more to her liking."

"Surely she writes to you."

"Aye, she writes occasionally." Andersen didn't tell her that now and then, he received a letter from Italy or Greece, asking him for money. Somehow he would have to find a way to keep his mother supplied, for she wasn't the type to understand it possible to run out of funds.

"Certainly she remembers you on your birthday," she said, smiling, while she thought of the elaborate festivities Mama made, even when there were only her parents and her to celebrate.

"I fear that my mother found it convenient to forget birthdays for the older my brother and I grew, the more years she had to add to her own calendar."

"I cannot imagine it."

"Don't judge her too harshly, Miss Grimsley. She was a Norfolk Andersen. The women were beautiful and very high ton. They seldom had large families. Yet, for three sequential years, my mother bore a son. All of us were born in April, all of us received the name of Andersen. My two older brothers died at birth. You can see that she was a persistant woman, and when I survived infancy, she proclaimed her duty done. Then Bertie came along, neither expected nor wanted. I am the only one left to carry on the family name, until my nephew comes of age."

"Goodness! If those are the circumstances, my lord, you should have offered for Miss Bennington today."

Andersen's jaw tightened. "That was my purpose, Miss Grimsley, before I got lured into this God-forsakened place. Since that is impossible, now, I can only hope that my Banbury tale about having to attend an ailing widow will suffice as an excuse for my absence at dinner."

"I still think you should have made more of an effort to return to the castle this evening to propose to Miss Bennington."

"Have you noticed, Miss Grimsley, there is a storm outside? I would not be surprised if it snowed. In fact, I would not be surprised if we had an earthquake."

Sarah looked at him, startled. "Not really! Do they have earthquakes in this part of Devonshire?"

With the toe of his boot, the baron kicked a stick toward the fire, catapulting it over the flames onto the hard rock beyond. "Not in the last several hundred years, Miss Grimsley, but the way my life has been turned upside down of late, I would not even count that possibility out."

"I'm sorry."

"For what? That there will be no earthquake, or that I will lose the entail if I don't get back to the castle in the morning?"

She told a little lie. "That you are stuck with me here in the cave."

"Save your pity, Miss Grimsley," he said, glancing over at Dog. " 'Tis not your fault. I cannot blame you, altogether."

Sarah turned her face up to him, her hood slipping onto her shoulders. "But, I feel it *is* partly my fault. I made up the schedules, and perhaps, if I had organized things better . . . But, who would have thought that Miss Martin would take a liking to Mr. Ripple—or that Lady Caroline would be afflicted with sleepwalking? Of course, you, yourself, crossed Miss Tremain off the list, so you cannot blame me for that."

She couldn't tell by the way the baron drew his lips in

a straight line, whether he was agreeing with her or not. "I cannot understand why you did not consider Miss Tremain, my lord." For a moment, Sarah thought she'd overstepped the bonds of propriety and that the baron wasn't going to answer.

"There was another problem which came up unexpectedly. I've told no one except Mr. Trummel, but I think you will understand, because your own circumstance was much the same. To pay my creditors, I need a great deal of blunt."

"But you are very rich—"

"A sudden reverse in my circumstance make it necessary for me to find a wife with a goodly portion."

"And Miss Tremain could not bring in the needed funds, and Miss Bennington could?"

"I am not proud of that decision, Miss Grimsley. In fact, if it were not for the necessity of keeping the entail in my control until my nephew is of age, I would not give one whit whether he gets the estate or not. In its present state, it doesn't amount to much."

"Then it is only a matter of finding a wealthy bride?"

"No, not just a wealthy bride, Miss Grimsley. I wished to find someone that I rub well with. I plan to take very good care of my wife. It is only that my birth date leaped upon me sooner than I expected."

That made Sarah feel better and she thought of her own dowry. Her father had told her he'd planned on giving her three thousand pounds when she wed, and she would receive an annuity of three hundred pounds a year from her maternal grandmother's estate. Dared she dream of it? Would he look on her differently if she offered it to him? He could pay off his debts and perhaps someday, he would even come to love her. "How much do you need, my lord?"

"My debts run well over one hundred thousand pounds, Miss Grimsley. I will need at least a quarter of that amount to stave off my creditors until I can rebuild the principle."

Sarah sucked in her breath. He needed at least twenty-five thousand pounds immediately. "And Miss Bennington—?"

"He father has hinted that her dowry will exceed that amount by several thousand pounds. The untitled are becoming the landowners of this country, Miss Grimsley, and their wealth far outreaches those who are encumbered by tradition to not soil themselves with trade."

Well, evidently the Benningtons were much richer than the Greenwoods. "I think Miss Bennington will make a proper Lady Copley," she said, trying to sound happy for him.

"Leave it be, Miss Grimsley. It is over and done with. Only one day remains before the hatchet falls."

Sarah settled back into her former position against his chest. "Well, at least I want to tell you that if I had known, I would have planned a birthday party for you. Everybody should have a party to celebrate the day they were born. A baby is so special."

That statement touched Andersen in a way none other had, and he pulled her closer. Once he'd noticed what nice eyes she had, now, he had the occasion to study her lips, only a few inches from his. "Miss Grimsley," he said, "I do believe I am going to kiss you."

And he did.

Kissing Miss Grimsley proved to be so pleasant, that Andersen decided to do it again, this time, longer.

Sarah felt tears forming and closed her eyes. She didn't want his lordship reading what was in her heart.

Andersen cleared his throat. "That was uncalled for on my part, Miss Grimsley, and I ask your forgiveness. In the morning, I shall try to make my way back to the castle to get help."

"I'll go," Sarah said huskily.

"I told you that you will stay here with Dog."

She lay her head back against his chest. "As you say, my lord."

Lord Copley knew that he should, but he wasn't ready to let her go. He'd thought her too plump, but holding her was like hugging a pillow. Miss Grimsley, he decided, was a very comforting lady.

He wondered if embracing Miss Bennington would be as pleasurable. Thinking about A, didn't do to him what Miss Grimsley's closeness was doing. But then, Anne was an innocent, and Miss Grimsley was . . . He really didn't want to contemplate on that, he thought sadly. Now that he had time to dwell on the matter of Miss Bennington's charms, not once had she encouraged any contact beyond his kissing her fingers. Yet, she'd followed willingly enough when he'd invited her and her father into the library. She had to have known what his intentions were. Yes, he was certain Miss Bennington would be a biddable, virtuous wife. Never disobeying her husband by going off into some God-forsaken land of bogs and rocks.

The woman in his arms was so quiet, he thought perhaps she'd fallen asleep. "Miss Grimsley?" he said brusquely.

Sarah startled by his address, jumped.

"I wondered if you were awake."

"I was only thinking, my lord, that if no one ever commemorated the day of your birth, have you ever had a birthday party?"

"Never."

"Then you have never had a birthday cake?"

"When one of our cooks found out that our parents were too busy to remember, she would bake Bertie and me a special cake on her own birthday. Why do you ask?"

This started Sarah thinking about the children she would have someday. Of course, for that she would need a husband, wouldn't she? Perhaps, when Lord Copley married Miss Bennington, she would continue her journey on to London to have her Season after all. She felt the warmth as well as the hardness of the chest of the man she sat beside. The idea of looking at other men, pleased her less than ever now. "If you were my child," she said, "I would have given you a grand gala every year."

The baron rested his chin on the top of her head. "You are very kind, Miss Grimsley."

Sarah wanted to be more than kind, but she didn't know how to go about it. She was getting very sleepy and all that she could think about was that his lordship didn't even know who she was. She nestled her face against his chest and closed her eyes. What would he think if she suddenly declared, *"I am not Miss Grimsley, I am Sarah Greenwood of Elmsdale?"*

But Lord Copley wasn't even noticing her, he was looking at the sleeping lion. "If Dog gets well, it will be all the gift that I ask for, Miss Grimsley. I regret to think that much of my rescuing of mistreated animals, may have been for selfish reasons as well as humanitarian ones. For I know now that much of my pleasure has been derived from my own satisfaction . . . a getting back at the world, so to speak, for Bertie. I didn't really realize that beasts could feel so deeply, too. Do you think I have been selfish, Miss Grimsley?"

When Andersen got no reply, he looked down. Miss Grimsley was asleep in his arms. He didn't know how much she'd heard of what he said. He kicked another piece of wood into the fire. Then wrapping the cape tighter around them, he leaned his head back against the hard wall. The vigil would be a long one. The lion lay, licking his lips in his sleep, his sparse ribs rising and falling with each breath. For one so sick, Dog looked quite peaceful.

It was the scolding *churr* of wrens which awakened Sarah. Her head lay on Lord Copley's chest. His head rested against the wall, his arms relaxed down around her hips. He slept.

On the floor beside the dying fire, lay his coat. The spot where the lion had lain was now empty.

"Lord Copley!" Sarah exclaimed, "Dog is gone."

Sixteen

Andersen awakened instantly, and leaping to his feet, sent Sarah flying. "Gone where?"

Sarah caught her balance, reminding herself to never startle a man out of sound sleep. "How do I know? Perhaps he went back farther into the cave."

Andersen lit the lantern. "I doubt that," he said, but they searched anyway.

No amount of calling Dog's name got any response.

"Listen," Sarah said, "the wind has stopped."

The baron shook out his coat and put it on. "The first thing we must do is get back to the castle before everybody rises and discovers we were gone all night. I'll send Jacob out with some men I can trust to search for Dog."

It took them just under an hour to return to the castle, for not only had the storm blown over, but the day already promised to be more like spring.

Jacob met Lord Copley outside his bedchamber door. Only a slightly raised eyebrow gave any indication he was surprised by his master's disheveled appearance. "When I checked at daybreak, Dog was in his room."

The baron started down the corridor. "I want to see him, Jacob. He is very ill."

"Oh, I don't think so, milord," the servant said, inserting the key in the lock after removing the bar.

Copley pushed open the heavy timbered door.

In front of the fire, Dog noisily licked the sides of his empty bowl.

"I filled it, twice," Jacob said.

The baron studied the lion through narrowed eyes. "Undoubtedly, he has had a remarkable recovery."

The servant smiled from ear to ear. "He's right as rain, all right."

"Well, I have precious little time to contemplate the reason for Dog's good health. It's important I be shaved and dressed before my guests come down to breakfast. I trust you can keep guard over the beast."

"Oh, aye, milord."

As soon as Andersen had completed his toilette, he sent Fletcher to assure Miss Grimsley that the lion had returned safely. Then wishing to be the first to arrive in the Great Hall he hurried down the stairs. He'd no sooner reached the high-vaulted Great Hall than the marquis rose from where he'd been seated on a settle before the hearth.

"Good morning, Copley. I got up early to catch you before the others came down. I wanted to tell you that Penny, Twist, and Genevieve kicked up such a dust about ghosts and goblins, that I promised I'd carry them all back to London today. I'll leave after breakfast. But first, I want to study the Copley charm when you greet Miss Bennington."

Andersen crossed his arms over his chest. "And what do you mean by that, Wetherby?"

The marquis flicked an imaginary piece of lint off his coat sleeve. "Sore throat or no, Mr. Bennington talked everyone under the table at dinner last night, dropping hints as fast as Basil dropped his eating utensils. He all but said, there would be an important announcement today."

"I will not have you embarrassing Miss Bennington."

Lord Wetherby's eyes sparkled with amusement. "And here I wanted to find out why Lady Caroline threw me over for a baron."

"I would much prefer your not being there."

The marquis refused to move. "A little touchy, this morning, heh? I think I have paid you well for the best seat in the house."

Above them from the balcony of the East Wing, voices floated down.

Andersen couldn't help smiling. "If you insist, Wetherby. I should probably be pleased that you are removing three potential bombs from our midst, by taking your little paramours away from here. But don't muck up my chances with the Benningtons by saying anything about their son's late night folly."

The young marquis grinned back. "Wouldn't think of it, old chap. Here come your intended bride's mama and papa right now, and if I'm not mistakened, Mrs. Bennington is up in the boughs about something. I hope her young whelp didn't spill the beans to her already."

The lady in question posed in the middle of the stairway, holding a handkerchief to her mouth. Beside her was one of their serving maids, whom Andersen recognized as Anne's abigail. Mr. Bennington, his face florid from trying to keep pace with his wife, followed.

"Ah, Mrs. Bennington . . . sir," Andersen exclaimed with exaggerated cheerfulness, hoping that Elroy's indiscretions hadn't been uncovered. "Is something the matter?"

Mrs. Bennington fanned her face with her handkerchief. "Oh, your lordship. Tina has just told us the most shocking news . . ."

Before she could finish her sentence, Mr. Bennington looked over his wife's shoulder and rasped, "Our daughter has eloped!"

A sense of impending doom hovered over Lord Copley. "Explain yourself, madam."

The maid began to sob.

Mrs. Bennington clasped a hands over her bosom. "Tina came to my room only a few minutes ago."

The tearful girl looked up at him. "She made me promise, your lordship."

Confusion threatened to erase Andersen's affable smile, but he managed to ask calmly, *"She*—I take it you mean Miss Bennington?"

The abigail nodded.

"Made you promise what, Tina?"

"She said I wasn't to say anything until I heard others were awake."

Mr. Bennington, his voice still no more than a croak, butted in. "They didn't even go to bed last night. Already had their bags packed and the carriage at the ready."

Andersen looked back and forth between Mr. and Mrs. Bennington. "They, who?"

"Anne and Mr. Smith, of course," Mr. Bennington snapped.

"He kidnapped our daughter," Mrs. Bennington wailed.

"Oh, no, ma'am," Tina interjected. " 'Twas Miss Bennington who made all the plans. That's why they took your coach and four. She said 'twould be faster."

Oh, my God! thought Andersen, what else can befall me? He ordered a footman up to find Mr. Smith's valet immediately. While they waited he questioned the abigail. "Where did they go, Tina?"

The maid shook her head. "She said if I didn't know, I couldn't tell."

"Where else would runaways go?" Mr. Bennington said. "Over the border to Scotland."

At that moment, Henry's man arrived carrying a piece of paper. "Mr. Smith said, I was to delay giving this to you as long as possible, your lordship."

Andersen tore opened the missive and scanned the page. It began:

> By the time you read this, Miss Bennington and I will be half way to Gretna Green.

There followed several lines of explanations, crossed out words, blotches where the ink had dripped while Henry had probably pondered his next word. It finished:

> Sorry, old chap, but we knew that once Anne's parents received an offer from a baron that I, a mere mister, would have no chance of marrying the woman I love. So we have chosen this means as the only avenue to finding eternal bliss.

Handing the letter to Mr. and Mrs. Bennington, Andersen took out his handkerchief and wiped his brow. He'd never known Henry to be so prosy, but he was discovering that love seemed to bring out some truly amazing characteristics in a man. Romantic spells had enveloped everyone at Roxwealde—everyone except him.

"My word," Mr. Bennington said, looking inquiringly at Copley. "I was right. You *were* going to ask—?

"For Anne." Mrs. Bennington dabbed her eyes with her handkerchief. "You must go after them, your lordship."

Just then, Basil and Beverly strode in from a side corridor, their ruddy cheeks attesting that they'd been outside.

"Go after whom?" Miss Martin asked.

"Anne and Henry have run off to Gretna Green," the marquis explained.

"Oh, Mr. Ripple," pleaded Mrs. Bennington. "With your riding skills, I am certain you can save our daughter."

Basil turned pleading eyes to the baron.

Lord Copley shook his head. "I am afraid even with Mr. Ripple's expertise as a bruising whip, there is no chance of his catching them now, Mrs. Bennington."

"Too cold anyway for my sweeting," Beverly said, putting her arm around Basil. "Freeze a man's eyeballs shut. Don't want that now, do we? We were just ordering our coaches be made ready to leave before noon. I want to tell his parents what a splendid bit o' blood they bred."

By now, the other guests had joined the group and were filled in on the latest on dit.

"How romantic to elope," Miss Tremain exclaimed. "Don't you think so, Peter?"

Peter raised his eyebrows and looked at Copley.

Miss Glover only shrugged. "Any tomfool could have seen those two were head over heels about each other."

The baron looked from one guest to another. God! What was this lunacy called love that made fools of everyone? It had been going on right under his nose, and he hadn't recognized it. He was beginning to think he never would. There had to be a solution, but right now with every one at sixes and sevens he couldn't think clearly. "Please, everyone. Why don't you all go into breakfast? We'll talk of this later."

Mr. Bennington coughed. "I say, Lord Copley, under the circumstances, m'wife says we should leave for Herefordshire as soon as we're packed."

"I am sure Anne will return there as soon as they do what they have their mind set on doing," Mrs. Bennington finished, dabbing her eyes with her handkerchief.

"By-the-by," Mr. Bennington lowered his voice, "I have two more coming out this year. You don't think you would be interested, do you?" he said hopefully.

Copley shook his head. "It's a little late for that now."

Peter pulled him aside. "What are you going to do now, Andy? I hate to leave you like this, but I promised Edith and Miss Glover that we would start back immediately. She wants to tell her folks the good news, but I'm sure she won't object if I ask her to stay."

"There's nothing anyone can do, Peter. Thanks anyway. There are matters of business, however, which I must attend to." With that, Andersen headed for the library. Just as he entered the room, from somewhere in the castle, he heard a clock strike ten. Fourteen hours were all that he had between freedom and debtor's prison. How had he ever let himself get to such a point?

Every one of his choices had been plucked right from under his nose. The only unmarried females left in the party were Lady Martin and Miss Glover. Even the nonsensical picture of his proposing to little Miss Glover couldn't bring a smile.

How had rolly-polly Basil taken Bev Martin? Even Henry Smith, who Andersen admitted had more in the attic than Basil, was no catch as far as looks and lineage. Than why was it Miss Bennington chose him? Was it that for all their faults, they were honest and didn't pretend to be more than they were? Was that more attractive to women? Not Lady Caroline, though. Thank goodness he'd discovered her shallowness before it was too late. Heaven help him, Andersen thought, if he should have to put himself in a league with the earl and his daughter.

Regardless of his regrets over what could have been, he now realized that his only recourse would be to make sure that the inheritance was made safe until Rupert came of age. Copley opened a desk drawer to look for a clean sheet of paper. The packet with the special license lay on top. Any good it was to him now.

The baron had just reached for a pen when he heard a knock on the door. It was his steward.

"What is it, Proctor?"

"There is a man to see you, my lord. Name of Mr. Tooley. Says it's urgent he see you. Says he came all the way from London with important papers for you to see."

Good, God! He couldn't even wait for me to get back to Town. Andersen had to stall him to give him time to think what he should do. "Ask him to wait in the solar, Proctor. Stall for about half an hour. Then offer him some lunch. Tell him—tell him you found out I'd left the premises and you aren't certain when I'll be back."

"Very good, my lord." Proctor started to leave, then said,

"Oh, and, I forgot, here comes Miss Grimsley. She said she would be by to see what orders you have for her today—seeing that most of the guests will be leaving."

Sarah hurried into the room. "Oh, Lord Copley, I just found out about Mr. Smith and Miss Bennington. Whatever are you going to do?"

The baron looked up wearily to see a blue cloud descending upon him. The same vision that had assaulted him the first time he'd seen her, only this time she didn't hold a weapon above her head. No, she looked quite lovely in the floating gown, that ridiculously large blue gem shining from the center of her turban. She'd saved him on more than one occasion, would she do so again?

"Miss Grimsley, you must marry me."

Andersen took her wide-eyed, noncommital response as a positive one. He didn't have time to put any other meaning into it.

Sarah, numbed by the baron's words, worked her mouth, but no words came out. She watched in dumbfounded silence as he rang for a servant, ordered his carriage readied at a back entrance, and grabbed a packet from the desk. She wondered if he'd forgotten her altogether when he threw his coat over her shoulders and hustled her out the back entrance.

Once seated in the carriage facing each other, Lord Copley threw his head back against the squabs, gave a great sigh, and closed his eyes.

Sarah stared at him. Now was the time to confront him with what he'd done. But she couldn't very well speak to a man who sat with his eyes closed and a smile on his face. Did she want to marry him? More than anything in the world—but not like this. Besides, she couldn't marry him as Miss Grimsley. The marriage wouldn't be legal.

Andersen's eyes remained shut. While in London, he'd inquired into the estate of Miss Grimsley's family. Her cousin who had inherited the title had lived only a few years after he'd usurped her father's lands. He'd gambled away what little funds there were, and left the country to escape his debtors. There was the on dit that he'd died somewhere in France. Andersen didn't think the knowledge would make Miss Grimsley any happier from hearing it, so he hadn't told her what he'd found out. "You know, you are saving my life, Miss Grimsley."

This made Sarah pause a minute. "But, you don't really know me at all. How can you want to marry me?"

He opened his eyes then and looked at her, really looked at her. Her looks had grown on him. She was not only an original, but she was pretty and clever. A rare combination in a woman. He didn't regret his decision. In fact, once overlooking Miss Grimsley's colorful past as hostess to the duke, Andersen found her fascinating. He felt he knew her far better than he'd ever known any woman before. Her family line went back farther than his in the peerage. He doubted that Miss Grimsley would be accepted by the ton, but from what she'd revealed to him thus far, she had no real interest in the life of the upper orders in London. She would be content to remain at Roxwealde Castle. From the way she'd kissed him in the cave, he knew she had some feelings for him. He was beginning to get an idea of what old Percival had found so entrancing about Roxwealde. Perhaps it was a magical place after all. "I know more about you than you think, my dear."

Sarah doubted that, and she was just about to tell him so, when the carriage pulled to a stop and the driver called down, "The vicarage, your lordship."

Several minutes later, Sarah found herself standing in the pleasant little parlour, the vicar's wife insisting she send for some refreshments.

"Ah, Lord Copley," the vicar said, coming in to greet them, "I wondered that you were ever coming. The month is about over."

The baron pulled out the leather packet. "I explained earlier that my fiancée and I wanted a quick and simple ceremony. We will have more elaborate festivities at a later date," he said, putting his arm around Sarah's shoulders. He liked the feel of her.

"Well, then," the vicar said, spreading the papers out on his desk and reaching for a pen, "the lady will just have to sign her name here—"

Sarah stared at where the clergyman pointed. She couldn't sign Miss Grimsley's name, and yet it dawned on her, they both had the same initials, S, G. If she made a big flourish of the first two letters, she could scribble the remainder of her name in such a way as to make it barely legible. They would put it down to bride's nerves. She would have to explain sometime to the baron, but he seemed dead set on getting a wife. Sarah picked up the pen and wrote.

Andersen checked the wall clock. "Can we hurry this up, vicar?"

The clergyman coughed and began the ceremony. When he came to the part of the exchange of vows, he picked up the paper and frowned.

Sarah had thought it seemed such a simple solution, until she realized she had to repeat her name aloud. She felt the tears forming. "I cannot."

The baron gave her hand a squeeze. "You don't need to be afraid of me, Miss Grimsley."

She kept her face down. "You don't understand. I am not Stanhope Grimsley."

"You . . . are . . . not . . . Stanhope Grimsley."

"I am Sarah Greenwood—of Elmsdale," she sniffed, looking up at him. "I didn't mean to deceive you, your lordship. I thought it only a harmless charade, you see." She threw up her hands. "Oh, it is a long story."

"You . . . are . . . not . . . Stanhope Grimsley," he repeated. He seemed to recover quickly from his daze, and forced a laugh. "It is a little jest we have between us, vicar. Now, dear Sarah, answer the vicar, so that we can return to the castle."

The baron's eyes still had a glazed look when they

climbed back in the coach for the ride back to Roxwealde, and although the set line of his lips gave every indication that he might be put out with her, Sarah did try to explain how she came to call herself Miss Stanhope Grimsley. The longer he remained silent, the more Sarah prattled on, until her story sounded more and more bizarre, even to herself.

Finally, Lord Copley looked at her and barked, "Enough, Miss . . . Greenwood! When we arrive at the castle, I must meet with a Mr. Tooley, my solicitor from London. He will be shown the marriage certificate, but as far as the rest of the household staff knows, everything is as it was before. You will still be Miss Grimsley. Do you understand?"

Sarah nodded. She wondered if he'd heard anything she had said.

The minute they walked into the castle, Proctor directed them to the solar. After the steward had withdrawn and he'd introduced Sarah, Andersen lost no time in handing the marriage certificate to Mr. Tooley. His humor was a great deal restored by the look of frustration on the solicitor's face.

"But that is what I came to tell you, your lordship, you were right all along. Your thirtieth birthday is still a year away."

"What?" Copley bellowed.

"It is totally my error, my lord. I take complete responsibility. Here, I have brought your birth certificate to prove it. I mistakenly took out the papers of one of your deceased brothers, Andersen. Here," he said, handing a portfolio to the baron. "I know you will want to go over these. And now if I can be shown to my room—I've been waiting a long time, your lordship."

"Of course, of course," the baron said, ringing for a footman. "Dinner will be served at . . . ?" He turned to Sarah.

"Dinner will be at seven, your lordship."

Lord Copley waited until Mr. Tooley had left the solar

before he grabbed Sarah around the waist and swung her in a circle. Setting her down her threw back his head and laughed. "I cannot believe it. Freedom for another year. We will have the marriage annulled, of course, and you will be able to continue your journey to London. You will not miss your Season after all, Miss Greenwood."

Sarah didn't want her Season in London. She wanted to be married to Lord Copley, but when she saw the ecstatic gleam in his eye, she said nothing.

"We must get you to your great-grandmother's without too much delay." He looked at her and guffawed. "There, you see, I did hear every word you said to me in the coach."

Sarah saw a flicker of something pass through his thoughts before he continued. "I daresay, I shall miss Miss Grimsley's costumes, but I am afraid they would look quite out of place on a young maiden making her debut. You are not laughing, Miss Greenwood."

"It is only that I am tired, my lord. And there will be much to tend to tomorrow."

The baron turned serious. "I shall straighten out matters with the authorities on the circumstance of Miss Grimsley's death. From what I found out about her past, she had no living relatives."

"What shall I do with Miss Grimsley's belongings?"

"I see no reason why you cannot keep what you will. Her jewelry is clearly paste and far too ostentatious for a young deb making her come out, but you may want to keep some of it as a memento of your adventure."

"Yes, thank you. I should like that," Sarah said, fingering the brooch on her turban. The large blue stone would always remind her of the golden-haired baron.

That evening dinner was a stilted affair. With Mr. Tooley the only guest, they supped in the smaller dining room, and leaving the men to their port and cigars, Sarah returned to her room to pack.

Nooney was much quieter than usual. "We're sorry that you are leaving, Miss Grimsley."

"I am sorry too, Nooney."

The girl shuffled from one foot to the other. "We were all thinking—well, the way you and his lordship ran off so fast to Danbury Wells—the coachman said—we were all hoping . . ."

"We only paid a courtesy visit to the vicar and his wife."

Sarah couldn't tell if the girl looked disappointed or skeptical, but she said no more. They sorted out Miss Grimsley's dresses. Now that Sarah had seen samples of the present fashion on their guests, Nooney told her she could make some adjustments on the gowns for Sarah to take with her to London. The remainder of the clothing could go in the castle collection of costumes. She put Miss Grimsley's jewelry and her silver toiletry set in a box to take with her. Each piece brought a memory, until by the time Sarah went to bed, the tears were running freely down her cheeks. Tonight was to have been her wedding night, and instead the groom was probably in his chambers celebrating his freedom.

Andersen's nose twitched. Two large yellow eyes stared at him over the side of his bed. Already, the light which filtered through the leaded glass windowpanes announced morning had come.

"Go away, Dog!" he groaned, pulling the pillow over his head. The baron had spent a boring evening listening to Tooley digest and redigest all the reasons and excuses he could think of for his faux pas on mixing up the birth dates.

After Miss Greenwood had left the dining room, looking so solemn and so pretty, Andersen could think of nothing else but what a mess he'd made of things. He was in love.

He didn't care what her name was. Names, he was finding out, mattered little. In the few weeks he'd come to know her, she'd wriggled her way into his heart. Now, he must give her up.

The first elation he'd felt at hearing he didn't have to marry for another year soon fell flat when he watched her leave the room. With her went the sunshine, the humor, his Miss Grimsley.

Strange, now that he had his wish to be free for another year, he realized that he really didn't want to annul the marriage. He also realized that it was the only honorable thing to do. He'd forced Miss Grimsley—rather, Miss Greenwood—to marry him. But it was too late. She must hold nothing but contempt for him, the cavalier way he'd treated her.

He'd spent a restless night trying to get to sleep. Now that he finally had fallen into a deep slumber, that pesky lion had to waken him. "Good God!" Andersen exclaimed, throwing off his pillow. Dog cocked his head to one side, viewing his master from another angle. "How did you get in here?"

The lion's head disappeared immediately.

Andersen flung off the comforter, and ignoring the step-stool, leapt off the bed just in time to see Dog's rear end wriggling under the bed. Flinging himself onto his stomach, the baron raised the bedskirt and peered into the blackness. As the shuffling and scraping sounds grew fainter, Andersen followed, until he found the opening in the wall.

So that was how the animal was doing it. The old medieval beds sat a good two feet from the wall, the space between covered with a thick, wooden headboard from which the heavy curtains draped overhead. If the opening was large enough to accommodate a lion, it was big enough for a man. It was only a matter of a few feet before the baron was able to stand upright. His hands explored the stones. He was on the inner wall of the tower. Narrow steps led both up and down. He heard the snuffling breath of the beast ahead of him and followed the sounds downward.

"Wait until I catch you, you lop-eared clown. I'll put an end to your gallivanting once and for all."

Seventeen

A very naughty word awakened Sarah. It sounded as though it came from beneath her bed. Sleep had only come to her in the early hours of the morning and her senses were still drugged. The scent of cinnamon buns and hot chocolate attested that Nooney had already come and gone.

In front of the table sat the lion facing the tray of pastries. Sarah was about to praise Dog for his restraint, when again she heard another mumbled oath. She hadn't been dreaming. The strange sounds *had* come from under her bed. She sat upright and pulled the sheet up around her neck and watched in horror as a ghostly figure rose at the foot of her bed.

Sarah, not usually squeamish of character, was so taken aback that she screeched.

The baron, his eyes not yet adjusted to the light, squinted and thrust his head toward the unpleasant noise. "Miss Grims . . . Miss Greenwood? I beg your pardon. It was Dog. He found the panels under the beds."

They both looked toward the window. The animal was nowhere to be seen.

Just then the door flew open. Nooney's face appeared. "Oh, ma'am, is anything wrong? I heard you scream—" She stopped short, as Jacob's face appeared over her shoulder. "Miss Grimsley. Dog has got out again."

Both servants stood staring.

"Beg yer forgiveness, yer lordship," Jacob said, grinning.

As soon as the door closed, Andersen looked at Sarah. "Well, I am certain the gossip will be all over the household in a few minutes."

"Whatever will they say?"

"That it is true that the master and Miss Grimsley were married in Danbury Wells."

"Well, that is true, isn't it?" Sarah said with a mixture of relief and apprehension. "It is not as if we were—but we really aren't—are we?"

"Only if you want to be."

"Be what?"

"Be married."

Sarah couldn't believe he was even asking such a question. "Do you want to be married?"

"Didn't I practically kidnap you to take you to the vicar's?"

"Well, yes, but that was when you thought you had to have a wife to save the entail."

"And now I don't. So doesn't that make a difference when I say I want to be married to you now?"

Oh, Sarah hoped so. "I suppose it does."

The baron looked hungrily at the picture she made with her curls cascading over her shoulders. "I am very tired, Lady Copley—"

"Lady Copley. That sounds strange."

"You will get used to it. Now, may I come to bed? I had very little sleep last night."

Sarah still held the coverlet up to her chin. "You are not going to get into my bed with that dirty nightshirt on, my lord."

"That is just fine with me," Andersen said, shedding the dusty garment in one motion and tossing it over his head.

My, he is more magnificent than Mercury, Sarah thought, as she moved over to make room for her husband.

With a flying leap, the baron took the shortcut over the foot of the bed and burrowed under the warm counterpane.

As he pulled her to him, Sarah squealed, "My lord, your feet are cold!"

"I think, my dear, Lady Copley, it is time you started calling me Andersen," he said, burying his face in her sweet-smelling hair. "Though, I know it will take me a time to get used to calling you, Sarah, for there will always be apart of me that thinks of you as *my Miss Grimsley.*"

"I don't believe Miss Grimsley would mind at all, your lor . . . Andersen. She was a very generous woman."

With a chuckle, he gave her a pinch on her soft derriere. "In more ways than one, I understand."

Sarah squealed and grabbed his hand.

"Now, come here, my little chatelaine," Andersen said, pulling her gently against the full length of him. "Let me show you how my keeper-of-the-keys has unlocked my heart as no other woman has done."

The kiss he gave Sarah quite took her breath away.

"I love you," he said.

That opened her eyes. "Truly?"

He laughed. "Truly. I only hope that someday you will feel the same toward me."

"But, I do, Andersen," she said, shyly exploring his shoulders with her hands. "I have loved you from that day in the library." She felt a shiver run through his entire body. "Did I hurt you, my lord?"

"Ah," he sighed, closing his eyes. "Not at all. And, here I thought that I should have a devil of a time of it, after I saw how properly you insisted on clothing poor Mercury."

Sarah felt her nightgown being eased up her body and over her head and giggled. "You are teasing me."

Andersen wrapped his arms around her. "I would never tease at a time like this, my darling."

There was a shuffling sound under the bed.

Sarah sat upright. "Dog, go back to your room!"

There was a shake and a scrape and then silence.

"Remind me to have all those panels nailed shut," Andersen said, pulling Sarah back down, "or I am afraid our children will make life havoc for us someday when they discover them."

About The Author

Paula Tanner Girard lives with her family in Maitland, Florida. Her first Zebra regency romance, LORD WAKE-FORD'S GOLD WATCH, is available at your local bookstore. Paula is currently working on her next Zebra regency romance, which will be published in December 1996. She will also have a short story in Zebra's regency collection, LORDS AND LADIES, to be published in May 1996. Paula loves hearing from her readers and you may write to her c/o Zebra Books. Please include a self-addressed stamped envelope if you wish a response.